CONSTEL

O

SCARS

MELISSA ESKUE OUSLEY

CONSTELLATIONS OF SCARS

Published by Midnight Tide Publishing.
www.midnighttidepublishing.com
Cover Art and Graphic Design by Mila
www.milagraphicartist.com
Interior Formatting by Book Savvy Services

This is a work of fiction. Names, characters, brands, trademarks, places, and incidents either are the product of the author's imagination or are used fictitiously. Any resemblance to actual events, locales, organizations, or persons, living or dead, is entirely coincidental and beyond the intent of either the author or the publisher.

Constellations of Scars/ Melissa Eskue Ousley – 1st ed.
ISBN 9781953238238
eBook ISBN 9781393722533

CONSTELLATIONS OF SCARS

MELISSA ESKUE OUSLEY

Flecti Non Frangi

1

Blood got everywhere and Mother wasn't happy about it. As I stood under the showerhead, rinsing blood from my skin, I could hear her grumbling. She was kneeling on the bathroom floor, scrubbing the tile. The coppery smell in the air faded, replaced by the pungent stench of bleach.

This was our monthly ritual—me, hurrying to shampoo blood out of my hair so I could help her clean up, her angrily wiping down tile and walls and the countertop with its cracked porcelain sink.

Hot shame washed over me as I heard her curse over the trail of blood I'd left in the hall. I hadn't meant to make such a mess, but sometimes my illness surprised me. She'd be livid when she realized I'd been sitting on the couch when I started bleeding. I prayed there wasn't a stain.

I had raced to the bathroom as fast as I could, stripping off my clothes and jumping into the tub to contain some of it, but still—the bathroom looked like the scene of a murder. As much blood as I lost each month, it was amazing I wasn't dead. If I wasn't such a freak, I guess I would be.

I tilted my head back, letting the warm water run over my

scalp, and then shut off the water. As I reached out from behind the shower curtain and grabbed a towel, I spotted Mom standing in front of the sink, counting this month's yield. It must have been a good one, because she stopped scowling. She gently rinsed the pearls under the tap, laying them out to dry on the hand towel she'd placed on the countertop. Her rage was pacified, for the moment.

I hurried to dress in the clean clothes she'd brought me. Maybe if I finished cleaning the bathroom, she wouldn't lock me in the attic this time.

Mother patted the pearls dry and then took them to her room, to store them in the safe. I got to work scrubbing the wooden floor of the hallway. I had finished by the time she came back, and to my relief, she didn't say anything when I checked the couch for a bloodstain. She just sat in her recliner and watched *Wheel of Fortune* on TV.

We didn't talk about my illness any more that night, but normally we talked about it a *lot*. Argued about it, mostly.

Mother often said my condition was a gift. A blessing.

I disagreed. "It's a curse," I told her.

"Don't be melodramatic, Amelia," she said, narrowing her eyes. "It's put food on our table. It's going to pay for your education."

We'd had this same discussion for months. I'd gotten my GED three years before, and wanted desperately to go away to college, far from Roseburg, Oregon. I'd just turned 21. Some of the kids I grew up with would be graduating from college soon. But not me. There would be no college for me, no moving out. Mother always found a reason for me to stay.

At first, she said there wasn't enough money to pay for tuition. That was a lie. I knew how much the pearls went for. I knew what our household expenses were. It was just the two of us. There was plenty for college and then some.

"It's dangerous," Mom said, the fifth time I asked. "If someone discovered what you can do, they'd lock you up and use you to get rich."

There was truth to her fear. It was why, when we'd first discovered my so-called gift, she'd taken me out of sixth grade at Fremont Middle School and begun homeschooling. We couldn't risk someone seeing my scars when I changed for gym. "People wouldn't understand," my mother told me. "They'd think I did that to you. They would take you away. I'd go to jail."

I started wearing long-sleeve shirts year-round to cover my upper arms, shoulders, and back. No spaghetti straps—ever. Looking back, I think people around town thought Mom had turned religious—that she was scared of me being corrupted and forced me to dress modestly and do school from home. I lost contact with my friends. I didn't date. It was just me and her, all day, every day. Except for the days when she left me alone to meet with the buyers. On those days, she locked me in our stuffy, windowless attic.

"It's for your own good," Mother said. "I can't have you sneaking out."

"I wouldn't leave," I promised her. I hated the attic. The cramped space made me feel claustrophobic and I was terrified of rats. I'd seen their droppings on the floor of the attic and on the lids of the dusty boxes Mom stored up there. "I'd just go out in the backyard. No one would even know I was there." With our wooden fence and tall, rhododendron bushes planted along the perimeter of the grass, someone would have to go to a lot of trouble to peer into the yard. I wanted to sit in the sun, feel warmth soak into my skin. It helped with the pain.

"No," she said. "Someone might see you. The mailman could stop by. It's not safe. You know that." With that, she closed the attic door. The click of the lock sounded as ominous as the locking of a jail cell.

The first lump had formed on my left shoulder, right after my twelfth birthday. Red, inflamed, and hot to the touch. There was a white head on the blemish. It hurt, and it scared me a little. Mostly though, it grossed me out. It looked like a giant pimple.

Mom thought so too. After inspecting the bump, she sighed and shook her head. "Adolescent acne. Sorry, kiddo. That's puberty for you. Don't pick at it, and it'll go away in a few days." Seeing my grimace, she added, "Don't worry. By the time you're grown, you'll have great skin. That's how it was for me."

The lump grew bigger and spawned more bumps. Soon my upper arms and back were covered. I felt feverish. Mother worried about infection. She considered taking me to see Dr. Neilson, but it was hard for her to get time off at the Stop & Go. Besides, we didn't have health insurance, and couldn't afford to pay a medical bill out of pocket. Instead, she made me a warm compress and gave me a couple of Advil.

I left the bumps alone as much as I could, not scratching even though they itched like crazy. They didn't go away like Mom promised. Later that week, as I was getting ready to shower, the skin on my left shoulder ripped as the first blemish opened. I cried out as something dropped to the floor, landing on the tile with a clink.

Horrified, I stared at my bleeding shoulder for a moment before dabbing at it with a wash cloth. Then I bent over to clean up whatever had fallen on the floor. It was a pearl the size of a marble, perfectly round with an iridescent sheen. I rinsed it off under the tap and dried it with the hand towel next to the sink.

The pearl looked luminous—it seemed to glow under the harsh light of the bare bulbs in the rusty fixture over the mirror. There was something almost magical about it. It had come from my body, which was a revolting yet thrilling thought. I slipped the pearl into a cabinet drawer, hiding it until I could figure out what to do with it.

Two days later, other lumps on my shoulders and back swelled and festered. I would have wondered if they too contained hidden treasures, but my body ached so bad, I could barely think. The slightest movement sent tendrils of pain down my spine. I stayed home from school.

Mother drew me a hot bath and was helping me undress when it happened. The sores opened, one after another, spilling new pearls to the floor. Mom jumped back and shrieked. I groaned with relief as the blinding pain suddenly eased.

Mom picked up one of the pearls, still slick with blood. "Is this what I think it is?"

I nodded. "I'm a human oyster." I didn't feel human though. I felt like a sideshow freak.

Mother's eyes were fearful, but her tone was angry. "Don't be ridiculous." She gingerly placed the pearl on the countertop, as though it might bite.

"It's true." I opened the drawer where I'd stashed the first pearl. I held it out to her.

She touched it and then shook her head. "No, they're not pearls. They're part of the infection you're fighting. Some kind of organic…" She didn't finish the sentence. She just stared at all those pearls on the floor. Including the one I held in my hand, there were 43 of them.

Mom decided to have the first pearl assessed. It was the only time she took me with her.

Mr. Whittier, the jeweler, studied it, gauging its worth. "Big one, isn't it? Fourteen millimeters. High luster…round…free of any defect I can see. Where'd you get this, Denise? Indonesia? The Philippines? Looks like a South Sea pearl to me."

"How much is it worth?" Mother asked. There was a hunger in her eyes I'd never seen before. It scared me.

The jeweler held the pearl up to the light. "I'd give you a hundred bucks for it."

"That's all?" Mom asked.

He handed the pearl back to her. "Well, for one pearl. If you had enough for a strand, it'd be worth more. I'd pay three grand for something of this quality."

It turned out my first crop had just enough pearls to make a matinee-length necklace. It sold for twice the appraised value, five times more than Mom's monthly paycheck.

My wounds healed in days, but a week later, new bumps formed. I soon realized they corresponded with my monthly cycle. After that first year of harvesting pearls, my skin had constellations of scars. I avoided mirrors. The one comfort to my isolation was no one could see my monstrous skin.

Mother quit her job so she could stay with me and do my schooling from home. Years passed. With each crop of pearls, we grew richer, but we were careful to be frugal. Mom was afraid big spending would draw attention to us, and she would not have welcomed a tax audit. She also worried I'd reach an age when the pearls didn't come anymore.

The pearls didn't stop forming under my skin. The pain didn't ease, but I got used to it, I guess, the way people do when they're sick for a long time. It *was* a sickness, and that was something Mother never understood. I was afflicted with a disease so rare, almost no one knew about it.

On one of the days when Mom was out, I learned how to pick the attic lock. I'd never actually picked a lock before, but I'd watched a lot of movies. How hard could it be? Harder than it looks, as it turned out.

Once I'd figured out how to escape the attic, I used her computer to research my condition, looking for a cure. There was only one recorded case I could find, a 1935 article from *The Queenslander*, a publication from Brisbane, Australia. It told of a man who underwent a kidney operation. His doctor discovered tiny pearls had formed in the organ, causing him pain. His story and his pearls were nothing like mine.

No surgery could cure me. I'd never be free of the pearls. As I grew up, I realized I'd never be free of Mother either. She wouldn't let me go away to school, and she'd never give me the money from the pearls I bled to earn. She kept the profits out of my reach. What cash she kept on hand was locked in her safe.

For years she told me she was making sure no one abducted me because of my gift. Truth was, *she* was my captor. I had made her wealthy and there was no way she'd let me go.

The moment I understood that was the moment I decided to escape.

I planned to hoard a few pearls each month, hiding them until I had enough to buy a bus ticket out of town. I'd pack a bag, see the jeweler, and run away. Only then would I be free.

2

How many pearls would I need to save before I could escape? If I could sell 30, that would net me a few thousand to buy a bus ticket, head to Portland, and find a place to stay. If I timed it right, just before another pearl harvest, I'd have a whole crop to sell as I got settled.

I decided on Portland because it was a five-hour bus ride north and the ticket would be affordable. It was a big enough city to get lost in. Mother wouldn't be able to find me. I'd travel light. I'd only take enough clothes to fit in a backpack. Anything else I could buy when I got there. It's not like I lived extravagantly anyway. Mom and I had lived on the basics for years. I knew how to be frugal.

The tricky part was deciding how many pearls I could save each month. If I could hide five pearls from every crop, starting in September, it would take me six months to leave. But I couldn't afford to be so predictable. Mother would suspect something. The number of pearls I shed varied from month to month—sometimes as few as 35, and other times, as many as 60. Mom always wanted at least 43 to make a strand to sell. She got more money that way, rather than selling individual pearls. As long as the crop was large enough to make a strand, I had leeway to put pearls aside.

Problem was, Mom liked to be present when I harvested the pearls. She didn't trust me, even though I hadn't given her a reason not to. As far as I knew, she didn't know about me escaping the attic and she hadn't discovered my research on her computer. I always erased my browsing history before shutting the computer down.

I had to buy time to shed the pearls in private. It would have been great to have been able to create a diversion, maybe enlist the help of a friend. I didn't have any friends. Not after being hidden away for so long. My only friends were the books and old black and white monster movies Mom brought me from the library.

The first month I tried to save pearls, I waited as long as I could before they were ready to burst from my skin before trying to force them out. Mother and I were eating pork chops with mashed potatoes in front of the TV, watching her favorite show, *Jeopardy*. She liked to try to guess at the answers, testing her knowledge of the world. When she seemed completely engrossed in the show, I pushed my TV tray aside and excused myself to use the bathroom.

I locked the door and removed my shirt, inspecting the large welts on my back. Most of the pearls were still growing, but there were a few on my lower back that looked ready to burst free. I prodded them gently, observing how the skin encasing them was thin and stretched. Then I took the steak knife I'd smuggled from dinner and sliced into my skin. After making the incision, I pushed on the skin around the pearl, trying to dislodge it. It wouldn't budge at first. Then, suddenly, it popped free and fell onto the countertop next to the sink.

The doorknob rattled, and I looked over at the door, startled.

The lock was ancient, and I was scared Mother would burst in and catch me.

"What are you doing in there, Amelia?" Mom called.

"I'm on the toilet," I called back, panicked at almost being discovered.

"You've been in there a long time," she said, her voice muffled by the door.

"I'll be out in a sec!" I shouted, exasperated. She absolutely would have walked in on me if I hadn't locked the door. I had zero privacy.

Wanting to hurry, I grabbed a wad of toilet paper, wet it under the sink, and held it to my wound to stop the bleeding. For a moment, I worried it wouldn't stop. There seemed to be more blood than when I shed the pearls naturally. Then, the flow of blood stemmed, and I threw the bloody wad in the toilet.

I inspected the pearl sitting on the counter. It had rolled several inches toward the sink when it fell, but thankfully, hadn't fallen in and gone down the drain. I grabbed more toilet paper to clean up the trail of blood it had left on the countertop. With disappointment, I noted the pearl was small and shriveled-looking. It hadn't been ready for harvest. I should have given it a few more days. By forcing the pearl out early, I'd wasted it.

Frustrated, I cleaned up the mess, folding the pearl into toilet paper. Then I flushed it down the toilet and washed off the knife under the tap, carefully sliding it into the back pocket of my jeans. I threw my shirt back on, made sure the knife was hidden, and opened the bathroom door.

Mother was there, pacing in the hallway. "Is it the pearls? Are they coming?"

"No, Mom," I said. "I was constipated."

"Don't be crass," she said with a scowl. "Let's have a little less attitude, young lady. I was worried about your health. Now go finish your dinner."

"No thanks," I said. "I've lost my appetite."

3

She wasn't the worst mother in the world. I want to make that clear. You hear stories about kids who are physically abused, molested—there was nothing like that. My mother never laid a hand on me, and she made sure no one else did either.

Education was important to Mother, because she never finished hers. We always had books in the house, and she started taking me to the library when I was a toddler. I learned to read early, while I was still in pre-school. At night, we'd curl up in my little bed and read nursery rhymes:

Jack be nimble,

Jack be quick,

Jack jumped over the candle stick.

or

Peter, Peter, pumpkin eater,

had a wife and couldn't keep her.

Put her in a pumpkin shell,

and there she lived, very well.

My favorite was the one where the cow jumped over the moon.

Hey, diddle diddle,

the cat and the fiddle,
the cow jumped over the moon.
The little dog laughed,
to see such a sight,
and the dish ran away with the spoon.

I didn't know what that nursery rhyme meant, but the idea of a cow jumping that high made four-year-old me giggle, and the rhythm of the poem felt familiar and comforting. When I'd wake up at night from a bad dream, I'd whisper that rhyme like a prayer of protection against any monsters that lurked in the darkness of my room. Then I'd fall back asleep.

My mother enjoyed fairy tales and fables. She read me all the well-loved classics—the stories of Cinderella riding to the ball in an enchanted coach made from a pumpkin, Snow White revived by her true love's kiss...but also lesser known tales like *The Twelve Dancing Princesses*. As a child, that story was scary to me. The king tasks suitors with finding out how the princesses escape a locked room each night and dance through the soles of their shoes. Those men who were unlucky and didn't solve the mystery were beheaded. Mother didn't believe in sugar-coating things.

My favorite tale was *The Goose That Laid Golden Eggs* because I didn't have a dog or a cat or even a goldfish, and I thought it would be neat to have a magic goose. Mom said I wasn't responsible enough to have a pet. Still, she'd tell me the story over and over, as many times as I asked, how a poor man and his wife get a goose that lays golden eggs and they become rich. But then they get greedy. Thinking the goose must have much more gold inside her, they decide to kill the goose and take all the gold at once. To their surprise, the goose is no different from any other goose, and rather than gaining all their wealth at one time, they lose their chance at more riches.

As I got older, I found myself relating more and more to that story. I had become my mother's golden goose, and had made her a wealthy woman. But we weren't always rich. There were times when we could barely afford groceries.

When I was born, we lived with my grandfather. My grandmother had died years before in a car accident, and my mother, worried that Grandpa would fall into depression and wouldn't make it on his own, never left home.

She went to the local community college on and off for a few years, working part-time to pay bills and coming home each evening to cook for my grandpa. He had never learned how to cook—Grandma always made his meals. When Grandma died, Mom was only seventeen, and she had to step in to help out. Grandpa's pension working for the city of Roseburg's water department was meager, but the loan for our one-hundred-year-old farmhouse had been paid off, so they survived. Then Mom met a boy at school and got pregnant.

Mother always said that was what broke Grandpa's heart. I never knew him because he died of a heart attack when I was two years old. Trent, the boy my mother fell in love with—my father—didn't stick around for my birth. Grandpa had wanted a better life for Mom than the one he'd had. Seeing her saddled with a kid at such a young age, her heart shattered when my dad left—that was what killed my grandfather, Mother told me.

"He couldn't bear the thought of me repeating the same mistakes he'd made in his life," she said. Unlike my father, Grandpa had married my grandmother when she got pregnant. "But he was never happy," Mom told me. "He did right by me, but he was never truly happy." I sometimes wondered if she was talking about herself too—if, by taking care of me, she had sacrificed her own happiness.

Mom never talked about my father. I sometimes asked about him, and she shushed me up quick. I don't think she ever got over him. At some point, her love for him turned to hate, the kind of hate that erodes your soul and rots you from the inside out. She blamed Trent for the way her life turned out—for her father dying, for us getting stuck with Grandpa's house and his debts, for her never finishing college. She never said it, but looking back, I think she blamed me too. Most of all, she blamed the girl Trent left her for.

I didn't even know Alexandra existed until I found the photograph. I was fourteen, and I'd never seen a picture of my father. Then, one day, when my mother locked me in the attic to sell pearls, I got bored doing my civics lesson and started looking through the boxes she kept up there. It was mostly my grandpa's stuff—things Mother couldn't bear to throw out, like his old bowling shirt and the trophies he'd been so proud of—but also boxes from her childhood. Old toys, an antique rocking horse I'd never been allowed to ride, and photo albums. I pulled out one of the more recent albums and began thumbing through it. There was a loose photograph tucked between the pages.

The colors were faded, but the photo was of my mom at a Luau-themed party, surrounded by friends. She couldn't have been more than 20. She was grinning at the camera, a pink lei around her neck, holding up a drink in a brown plastic cup shaped like a coconut. There was a tiny yellow umbrella in the drink. A handsome, dark-haired boy wearing a Hawaiian shirt had his arm around her, and it looked like he was laughing. His eyes were pale gray, like mine. I knew, in my gut, that he was my dad. I felt an ache in my heart—I knew nothing about him except that my mother loathed him. What had he been like? Did we have anything in common? Where did he go after he left us?

The fact that Mom never talked about Trent made me even more curious. The topic of my father was as forbidden as the fruit in the garden of Eden. I gave into temptation to satiate my curiosity.

I should have known better—it wasn't the first time

curiosity would get me in trouble, nor would it be the last. Mother used to chide me for being nosy, saying, "Curiosity killed the cat, Amelia." As though that were a deterrent. I was more worried I'd die of boredom if I never got to leave that house.

When my mother got home and unlocked the attic door to let me out, the first thing I did was show her the photograph. I pointed at the boy. "Is that him?"

She glanced at the photo and a dark look crossed her face, like a cloud blocking out the sun. "Where did you get that?"

I gestured to the box of photos. "It was in one of those albums. Is that my father?"

"Yes," she snapped. "Put that back. I never gave you permission to go through my things."

"I want to know what he was like," I persisted, knowing I was pushing her buttons and I'd regret it later. "I don't know anything about him. You never talk about him, and he's my *dad*."

She snatched the photo from my grasp. "You want to know what he was like? He was a lying cheat, that's what he was like." She stabbed at the photo with her finger, pointing out a pretty girl with black curly hair standing off to the side, behind her and my dad. "And that's the slut he cheated with."

At the time, I wasn't entirely sure what the word *slut* meant, but I could tell by her tone it was something bad. "Who's that?"

"Alexandra St. John," she spat. "From San Diego." Her tone was derisive. "She thought she was better than everybody, but she was nothing but a filthy whore. She shouldn't have come to this town."

I stared at my mother, shocked by the naked hostility in her voice. I'd heard my mother say plenty of cruel things before, but the venom in her tone dripped with pure hate. "Where are they now?"

"Where are they *now*?" Mother stared at me, exasperated.

"You're just going to keep pushing, aren't you? Fine. I get it. You hate me, you want to go live with your dad."

"That's not what I was saying," I said quietly.

Mom wasn't listening. "Well, too bad, so sad, because he left and he's never coming back. I don't know where he is, and frankly, I don't care. He's probably in San Diego, living on the beach like a bum." She stuffed the photo into an album and glared at me. "There. Now you know. End of discussion."

It was the first and only time we ever talked about my father. She never even told me his last name. I tried searching for Alexandra once, using Mom's computer when she was out. I found records for a lot of women with that name, but none who looked like the girl in the photograph. Eventually, I gave up. It wasn't that I'd wanted to go live with my dad, like my mom feared. I just wanted to know about him, to know my history. But I'd never know, because Mom refused to tell me anything more. Maybe the reason she hated him so much was some part of her still ached for him. He was the only man she ever loved, and she never let herself be that vulnerable again.

The last time my mother went on a date had been years before, when I was ten. A man with a nice smile named Steve took her out to a fancy restaurant. I remember she was excited about the date, and took extra care to dress up. I watched her put her long, dark hair in a French roll and slip on her best Cubic Zirconia earrings. I remember thinking she looked beautiful. By that point, my mom wasn't leaving me with a sitter when she went out or to work. I remember feeling proud I'd managed to make my own dinner of mac 'n cheese, so Mom didn't have to.

When they returned from their date, Mom invited Steve in for a slice of pie. She left Steve in the living room, where I was watching TV. Steve asked me if I wanted to see a magic trick.

"Sure," I said.

He beckoned me over and had me sit on his lap. I don't

remember much about the trick—something involving a disappearing coin. What I do remember is his hand on my knee, inching up my leg, under the hem of my nightgown. Then, Mother, coming out of the kitchen with a slice of cherry pie.

I remember her screaming at Steve, and him holding up his hands, proclaiming his innocence. "I didn't do anything to her, Denise!" he said. "I swear I didn't!"

I slid off his lap and onto the floor, my nightgown creeping up to my thighs. I looked from Steve to my mom.

As I tugged the gown down, over my knees, Mom threw the pie at Steve, plate and all. He ducked, and the plate hit the wall behind him, shattering and leaving a streak of red sliding down the wall. Cherries and chunks of pie crust landed on the couch. I crawled away and hid under the coffee table.

Steve, unscathed except for a blob of cherry juice on the collar of his shirt, ran out the front door, never to return. Mom chased after him, screaming the kind of words she told me never to use.

I stayed under the coffee table for a while. Mother came back in and sank into her favorite chair, crying. I thought she was mad at me, so I went into the kitchen and got a dishrag to clean the pie off the wall and the couch. After a while, Mom got up and found the broom and dustpan, and cleaned up the pieces of the glass plate in silence. When she tucked me into bed, she gave me a sad smile. I guess that meant she forgave me. We never talked about it again.

That wasn't the first time I'd heard Mom scream at somebody. She shouted at people in traffic. She chewed out the repairman over fixing our washer. Mostly she yelled at me, when I didn't get ready for school on time, or I made a mess and didn't clean it up. I thought that was how things were between moms and kids.

The first time I realized other people's families were different from mine was when I was eleven and stayed the night at my friend Janelle's house for her birthday sleepover. Her dad ordered delivery pizza and told us jokes that made us laugh even though they were dumb. Her mom made Janelle a birthday cake with a purple unicorn on it, and in the morning, she cooked us pancakes. My mom didn't like to bake, but she always remembered my birthday, bringing me an ice cream sandwich from the frozen food section of the convenience store where she worked.

What surprised me most about Janelle's family was the lack of yelling. When we stayed up too late giggling, I thought for sure Janelle's mom was going to come upstairs and scream at us to go to bed. She didn't. She just told us, "Lights out, girls," and went back to bed. Simple as that.

I hunkered down into my sleeping bag and thought about that for a long time. It was a moment that would stay with me after the pearls came and I was no longer allowed to spend the night with friends.

4

My mother *hated* messes. Grandpa's farmhouse might have been old and falling apart, but she was obsessive about keeping the place clean. She'd vacuum twice a week, whether the worn shag carpet needed it or not, even though it was only me and her and we didn't have pets. She washed our sheets and towels at least once a week, and put me on toilet cleaning duty, while she scrubbed out the bathtub and sink.

Our kitchen was spotless. She cleaned while she cooked. She'd have soup simmering on the stove and unload the ancient dishwasher and wipe down the countertops. Then, as soon as we were done eating, dishes went straight into the dishwasher. With just the two of us, we didn't have many dirty dishes.

Shedding pearls is *messy*. It didn't matter how careful I tried to be, blood got everywhere—on the floor, my towel, my clothes. I'd learned to sit naked in the empty tub so the pearls would land there. That way they were easy to wash off and collect, and then we could clean the tub afterward. Mother insisted on being present for this ritual, even though I didn't have a stitch of clothing on.

When I was a kid, it didn't bother me so much, but as I grew into my adult body, her being there, watching me shed the pearls, felt more and more intrusive. It wasn't just being naked in front of her. Every time the pearls burst from my skin, I felt sick with a fever and nausea, and I wanted to be alone. But Mother didn't care about my privacy, even though I begged her to let me deal with my illness behind the closed door of the bathroom.

"You'll make a big mess, and I'll have to clean it up anyway," she said. "I might as well be there to help you."

"I can clean up after myself," I assured her.

"You won't," she said. "You never do. The last time you shed, you got blood all over the bath rug, and guess who had to clean that up? That's right, me. Do you know how hard it is to get blood out of a shag rug?" Why we had so much shag carpeting, I'll never know.

I tried to be careful, I really did. But inevitably, as I tried to cleanse my wounds, there would be blood on the washcloth, blood on my bath towel. Sometimes it took a while before I stopped bleeding.

I'd try to help her clean after the pearls came, but she'd dismiss me. "Just get yourself cleaned up," she'd say with a huff. As I washed off in the shower, I'd hear her talking to herself, muttering that she didn't know why our house was always so messy and she was the only one who cleaned it.

I could never please her. Whenever I tried to clean, she'd take over, pointing out how I was doing it wrong. If I gave up trying, she'd yell at me for being lazy. I couldn't win.

That was why I was so careful the next time I shed the pearls. I woke up in the middle of the night, feeling feverish, a sure sign the pearls were coming. I glanced at my bedside clock—it was three in the morning. I laid there in the dark, holding my breath, listening to Mom snore in the next room.

Stealthy as a cat, I left my bedroom and went downstairs. I grabbed two plastic sandwich bags from the kitchen and stole into the bathroom. I locked the door, took off my clothes, put the rubber stopper in the drain, and sat down on the cold porcelain bottom of the tub to wait for the pearls.

A familiar ache ran up and down my spine, sharp pain spreading out like tendrils across my back. I gritted my teeth as the first pearl burst free and landed in the tub next to me. Then, with a faint popping noise, my skin ripped open as pearl after pearl dropped with a clink onto the surface of the bathtub. The air filled with the smell of copper.

When I was finished shedding the pearls, I stepped out of the tub, careful to kick the bath rug out of the way so I didn't bleed on it. I pulled the stopper on the sink and filled it with warm water to wash the pearls. I laid them out on a washrag to dry while I cleaned myself up.

Once I made sure the bathroom was spotless, I counted the pearls. There were 52 of them, and they were perfect—large, round, and luminous. I selected seven and put them in one of the baggies—those were the ones I was saving. I put the rest in the other baggie for my mom. She would be happy to have 45 pearls.

Then I snuck back up to my room, pausing outside my mom's door to make sure I hadn't woken her. I could hear steady snoring. Good.

Silently, I slid out the bottom drawer of my nightstand and placed my pearls on the floor below. I replaced the drawer and then rocked back on my heels to inspect my work. The bottom of the nightstand was flush with the floor, so you couldn't see underneath it. Still not satisfied, I stood and walked over to my bedroom door, taking in the nightstand from that angle. It looked all right. Unless Mother suspected something and ransacked my room, she'd never know I'd hidden the pearls. Seven down, 23 to go.

I put the other bag on top of my nightstand and went back to bed.

Mom shook me awake the next morning, annoyed that I hadn't told her about the pearls.

She held up the baggie I'd placed on top of my nightstand, assessing the crop my body had yielded. "Why didn't you tell me the pearls were coming?"

I frowned. "It was three in the morning, Mom. You were fast asleep."

"Well, wake me up next time," she told me. "And make sure you clean the bathroom."

"I did."

"There was blood in the sink," she said.

There wasn't. I'd been thorough about cleaning every surface, erasing every trace of blood. I was sure of it. But I didn't argue. "Okay. I'll take care of it."

I pulled the covers back over my head, waiting for her to leave the room. When she did, I breathed a sigh of relief.

5

It took until February before I collected enough pearls to leave. In October, I was only able to save two pearls, giving my mother the other 44. The month after, my body produced 53 pearls, so I saved five. I tried to vary the number I gave her, to make the amounts seem arbitrary and natural, and to reflect yields from years past.

It was difficult because Mother still insisted on invading my privacy. I got lucky in December, hiding four pearls under the washcloth next to me while she collected the others. In January, the pearls came in the middle of the night again. I waited to wake Mom up until after I had shed the pearls, placing a baggie at her bedside. She looked at the clock, saw it was two a.m. and then waved me back to bed. I guess she wasn't into getting up that early after all.

January was a banner month. I saved eight pearls, the most I'd been able to collect at one time. The yield in February was smaller, so I could only save five pearls—but that was enough. I had 31 pearls to sell. Still, I waited until mid-March to leave. I wanted to time my trip to be close enough to the harvest of another batch of pearls that I'd have more to sell once I reached my destination.

Mom went grocery shopping on Wednesday mornings. I packed my bag in the early morning hours, long before sunrise: two shirts, two pair of pants, socks, underthings, a heat pack to ease the pain in my aching back, and a suspense novel for the bus. I saved toiletries and the pearls for last, to pack after Mom left. Once she was gone, I sprang into action, raiding the little jar above the fridge where she kept spare change and a few dollar bills. I tucked the money and my state-issued ID into my grandfather's old leather wallet, and shoved that in the back pocket of my jeans.

I didn't have a cell phone—Mom never would have allowed it, and besides, I had no one to call. If I decided I needed one for my new business of selling the pearls, I could buy a cheap burner in Portland.

The most sentimental thing I took with me was my backpack, a relic from my days in middle school. It looked like a little kid's bag, with iron-on patches of a unicorn and a rainbow. It didn't matter. I could buy something in a more grown-up style once I found a place to stay.

I grabbed my hoodie and winter jacket and was out the door within fifteen minutes, walking toward the jeweler's. I stayed off the streets Mom might drive down, not running, but walking fast.

Mr. Whittier gave me a suspicious look when I showed him my haul. "You didn't steal these pearls, did you?"

"No, sir," I told him. "They're mine to sell." He had no idea how true that was.

"All right. I had to ask," he said, still hesitant to do business with me. He studied my face. "Do I know you?"

I didn't want to tell him the truth about that, so I held out my hand for him to shake and said, "Jessica Smith. I'm from around here. We've probably bumped into each other before." I tried to sound more confident than I felt.

"Well, that explains it," he said. He hadn't seen me in almost a decade, but I looked enough like my mother that he'd notice the resemblance if I told him who I really was. No chance of that.

"How much would you be willing to give me for these?" I asked. "They're South Sea pearls, and as you can see, they're of a fine quality. They'd look lovely as a pair of earrings or a bracelet." I didn't have enough pearls to make a strand for a necklace, but I crossed my fingers he'd still be interested.

"Hmm…they *are* fine quality," he said, murmuring his agreement as he assessed the pearls. "Not the best I've seen, mind you, but fine enough."

I held my tongue, trying not to take the slight personally. There was no way he could know these pearls came from the same source as those my mother sold him. The pearls he was looking at were of the exact same quality. He was employing a bargaining tactic.

"How does $2,500 sound?" he asked.

He was low-balling me on the price. The pearls were worth more than that—at least $100 each, but I was in a hurry. More so when I saw a silver car that looked a lot like my mom's Civic drive past the jewelry shop windows. "Sounds good," I said.

I wasn't sure that would be enough to rent an apartment in Portland, but it would be enough to buy my bus ticket and pay for a hotel room until my next crop of pearls arrived in a few days. Maybe I'd find a jeweler in the city who would give me a better price.

Mr. Whittier counted out the cash in twenties, and I was on my way, putting sixty bucks in my wallet and the rest in my backpack.

I made it to the bus station with little time to spare. It was eleven a.m. and my bus was leaving in a half hour. I realized my first mistake as I purchased my ticket. When I had mapped out my trip to Portland, I had planned on a five-hour drive. Going by bus took longer than if I were driving my own car, because of stops along the way. I'd reach the bus station in Portland around seven that night.

That worried me. I hadn't booked a hotel because I needed a credit card to do that online, and I didn't have one. I didn't like the idea of wandering the city after dark. I just hoped I could find a place to spend the night that took cash. Luckily, my bus ticket only set me back $32. If I had a car, gas alone might have cost that much.

I thanked the ticket vendor and hurried to the station gift shop to buy snacks for my trip—a sandwich, a candy bar, and a bottle of water—nothing too fancy. I had to be frugal and make my money stretch. I was surprised by how much food cost—I wasn't sure what to expect since Mom was the one who did the grocery shopping.

I kept an eye out for my mom, convinced she'd show up at any moment and make me come home. My anxiety didn't ease until I was safely on the bus and it was pulling away from the curb. Guilt washed over me. I hadn't even left Mother a note. What would she think happened to me? Would she be sad I'd left? Or just sad to lose the pearls?

Plagued by bad thoughts, I focused on the passing landscape, watching as it turned greener the further north we traveled. I didn't want to think about the past, and the future was frightening, with too many unknowns to predict what might happen. I munched on my sandwich and escaped into my novel. Eventually, the motion of the bus lulled me to sleep. That was good, because I hadn't slept much the night before, and I certainly didn't sleep well during the nights that followed.

6

When I exited the bus station in Portland, visitor's map of the city in hand, one of the first things I saw was the red brick Union Station clock tower. The sky above it was dark and heavy with clouds, and as I stepped out on to the sidewalk, rain began to fall. I pulled up my hood and started walking south on Sixth Avenue toward Glisan Street, thinking I might find a hotel. I had mapped out a few possibilities as I planned my trip, but actually being in the city was more intimidating than I thought it would be. It took me several minutes to get my bearings.

The city was louder than I was used to—Roseburg was smaller, with less traffic. The smells were different too—fresh bread from a bakery and exhaust from a passing truck.

As I waited to cross Flanders Street, I noticed bars on the windows of a deli, and a group of homeless people huddled together against a building. I started to wonder if I'd landed in a bad part of town. I shifted my backpack, making sure my straps were secure.

My fears were realized soon after that. I crossed Everett and moved to the other side of the street when I saw a trio of large men headed my way. They looked scary, but they weren't who I should have been afraid of.

As I passed an empty storefront, a bearded man standing next to the plate glass window grabbed my arm and pulled me into the shadowed alcove that served as the store's front entrance. He smelled like he hadn't showered in days, and his breath reeked of cheap alcohol. He shoved me up against the metal security bars of the door and held a hunting knife against my ribs.

"Your backpack now," he growled, "or I'll gut you like a fish."

I froze in fear, unable to move. He had a scar above his right eyebrow, and his eyes narrowed in anger when I was slow to comply. He pushed the blunt edge of the blade into my side, not cutting me, but showing me he was serious.

Terrified, I let the backpack slip off my shoulders. He ripped it away from me and drove his fist into my stomach. I doubled over in pain as he ran off, disappearing into the storm.

Trembling, I crumpled to the sidewalk, trying to breathe after getting the wind knocked out of me. Tears pricked my eyes, threatening to fall. I let them. I pulled my knees to my chest and cried, watching the rain fall. I felt defeated.

I hadn't been in the city a half hour, and already I'd lost everything I owned.

7

I had nowhere to go. I was stuck in a large city foreign to me, with a twenty-dollar bill and change in my wallet and the clothes on my back.

I left the shelter of the storefront and walked south, looking up and down the street for someone who could help me. I didn't see any friendly faces. People hurried about their business, not making eye contact.

I was cold and wet, and getting wetter by the minute as fat raindrops drummed on my head and shoulders. Even the hoodie I wore under my winter jacket felt damp, and my socks were getting soaked inside my sneakers. I sought refuge under the awning of a coffee shop as I tried to figure out what to do.

I couldn't spend the night in a hotel like I'd planned, not with the little money I had left. How could I have lost thousands of dollars, just like that? I felt hollowed out by the loss. I still had my state-issued ID, thank goodness. I'd stuffed my wallet in my coat pocket rather than put it in my backpack—otherwise it too would have been stolen. I don't know what I would have done if I'd lost my ID. It was the only thing I had to prove my identity, and I was lucky to have it. Mother wouldn't allow me to get my driver's license so I never learned how to drive. That was just another tool she used to keep me dependent on her. But she had to let me get my ID so I could test for my GED. I'd pestered her about it until she finally gave in.

I rubbed my hands together, trying to work feeling into my numb fingers, wishing I'd had the foresight to pack gloves. Portland was much colder than Roseburg. I thought March would be warm, but hadn't expected a spring storm. The icy wind whipping between the towering buildings bit through my damp clothes, forcing me up against the brick of the coffee shop, cowering against the cold. The sun had set, leaving me alone in the dark in this terrifying city.

For one awful moment, I missed my mom. I could call her, and she would come get me. She'd take me back home—no doubt about that—but would anything change? Would she allow me to have my own life, or would I be returning to a prison? She would consider my running away a betrayal and hold a grudge over my head as though it were a bludgeon. Home might be safer than where I was now, but here, out in the wide, dangerous world, at least I was free. Having tasted freedom, could I go home? No, I decided. I had to attempt to make this work, even if I froze to death trying. I pictured myself spending the night huddled under a bridge. Not what I had in mind when I'd planned my escape.

I started back toward the bus station. It didn't take long to arrive, considering I'd only gotten a few blocks when I'd been robbed, but walking into the wind slowed me down. I shuffled along hunched over, hands stuffed in my pockets, trying to keep the wind from stealing my heat. My efforts weren't successful.

By the time I blew into the station, I was shivering uncontrollably. I hurried into the ladies' room and hit the button on the hand dryer, kneeling down to warm up under the hot air. I'd kept my hood up, but my hair lay limp and wet on my shoulders. I squeezed moisture out of the strands and unzipped my coat to dry my hoodie and t-shirt. It helped—I was still cold, but could speak without my teeth chattering. I lifted my shirt—no bruise where the guy punched me, but my ribs felt sore where he'd dug in with the knife. It could have been worse. He could have stabbed me and left me for dead. That I'd escaped mostly unscathed was a small comfort. I tugged down my shirt and went to look for someone who could help me.

There was a woman at the traveler's aid desk. Maybe she would know of a place where I could stay for the night. She was about my mother's age and her name badge said, *Hi! I'm Mary.* She stared intently at the computer screen in front of her. I cleared my throat. "Excuse me, ma'am?"

She looked up, as if startled to see someone standing in front of her. "Yes? How can I help you?"

"Hi, I just got to Portland, on the bus, and some guy stole my backpack. All my stuff was inside."

"Oh! I'm sorry. Would you like me to call the police?" she asked, genuine concern in her eyes.

That was a bad idea—the police would call my mom and send me home. "No," I said quickly. I gave her a small smile, like losing the only belongings I had was no big deal. "It's not worth calling the police. I was just wondering if you knew of a place where someone like me could stay for the night. I, uh, don't have much money. He took that too."

The woman gave me a look of sympathy. "A shelter?" she asked. I nodded. She reached for a tabbed binder on her desk, found the section she wanted, and ran her finger down the listings. "Columbia Shelter might be able to assist you. They're on 4th and Washington, a few blocks south. If you like, I could give them a call and see if they have a bed available."

"Yes, please."

She picked up her phone and dialed the number. She

explained my situation and then held her hand over the receiver to ask, "Are you a minor?"

I shook my head. "No, ma'am. I'm 21."

"What's your name, honey?"

"Amelia."

"Ah." She put the phone back to her ear. "An adult female, yes. Any beds?" She listened and then nodded. "Yes, very good. I'll send Amelia right over. Thank you." She hung up and turned to me. "It's a cold night, so they're just about full. But they've got one bed left and they're saving it for you."

Relief washed over me. "Thank you," I said. "Thank you so much."

"You're welcome, sweetie," the woman said, giving me a kind smile. She retrieved a map, took out a pen, and circled the location of the shelter for me. "Stay safe and warm. I hope things go better for you."

The shelter was a hive of activity when I arrived, with people preparing to bed down for the night. There were men and women of all ages at the shelter, even a handful of kids. One old man spoke overly loud, trying engage two women close by, but most people kept to themselves, finding a place to sleep. I saw a haggard-looking woman tucking in a small girl, pulling the blankets to her chin. The child didn't look sleepy just yet, taking in the scene with wide eyes. She clutched a stuffed yellow dog to her chest as though she were afraid her toy could be snatched away at any second. I understood the feeling.

I was assigned a cot and given a clear plastic bag filled with hygiene products—a small bottle of body wash, a washcloth, a toothbrush, toothpaste, and a comb. A meal wasn't provided, but the worker doing check-in told me the shelter had coffee and tea available, and there was a food truck two blocks down that sold inexpensive sandwiches. I could have braved the cold again, but I was so grateful to get out of the storm that I ignored my growling stomach. Instead, I poured myself a cup of hot tea and sat on the edge of my cot, people watching. The tea heated my insides and the warmth emanating from the cup thawed my frigid fingers.

After I finished my drink, I shrugged out of my winter coat and spread it at the foot of my bed. Scared someone might steal it, I debated taking it with me to the restroom, but decided it wouldn't go far if someone did. Nobody wanted to be out in the freezing rain.

I grabbed the plastic toiletry bag and headed to the ladies' room to wash up. Standing at the sink, I combed out my wet hair and braided it, securing it with a black elastic band I found in the pocket of my hoodie. I brushed my teeth and headed back to my cot, relieved to see that my coat was still there. I laid out my hoodie to dry, slipped off my sneakers and socks and placed them under the cot, and crawled under the warm blankets wearing my jeans and t-shirt. After my long, exhausting day, it was no wonder I fell asleep in minutes.

I slept like the dead until I woke to a creaking noise, the sound of someone sitting up on a cot a row over. In the near dark, I saw a man throw off his blanket and saunter over to the restrooms. As he passed under the industrial light fixture marking the hallway leading to the men's room, the harsh glare of the bulb illuminated his face. I gasped, recognizing him. It was the bearded man who had hurt me and stolen my backpack.

Frightened, I sat up, clutching my blanket to my chest. I let out a ragged breath and looked over at his cot. There was a dark shape under his bed—a bag of some kind. My fear turned to anger—my backpack! I knew it was mine because I could make out the shapes of the unicorn and rainbow patches on the front pocket. I had to grab my bag before he came back—if he caught me, he might make good on his promise to gut me like a fish. I stuffed my socks into my sneakers and scooped them up, along with my hooded jacket and coat. Then I padded over to his cot, swept the bag out from underneath it with my bare foot, picked it up, and slipped the backpack over my shoulder before scurrying off to the ladies' room. I had a moment of sheer terror as I entered the hallway. I heard heavy footsteps in the men's room and then someone coughed. I ducked into the women's room and didn't look back, heading straight for the largest stall.

Once I had locked the door, I hung up my coat and hoodie and slipped on my socks and shoes, ready to run or fight if I had to. Then I inspected the backpack. It *was* mine, but most of my belongings were gone, probably tossed into a garbage can. I wouldn't have expected the cash to still be there—that was too much to ask—but it would have been nice to have a fresh change of clothes. Instead, I found part of a subway sandwich wrapped in butcher paper, several wadded-up dollar bills, and a bag of rolled up joints, probably pot.

Growing up as sheltered as I had, I'd never actually seen marijuana—it could have been cilantro for all I knew. Funny story —Mom had lectured me about the dangers of drugs over and over, trying to scare me into walking the straight and narrow, even though I never left the house. She would have had an aneurism if she saw me holding that baggie of joints, breathing in their strange aroma. The thought made me laugh. Still, I wondered if the pot had been financed by money I had literally bled for. I'm not ashamed to say I got sick pleasure from flushing the joints down the toilet. You take my cash, I flush your weed. That's fair, right? The half-eaten sandwich I threw in the trash.

After that, I put on my hoodie and coat, hiding the backpack between my layered clothing. Then I booked it. The digital clock over the front door to the shelter read five a.m. An early start to my day, but it's not like I could sleep after that, knowing the guy who robbed me had been camped out in the same room.

I got out my map and wandered the streets until I found a food cart that sold breakfast sandwiches and coffee for five bucks. The skies had cleared but the air was still brisk. I sat on the steps of Pioneer Courthouse Square, munching my egg and sausage sandwich and watching the city wake up. Joggers ran by, and a couple walked their corgi. I studied my map, planning my next steps. I couldn't go back to that shelter, and I only had enough money for a few humble meals.

The sun warmed the bricks on the steps. I raised my face to the light and closed my eyes. After being so cold the day before, I understood why reptiles basked in the sun. The heat felt good, especially on my back, which ached. It always ached, to be honest, but in the days leading up to a fresh harvest, the pain intensified. The only remedy was a heat pack, but since the one I'd put in my backpack had been taken, the sun would have to do. I figured I only had a day or two until the new pearls were ready. If I could hold out until then, I could find a jeweler to buy them and have money to find a safe place to stay.

I opened my eyes and looked at my map again, curious if any jewelers were listed in the business directory on the back. None that I could see, but then I spotted something else that might be of help: the Multnomah County Central Library. Not a bad place to spend the day, and I could use their computers to research jewelers and places to stay. It was only four blocks west. I rose to my feet and started walking.

8

The library was the most beautiful building I'd laid eyes on, with arched windows on the outside and marble pillars inside. There was nothing like it in the town where I'd grown up. We had some pretty Victorian houses in Roseburg, but nothing so regal as this. I tried not to let my mouth gape at the wonders I was seeing—towering ceilings with massive bronze chandeliers, grand staircases, and of course, books—more books than I'd ever seen in my life. I loved books. They were the one thing Mother never denied me.

She wouldn't let me attend school with other kids, but each month she brought me a stack of books from our tiny branch library. I read in my room after doing my lessons at the kitchen table. Mom was almost apologetic about this one extravagance, as though she were acknowledging, in her own, limited way, that I was a prisoner and she had to make up for it somehow.

I wasn't allowed to go out in my own backyard, but I could travel the universe through books, visiting times and places I'd never reach in real life. I'd escaped to hundreds of other worlds before I fled home. I bet Mother never imagined books could have given me the courage to leave. If she had, she would have shielded me from the stories of adventure I consumed like I needed them to breathe.

But I hadn't come to the Multnomah Library to read, much as I would have liked to. Given the chance, I could have happily lived and worked here, but of course, that wasn't an option. Instead, I went to the circulation desk and asked if I could use a computer to do research.

"What kind of research?" the man at the desk asked. "Maybe I can help." He looked about ten years older than me, and rather dapper in a vest and bow-tie. I felt underdressed in jeans and sneakers.

I was out of place, and it made me nervous. I forced myself to meet his gaze, squaring my shoulders like I belonged here in this gorgeous building. Of course I did, why wouldn't I? I was scared he'd peg me as a fraud and send me back to the street. "This woman doesn't have a library card!" he'd yell, alerting library security. Ridiculous, I know, but I felt like a fake, like everyone could tell I was an outsider just by the way I was dressed. I cleared my throat. "I'm doing a job search. I'm looking for a position in the jewelry industry."

The man smiled and his eyes were kind. He didn't push a secret button on his desk to call the library cops on me. Instead, he said, "Sure, I can help with that. Follow me." He led me over to a bank of computers and showed me how to access the browser and do a search for local jewelers.

"I'm looking for someone who specializes in pearls," I told him. "I used to work for a woman who sold them." A lie, but more believable than the truth.

"Okay," the librarian said, and quickly pulled up a list of jewelers in a two-mile radius. He printed the list and handed it to me.

"Wow," I said, studying the list. "You're fast."

He laughed. "Thanks. I do my best." He spotted the map

sticking out of my coat pocket. "You can use that to pinpoint the locations. Or Google, which is faster. If you need to use the printer again, that's fine."

"Thanks," I said, giving him a smile. "Do you know anything about apartments in Portland? Any place affordable to stay?"

He scoffed and then gave me a good-natured grin. "Well, there's the Pearl district, but that's not for the likes of us lesser mortals. Much too expensive."

I laughed, covering my surprise at the district's name. Given a fine enough crop, it might not be so farfetched for some of us commoners, but I couldn't tell him that. Besides, I needed to save my money and keep a low profile. Attracting attention was a bad idea—that's one lesson Mom taught me that I'd taken to heart. "Okay, anything for us peasants?"

"The further outside the city center, the less expensive it is for the most part. I found a decent place in Beaverton, and I ride the MAX to work. There's a station near my complex, and the commute's not too bad," he said. "Good way to catch up on reading."

I'd seen the light rail around the city and figured I might need to use it at some point. I was relieved he recommended it, because I was worried about using public transportation and getting mugged again. Maybe it was safer than I thought. "Sold. Now if I can just find that job."

"Good luck." He nodded to the computer. "Stay as long as you like to do your research. We're open until 6."

"Thanks," I said, taking a seat. He nodded and left me to my work. I didn't stay long. After he went back to his desk, I did a quick search for shelters, too embarrassed to do that kind of research in front of someone, especially a dashing older man. Given my lack of experience with men—or anyone beyond my miniscule circle of contact from home—social interaction was difficult.

I'd avoided interacting with people on my bus ride here and that didn't work out, did it? Perhaps if I'd made a friend on the bus, I wouldn't have been walking the city streets by myself. I'd left myself vulnerable because I was alone in a new place. But there was a difference between being alone and being independent. If I was strong, it wouldn't matter if I was alone. I could face whatever dangers I encountered.

If I was going to make it on my own, I had to be different than the person I'd been for the last decade, locked away in isolation. I thought about all the lives I'd lived through books, how the heroines in the stories I read met challenges with humor and insouciance. The kind of person who laughed in the face of danger and slayed adversaries with wit. I wanted to be that girl.

I would be, once I got started in my new life. But first, I needed to find someplace safe to stay until the next harvest. I found a few possibilities and marked them on my map.

I spent the afternoon walking the city, visiting shelters and jewelry shops. It did not go well. The first jewelry shop I visited had a poster taped to the front window saying it had gone out of business. The second one looked like a pawn shop, with electronics, katana swords, and guitars behind the iron bars of the front window. Peering in, I saw guns and knives displayed behind the sales counter. Given the unsavory characters hanging out on a nearby street corner, I decided it wasn't the sort of place I wanted to do business with. I didn't want to get cheated. Or stabbed.

I didn't even bother with chain stores—the sales associates wouldn't be authorized to make a deal with me, and the managers would want to promote their own brand. I'd learned from Mom that small businesses were best for selling our pearls, particularly jewelers who specialized in loose gems.

The third shop, closer to the famed Pearl District, looked decent. Elegant even, with an art deco façade and interior. The sign over the door said *Gatsby's*. I approached the woman at the counter, who wore her blond hair in a sophisticated updo. She looked like she was in her 50s, and she wore a choker of pearls around her throat. I took that as a positive sign.

I patted down my hair and introduced myself. "Good afternoon. My name is Amelia Weaver. I have a business proposition for you." I held out my hand to her.

She arched a sculpted eyebrow and shook my hand. "Margaret Beck. How may I help you?"

I tried to project the same confidence I'd shown the librarian. "I'm in the pearl business, and I'm looking for new buyers."

She looked me up and down. That was a bad sign. I wished, not for the first time that day, I still had a fresh change of clothes. The jeans and sneakers look wasn't selling this. It would have been better to dress up. "What kind of pearls?" she asked, skeptical.

I smiled. "I specialize in South Sea pearls, high luster. I'm in the import business."

"No offense, but you seem a bit young."

I nodded. "None taken. I get that a lot, but I've been in this field for nearly ten years. I started out in the family business, but recently moved to Portland to branch out on my own. We've sold thousands of pearls, and I've worked with several buyers across Southern Oregon." Technically, not a lie.

She scowled and studied my face, probably trying to figure out if I was for real or not. "Well, can you show me a sample?"

My smile widened. "I've got a shipment coming in a few days and could stop back in to show you. Would that be all right?"

She looked around the shop, gazing at diamond dazzlers and gold cuffs displayed on black velvet. "I don't carry a lot of pearls, but I might consider expanding my selection if the pearls were of high enough quality."

"They will be." I held out my hand again. "Thank you. I'll come back later this week."

She shook my hand absently. “Sure. We’ll see what you’ve got to offer.”

Buoyed by a potential buyer, I decided it was time to look for a shelter. I could feel the pearls working their way to the surface of my skin. My back was itchy and inflamed. Another two days and they’d be out. I’d need a clean place with some privacy to shed the pearls, preferably with a sink or shower to clean myself up afterward. I’d gotten to be pretty good at handling the pain, gritting my teeth to stay quiet, but the amount of blood involved would be alarming to anyone who stumbled upon the carnage.

9

I had zero luck finding a place to stay for the night. I tried four different shelters and all of them were full because the overnight temperature was going to drop below freezing. This was unusual for a night in March, and people were unprepared for weather that felt more like winter than spring. Nobody wanted to be caught in the cold.

I even went back to the shelter I'd stayed at the night before, but the guy taking reservations said I'd failed to follow check out protocol and they'd given my cot to someone else. Just as well—I didn't want to encounter my assailant again.

Frustrated, I forced one weary foot in front of the other, dragging myself back to the library for more research. By that time, it was nearly five, and I'd only have an hour to come up with other ideas before the place closed.

As I hunched over the keyboard at my computer station, I heard a crash behind me. "Finn!" a woman hissed, clearly agitated, but trying to keep her voice down. I peeked over my shoulder to see a woman kneeling next to a six-year-old kid whose arms were filled with picture books. Next to them was an upturned succulent in a cracked pot, soil fanning out from where the container had rolled to a stop.

The boy looked up at his mother with a scrunched-up face and tear-filled eyes. "I just wanted to touch it." The woman looked distraught—torn between wanting to comfort the child and chide him for knocking the plant off the window sill behind us.

I heard quick footsteps on the carpeted floor. "It's quite all right," a man said, the same librarian who had helped me that morning. "I've got this."

"Thank you," the mother said. "I can grab a broom or a dustpan or…"

The librarian knelt down and gave the boy a smile. "It's okay—don't give it another thought." He read the title of one of the books the boy was holding. "*The Day the Crayons Quit*. That's a good one. Have you checked out your books yet?" The man picked up the broken pot, gathering a couple of stray shards from the floor.

"No, we were just about to," the mother answered.

"Let's go do that, and then I'll finish with this," he said. He carried the pot to a garbage bin, carefully placed it inside, and headed toward the circulation desk. The boy and his mother dutifully followed.

"Need any help?" a young woman asked, approaching the desk.

"Sure, Tiff," the librarian said as he scanned the barcodes on the little boy's books. "Could you grab the vacuum cleaner from the custodian closet? I don't think Patricia will be in tonight to clean—she caught that flu that's going around."

Suddenly I knew where I was going to spend the night. Quietly, I closed my browser and slipped my backpack over my shoulder. The young woman—Tiff or maybe Tiffany—headed down the hallway toward a staircase. I trailed behind at a distance, stopping to admire an abstract painting on one of the walls so she wouldn't notice me following her. Then I watched out of the corner of my eye as she opened a door under the stairs. She reached in to flip a light switch and then grumbled under her breath when the light fixture in the closet stayed dark. She disappeared from my view for a moment as she stepped into the closet and fumbled around looking for something. She resurfaced pushing a vacuum cleaner that looked thirty years past its prime.

I waited for her to pass me and watched as she headed back to the main room to clean up the soil on the floor. Then I sauntered over to the closet. The door was ajar, and I inspected the knob to make sure I wouldn't be trapped if it locked. Satisfied, I looked around at the contents in the dim light from the hallway, memorizing the location of a shelf with cleaning supplies, a mop and yellow bucket with wheels, and a tower of stacked boxes. There was an empty space toward the back of the closet, behind the boxes. I slipped in and scrunched down, hiding from view. I could hear the roar of the vacuum, and then a few minutes later, the sound of its wheels clacking on marble tile as Tiff returned the vacuum cleaner to the closet. I flinched as she closed the door and I was left in complete darkness. Then I waited.

10

I'm not sure how long it took for everyone to leave the library when it closed for the day. Twenty minutes? A half hour? It was difficult to know in the dark. I waited until it was utterly silent and then waited some more, just to be sure. When I finally inched over to the closet door and turned the knob, it was almost seven, by the clock in the hall.

It seemed like the library staff had been a skeleton crew that day—maybe staff members had been out sick because of that flu the librarian mentioned. I stood perfectly still in the hallway by the storage closet, listening. Nothing. Everyone was gone for the night. The lights in the main room had been dimmed, but there was still a light on over the circulation desk. There were cameras too.

I'd noticed them earlier, in the main area of the library and above the circulation desk. I was sure there were more, and I didn't know if they were a live feed or who might be watching. I would need to be careful. I pulled my hood up and decided that looked sketchy even though it hid my face. I had to look like I had a legitimate reason to be in the library after hours. I peered back into the closet. I grabbed the mop, stuck it in the yellow bucket, and rolled it out, gripping the handle on the mop.

I realized I had my backpack on and that would seem odd for a custodian. I stepped back into the closet, took off the backpack and my coat, and then put the backpack on again, wearing it under my coat. I imagine it gave me a hunchback appearance, but I didn't want to leave anything behind to improve my disguise. If I got caught, I'd have to run.

I rolled the mop bucket along and went exploring, keeping my head down whenever I spotted a camera. Several rooms of the library had couches that looked comfy, but I was scared to sleep there. It felt too open and exposed. I needed some place where I'd have warning if I had a visitor. I made my way to the librarians' offices. The wooden door wasn't locked. Maybe whoever usually cleaned needed access.

The librarians' area didn't have cameras. It included a large office for the head librarian and work spaces for other staff, carved into a large room. Some desks were out in the open and others were partitioned off in cubicles. None looked like good places to rest, unless I wanted to squeeze underneath a metal desk that looked like it had been manufactured in the 60s. Then I stumbled upon the lounge, and miracle of miracles, it had everything I needed.

There was a shabby blue couch that was surprisingly comfy, in spite of a tear on one of the cushions where the stuffing poked out. There was even a throw pillow set on one end. There was a kitchenette on one side of the room, with a sink, microwave, and mini-fridge. An inspection of the fridge yielded treasure: a to-go box of Kung Pao chicken and chow mein, a banana, an apple, half a grilled cheese sandwich in a plastic bag, a bottle of water, and a carton of milk. My stomach growled at the sight of this feast. I hadn't eaten anything since breakfast. I was going to hell for sure for stealing food from librarians, but I was desperate. I promised myself I'd write down the address of the library and donate cash anonymously to atone for my sins.

In the cabinet above the sink, I found a coffee mug. I poured myself a glass of tap water and chugged it down, then filled the mug again. I'd save the other beverages for later, putting them in my backpack before I left. Then I nuked the Chinese food and ate until my stomach bulged. I didn't know how long it might be before my next solid meal, so I had to eat while I could. The sandwich and fruit would work for breakfast.

Before I settled in for the night, I found a humble staff bathroom with a pedestal sink. I used the toiletries I'd gotten from the shelter to clean up and wash my long hair, which was starting to feel greasy and unkempt. On my way back to the lounge I spotted a cardboard box filled with t-shirts with various slogans promoting reading, like *Reading Rocks!* and *The Book Was Better*. I found two in my size and swiped them, adding the cost to my growing library tab. I considered leaving a note of apology in the box, but didn't want to further incriminate myself.

As I lay down on the couch, adjusting the throw pillow for my head, I realized I didn't have an alarm to wake me up. It wouldn't be prudent to stay too long, risking the staff finding me sleeping the next morning—I imagined opening my eyes to find the library director staring down at me, shaking her finger at my t-shirt theft. It was a horrifying thought.

I didn't own a watch—I'd never had a use for one under Mom's roof. She set my schedule so there was no need for me to keep track of time. It's not like I had anywhere I needed to be, like a job. Mother made sure of that.

I sat up on the couch. There was a clock in the lounge, but not the kind with an alarm. I glanced over at the kitchenette. The microwave had a timer. I tested it—it would allow me to set the timer in four-hour increments. Not ideal, but it would do. I'd have to get up early anyway so I could slip out unnoticed.

I ended up waking at 4:30 in the morning without needing the timer. I'm not an early riser, but I'd been under a lot of stress and slept fitfully, worried about getting caught. I packed up the food in the fridge quickly and was on my way out of the offices when I remembered the mop bucket. I went back for it and then retraced my steps to the storage closet.

Hood up and head down, I headed to a side exit. I almost pushed through the door when I noticed a neon orange placard: *Alarm will sound.* I stared at it, hand on the push bar, and slowly backed away, as if I'd nearly set off a bomb. I had neglected to think this through.

I checked the main doors to the library and found I'd need a key to get out. They were probably similarly alarmed. I was trapped. I thought about it and decided to wait things out in the custodian closet. Once the library was open for the day, I could just walk out. No one would suspect I'd spent the night, unless they checked the security footage for the main areas of the library. And if they questioned my presence, fingers crossed, my role play with the mop bucket might dissuade them from pegging me as a trespasser. It was a risk, but I didn't have other options. I'd just never come back here again, which was a shame, because I would have loved checking out the books in their collection.

I sat crisscross in the dark closet, munching on the banana to pass the time. I still hadn't shed this month's pearls, so I had nothing to show the woman at Gatsby's, but I could try the other jewelers on my list. It wouldn't hurt to have backup buyers. I'd also have to find a new place to stay. Another stellar day in the City of Roses.

11

I struck out completely that day: no pearls, no deals to sell them, no place to spend the night. I did find a 24-hour diner called the Rose City Pancake Palace—I settled into a booth after ten, when I could no longer take the cold and the rain.

I managed to stretch out my cheap meal for an hour and then bought myself more time with a coffee. My server didn't seem to mind. Hardly anyone was out at that hour, and the few people who were in the restaurant seemed to be in similar straits, all of us with nowhere to go, avoiding the icy rain pattering against the picture windows of the Pancake Palace.

Just before midnight, a familiar pain arched up my spine, and nausea washed over me. I took a deep breath to settle my stomach, grabbed my backpack, and made a beeline for the restroom. The largest stall was unoccupied, thank goodness, and I grabbed a massive wad of paper towels as I rushed by. I'd shed pearls a hundred times since they first started growing, and it was never pretty.

I'd gotten better about handling the pain, gritting my teeth against sharp, biting pangs that felt like needles piercing me from inside, and then the ripping sensation as the pearls burst free from my skin. I could get through that part, because I knew the pain would stop.

Once the pearls were shed, the aches that steadily increased over the week prior would be gone, and I'd feel, not exactly healthy, but normal. Like a regular human being who didn't have to deal with this. I admit, I didn't really know what that would be like. The pearls and the pain consumed so much of my waking thoughts, I couldn't fathom my life without them.

I couldn't imagine not having to hide an essential part of myself. Dressing to hide my scars. Shedding in secret so no one would ever know what I was. Mother told me over and over that the pearls were a gift—like somehow that would make living like this tolerable—but I never felt special. I just felt alone.

I felt more alone than ever kneeling on the dirty floor of that Pancake Palace restroom, praying nobody would barge in while I was trying not to scream or vomit. I felt exposed too, because I had to remove my hoodie, shirt, and bra so I wouldn't get blood on them. I placed the wadded paper towels around me strategically, to catch the pearls as they fell. I couldn't risk them rolling away.

Afterward, I kept a paper towel handy to dab my open wounds. This wasn't how I wanted this to happen, but I didn't have access to first class amenities. There was no shower to step into, no rush of hot water to soothe my inflamed skin. I didn't dare risk leaving the stall to clean up at the restroom sink because if someone came in and saw me covered in blood, I didn't know how I'd explain it. I had my water bottle, so I used water from that to wet paper towels and wipe away the blood. I had to clean myself up as best I could, and hope I didn't introduce bacteria and end up with an infection. I traded my dirty shirt for one of the clean ones I'd stolen from the library. Then I gathered the pearls and wiped them off before placing them in my backpack.

There were 61 of them, my biggest crop ever. I didn't take

pride in that. They were a means to an end, sacrificing my health to pay the bills. There are better ways to make a living, but not many as lucrative for somebody who barely finished her GED. And it's not like I ever had a choice in the matter. The pearls would grow whether I wanted them to or not.

12

I felt feverish and dizzy after the shedding. I meant to return to my table for another cup of coffee, but after securing the pearls in my backpack, I sat down in the corner of the bathroom stall, trying to stop my head from spinning. I couldn't afford to get sick—not in my current situation. I promised myself that after I sold the pearls, I'd treat myself to a hot shower in a nice hotel. Then I'd sleep for two days at least.

I must have dozed off, because some time later—an hour, I think—I was awakened by someone knocking on the stall door.

"Excuse me, miss? Are you okay?"

I rolled to my knees and got to my feet, holding on to the tiled wall for support. I peeked through the gap at the stall's door and saw the woman who had served my meal. She looked concerned. "Yeah—just having a little stomach trouble," I said. "Be right out."

"Oh, okay. My shift is over, so I'll leave your check with the cashier."

Ah. Not a wellness check—she was worried I was going to skip out. "Yeah. Be out in a sec." What time was it? *Time to get a watch*, I told myself. *Ha ha ha.* I was a real comedian when I was sick and sleep-deprived.

I slipped my coat on, grabbed my stuff, and washed my hands and face. Then I headed out to pay for my meal. It was almost two in the morning, and my worst night in the city so far. There was nowhere I could go to sleep safely, so I wandered the streets, taking refuge in the stairwell of a parking garage for a while to get out of the rain and wind.

The nice thing about being out that time of night is hardly anyone else is. I was scared I'd encounter some drunk, but I guess most of the bars had closed. I spotted homeless people, huddled where they could find shelter from the rain, but they left me alone. They just wanted sleep too.

The streets were quiet, with barely any traffic. I climbed the stairs of the mostly empty parking garage to the roof on the fifth floor, and took in the lights of the city. The rain had transformed to mist, and the moisture felt refreshing on my flushed cheeks. Being in the city still felt strange to me, standing in a place where buildings towered around me, where giant bridges spanned the Willamette River. It was such a contrast to the town I'd grown up in. But I didn't regret leaving, in spite of the rough start I'd had in this city. I didn't know what challenges lay ahead, but I wasn't the same person I'd been when I got on the bus to come here. I felt stronger, more sure of myself. If I could survive the streets of Portland, I could survive anything.

I watched the sun come up, and then went down to the street level to scrounge up breakfast. I had nine dollars in my pocket, but that would change today. Today I'd sell the pearls and my new life would finally begin.

13

Selling the pearls did not go as expected. After all the jewelers I'd visited in the city, Gatsby's was still my best shot, so I went there first. I tried to make myself look as presentable as possible, hoping the well-dressed woman who managed the shop would forgive my appearance once she saw the quality of my pearls. Today Margaret Beck was wearing a black dress, a diamond pendant, and ruby earrings. Her hair was pulled back in a chignon and she looked effortlessly sophisticated. I crossed my fingers and sent up a little prayer.

There was a man in the shop, but he was browsing a case full of sparkling rings. The manager stood at the register, looking through a stack of papers, glasses perched on her nose.

"Good morning, Ms. Beck," I greeted her. She looked up as I approached. "Amelia Weaver. I spoke to you a few days ago about buying pearls. You mentioned I should stop back in when my stock arrived."

The shop manager looked down her glasses at me as though I were an uninvited pest, a mosquito that had flown in on a breeze to harass her customers. After a second, her annoyed expression changed to one of recognition. "Ah—yes, I remember." She eyed my backpack, frowning at the unicorn patch on the front. It wasn't something a professional would carry, but if I could just sell the pearls, I could afford an upgrade. I hoped my desperation didn't show on my face. "Are they in there?" she asked.

I nodded and opened one of the side pockets, drawing forth the pearl I'd selected to show her. I held it out, hardly daring to breathe as I waited for her reaction. As she took the pearl and held it up to the light to inspect it, her eyes brightened. She turned it back and forth, transfixed as she admired the sheen on the surface. Then she set it down on the counter in front of her. "Well, I'll give you this much, it is quite beautiful. How many of these do you have?"

I let out a long breath. "I have 61 now, and I'll have more next month."

"Are they all loose, like this one?"

"They are. I sell them loose so jewelers can use them in any setting they wish. The last jeweler I worked with strung them and sold them in a matinee length. They were a best seller." I wasn't exaggerating. The pearls always sold within days of being displayed. People couldn't resist their allure. I'd say they sold like magic, but the ordeal of growing them didn't feel magical to me.

Ms. Beck put a finger to her lips and tapped absently as she gazed past me, thinking. "I could see them as a pair of earrings, maybe a ring." She turned to me. "How much was your last jeweler willing to pay for each pearl?"

My confidence waivered. "He bought by the strand, so that comes to about $120 a pearl."

"Hmm. I'd have to put them in a setting, so there'd be an additional cost that would affect markup..." She took off her glasses. "Tell you what. I'll give you $500 for five. If they sell, we could consider a contract."

My heart sank. It wasn't as strong a sale as I'd hoped for. Still, it wasn't a no. And if the pearls sold quickly, she'd be open to buying more, and maybe I could renegotiate the price. I forced a smile. "Deal." I opened my bag and took out four more pearls, carefully lining them up along the counter. They were perfect—zero blemishes and remarkably similar in size and luster to the first pearl. I could tell by the look on her face that Ms. Beck was impressed.

She took two and held them up, as if imagining what they might look like as a pair of earrings. "Where did you say you got these?"

"I import them."

"Yes, but from where? Specifically? They look like South Sea pearls."

"They are, but I can't disclose my source."

She gave me a hard look. "But they're not stolen?"

That question again. This time I was prepared for it. I held her gaze. "Absolutely not. Ms. Beck, I realize I don't look like the kind of person you're used to doing business with, but I promise you I am honest and legitimate."

I sensed movement to my right and realized the man who had been looking at rings had drifted closer and was eyeing the pearls. Our eyes met and he looked away, suddenly intensely interested in an emerald necklace in the case in front of him. I flushed, wondering how much of the conversation he'd heard. It bothered me that the manager suspected me of being a thief, though I could understand why she did. I wasn't forthcoming with details. And, if we're being honest, I guess I *was* a thief, considering what I'd done at the library. But I intended to make that right.

Ms. Beck set the pearls back on the counter and turned to the register. "All right. I will take you at your word, and I sincerely hope my trust is well-placed."

"It is," I assured her.

She nodded, and wrote out a receipt, documenting our exchange. She gave me the carbon copy and then opened the register and counted out $500 in twenties. "Here you are, Miss Weaver. How do I contact you if I decide to purchase more pearls?"

I really needed to buy a phone. Thankfully, I had created an email address for my business venture. I gave her that, accepted the money, and stowed it in my backpack. Then I thanked her and left the shop, my mind swirling around the fact that I'd made my first real sale in Portland, and I could now afford a change of clothes and a cheap hotel room. I'd have to make the money stretch though, since a second sale wasn't guaranteed. I wondered how long it would take for the five pearls to sell, how long before I could sell the rest of them and obtain more permanent housing.

I was thinking about what the librarian had told me, about finding cheaper places to stay outside the city center, when I felt a hand on my shoulder. I whipped around, hands gripping the straps of my backpack, ready to protect it at all costs this time. I was not getting mugged again.

"Whoa!" It was the man from the shop. He backed away, hands held up, an apologetic look on his face. "Sorry—didn't mean to startle you."

I kept a firm grip on my bag. "You didn't," I said, though we both knew he had.

He gave me a small smile. "I don't mean to bother you," he said, "but I couldn't help overhearing your conversation in Gatsby's. You sell pearls?"

I looked him over. He might have been in his late twenties, closer to my age than I'd first thought. He had neatly combed blond hair and was well dressed, in a Columbia jacket, a white button down, and khakis. It didn't escape my notice that he was easy on the eyes too. I relaxed a little. "Yes. I'm hoping to get a contract with Gatsby's, but I'm open to other offers. Are you interested in buying some?"

"I might be." He held out his hand in introduction. "My name is Peter Fortunato. I'm in the process of opening a business with my dad on the coast. We're working on a tourist attraction in Seaside."

"Amelia Weaver." I shook his hand. "What sort of tourist attraction?" I asked, wondering what that had to do with pearls.

He looked up at the sky—it had started raining yet again—and then across the street to a café. "Can I buy you coffee? It would be good to get out of the rain."

That was a proposition I could get on board with. "Sure."

We ducked into Mother's Bistro and found a table. He took off his jacket and draped it over the back of his chair. He rubbed his hands together. "This damp cold—it gets into your bones, doesn't it?" He glanced at the menu. "I need soup to warm up my insides. Would you like a bowl too?"

I peeked at the menu. Tomato bisque was the soup of the day—my favorite. It came topped with sour cream and chives, with a side of bread. It sounded heavenly, and I sure wasn't going to turn down a free meal. "That would be nice. Thank you."

He grinned. "My pleasure." After relaying our orders to the server, he tented his hands. "So, like I was saying, my dad and I are opening a new business in Seaside. Are you familiar with the area?"

I shook my head. "I've heard of it, but never visited. I'm from Roseburg."

He nodded. "They have a zoo near there, right?"

"Yeah. Wildlife Safari. My mom took me to see the cheetahs once."

He smiled. "I went when I was a kid. I loved that place."

Our server brought over bread in a basket, and he nodded his thanks. My stomach growled at the smell of freshly baked bread, but I resisted the urge to grab a slice and stuff it in my mouth, letting him make the first move. He took a slice and passed the basket to me. As I buttered a piece of sourdough bread, he continued.

"Seaside is a tourist town. Things are pretty slow during the winter, but it wakes up in late spring when the tourists come in droves to the beach. There's a mom-and-pop aquarium where you can feed seals, Zinger's, where they make the best homemade ice cream, all kinds of shops where you can get salt water taffy, a t-shirt, that kind of thing. My father just bought a building on the main drag—he wants to create a sort of science museum."

I raised an eyebrow. "Sort of science?"

He laughed. I took a bite of bread and studied him. He seemed nervous, but I wasn't sure why. Maybe he was worried I'd think the tourist attraction he was building was a crackpot idea. "It *is* science-based, but the topic is a bit sensational. The museum focuses on human oddities."

I just about choked on my bread. I took a sip of water to clear my throat. "A freak show?" I could almost hear my mother sounding the alarm. *If people knew what you were, what you could do, they'd lock you up,* she had often told me.

He shook his head. "No, definitely not. We highlight mutations to talk about the science behind them, but we humanize the exhibits. It's part history, addressing how people with rare conditions have been alternatively idolized and demonized, but we also want to tell real stories about real people. That's why some of the staff we're hiring have oddities themselves. We want to talk about what it means to be human."

"Why?"

He opened his mouth to answer, but our server came over balancing our meals. Peter thanked her and waited until she was gone before answering. When he did, he kept his voice low. "My father knows what it's like to be ostracized for being odd."

Peter had captured my interest. "Go on." I tasted my soup—just as rich and creamy as I'd hoped.

Peter looked around the café and then back at me as though he was worried about someone overhearing. "Dad grew up in Union City, Michigan. He was born with webbed feet. His family kept his condition secret, out of shame. But when he was in high school, the kids had to shower after gym class and…"

My eyes widened in horror. "People found out." That was exactly what my mother had feared—it was why she hid me away.

Peter nodded. "They called him Daffy Duck after that. That wasn't so bad, but whenever he walked down the hallway at school, this group of older guys would quack at him. It was pretty humiliating. Then things went from bad to worse."

I set my spoon down, riveted by his story. "What happened?"

He stirred his soup absently. "There was a river that ran through town. One day, walking home from school, he ran into those guys on the bridge. They forced him to take off his shoes and ridiculed him for his webbed toes. Then they threw him off the side of the bridge."

I covered my mouth with my hand, holding in my shock.

"He didn't fall far—maybe ten feet to the water, but he couldn't swim. As he thrashed around, trying to stay on the surface, they threw rocks at him from the bridge," Peter said. He gave me a long look. "They were laughing and quacking the entire time."

"I'm so sorry. That's awful."

Peter nodded. "Yeah. He kept going under. He thought he was going to die. Luckily, one of the girls from school lived in a house next to the river. She heard my dad crying out and came to see what was happening. She *could* swim. She dragged him out of the water to the riverbank."

"Wow. Did they go to the police?"

Peter shook his head. "No. You don't go to the police in a small town like that, not when one of the perpetrators is the chief's son. My dad quit school and left town before those guys had another chance to kill him." He gave me a small smile. "But he married the girl, so it worked out for the best."

I returned his smile and grabbed another piece of bread. "Your mom?"

"Yes. She was quite a woman." He took a sip of his soup.

"Was?"

"She passed away five years ago. Cancer."

"I'm sorry."

He shrugged. "We made the most of the time she had. She's the reason we decided to create the museum. She tended to indulge my dad's crazy ideas, so I guess this is our way of honoring her. That and the mermaid."

I stared at Peter. He had a way of speaking in riddles, saying things that seemed to make sense to him, that I had no context to understand. I started to wonder if he was entirely sane. "You lost me—you're saying you have a *mermaid* at the museum?"

Peter chuckled. "Oh, no. Not a real one. More of an idea to promote the museum. My dad used to refer to my mom as 'the mermaid' because of how she rescued him. She could swim like a fish, and she had this long, blond, wavy hair. Dad said she was an otherworldly beauty. He's a bit of a romantic."

I'm not usually the kind of girl who giggles over romance, but that got me. "I guess so."

Peter grinned. "Anyway, this is where your pearls come into the picture. We've got this giant tank, and the plan is to have oysters—fake ones—resting on the bottom and on shelves carved into a rock wall. Some of them will have real pearls in them. Visitors to the museum will have the opportunity to pick an oyster and win a pearl. It's a game of chance, you see."

"And the mermaid?"

"We plan to have a girl dress up like a mermaid and swim down to retrieve the oysters. Kind of over the top, I suppose, but then, that's our shtick." He looked at me appraisingly. "Can you swim?"

"Me? I can, but…" But it had been a while—years—it's not like Mom took me to the YMCA pool after we discovered my so-called gift. I used to love to swim. It was one of the many things I missed about being a normal human being.

"I mean, you kind of look like a mermaid—like you could play the part," he said. He seemed oblivious to my inner turmoil. "It's an easy gig—smiling and waving at the guests underwater, diving down to get the oysters." He demonstrated by smiling and waving like a beauty queen. "You don't have to talk or anything. You just wear the costume, which is pretty cool, by the way. The tail is rubber and the top is covered with shells and glass beads—classy, you know. Old Hollywood glamor."

He seemed sincere, like he was paying me a compliment. I guess he was trying to tell me I was pretty, but I didn't know whether to be flattered or insulted. The job he was offering wasn't exactly on par with the image I was trying to project—that of a business owner, an independent and capable woman on her own. I pictured myself in a bikini top, baring my scars to the world, and frowned. Yeah, there was no way I was playing a mermaid. No way.

"Thank you, but I don't think that's something I'd like to do," I said quietly.

He looked flustered, toying with his napkin before laying it on top of his bread plate. "I—I'm sorry, I didn't mean to offend you."

I raised my chin and looked him in the eye, projecting confidence I didn't feel. "I'm not offended. But I'm not here to play a part. I'm here to sell a product."

He nodded. "I can respect that." He pulled out his wallet. "I'd still like to buy your pearls, if you're willing to sell them to me."

I softened, realizing he really had meant the job offer as a compliment. I didn't exactly look like a business woman, I knew —not with my t-shirt, hoodie, and raggedy winter coat. My middle school backpack didn't help my image either. He probably figured I could use the job. "I'm willing."

"Okay, give me a price. How much did that jeweler offer you?"

For a second, I considered jacking up the price to see how high he was willing to go, but then decided it was better to be honest with him. "One hundred bucks a pearl."

"And she bought five?"

I nodded, relieved I'd been candid. He'd heard more of my conversation with Ms. Beck than I'd thought.

"I'll double that," he said. I watched, my jaw dropping, as he opened his wallet and counted out cash in twenty-dollar bills, placing them in a neat stack on the table. "Ten pearls at $200 each."

It was my turn to be flustered. Once I managed to stop gaping at him like a fish, I said, "That's really generous."

He held my gaze. "It's worth it. Your pearls are better than anything I've seen on the market, and I've been looking for a while. Weeks." He stuffed his wallet back in his pocket. "If we can bring in as many summer tourists as I hope, our proceeds will be more than worth it."

I didn't know what to say as I reached into my bag and selected ten pearls for him. "Well…thank you." I'd gone from pocket change to $2,500 in the space of an hour. It was a dizzying amount of money to unexpectedly have in hand, and felt validating after all the trouble I'd been through since arriving in this city. Maybe I really could make it on my own.

He gave me a shy smile that I found just as dizzying. When he looked at me like that, it felt like the floor dropped right out from underneath me—a falling sensation that was foreign but not unpleasant. I'd never had a man look at me like that before. But then, I'd been locked away like Rapunzel in her tower, so it hadn't been easy to meet people.

"You could come visit us," he said. He glanced out the café window. "I know the big city is more exciting than a small town, but I'd love to show you what we're working on. And if things go well, we'll need to buy more pearls soon."

"A trip to the coast?" I'd never seen the ocean before. I would have gone for that reason alone, but the promise of selling more pearls sealed the deal. "Like, a business trip?"

He turned to meet my gaze. "Do you have a car?"

My mood deflated. "Uh, not yet. I just arrived in the city, so I've been using public transportation." And my feet. Mostly my feet. Besides, I didn't know how to drive.

"Hard to get to the coast without a car, though I guess you could ride the bus," he mused. I didn't tell him I'd had more than my fill of riding busses of late. He looked at his hands, thinking, and then made me a bold offer. "You could ride with me." He glanced down again, backtracking, as though he was afraid he'd overstepped his bounds. "But I'm leaving tomorrow."

"Oh. That's pretty soon." The disappointment I felt was unexpected—I'd just met this guy, but I realized I wasn't quite ready to end our conversation. It was more than the fact that he'd paid a generous amount for the pearls, or that he was handsome, or that I liked how he looked at me. I liked talking to him. I would have thought the idea of taking a road trip with a stranger would scare me, but it didn't. Funny how much I'd changed since leaving home.

"Yeah. I imagine you want to get settled in the city," he said.

I did, mostly because I was hoping to sell more pearls to Gatsby's. But I was worried about stretching my money after I'd been warned about high rent in the city. A thought occurred to me. I didn't have to stay in Portland. I could ship pearls anywhere. And, as a bonus, if Mother came looking for me, she'd never think to look in a small coastal town. “What’s the rent like in Seaside?”

He looked up at me, surprised.

“It’s just that I’m looking for a place here, and rent is pretty high,” I said. “Is Seaside more affordable?”

“It is. Where are you staying now?” he asked.

“A hotel.” Technically a lie, but it would be true soon enough. I couldn’t wait to sleep in an actual bed.

He nodded, considering. “You’re not committed to staying in Portland, but you could still do business here.”

“Exactly. I’d like to keep my options open, see what Seaside’s like.” I gave him a smile. “Since you’ve talked it up so much.” Oh goodness, now I was flirting with him.

He rewarded me with a grin that gave me that sensation of falling again. I felt reckless, and I didn’t care. “All right,” he said. “I’ll pick you up tomorrow at ten. It’s a two-hour drive, but I’ll show you around Seaside. See what you think.”

I held out my hand for him to shake. “Deal.”

He shook my hand and held onto it a few seconds longer than required. I didn’t mind. “Where should I pick you up?”

Crap. I had no idea where I was staying. “I can’t remember the address off the top of my head, but can I call you from the hotel?”

“Sure.” He retrieved a business card from his wallet and wrote his cell on the back.

He picked up the check and I thanked him for treating me. Then we parted. Nervous about the lie I’d told, I walked away from him as though I knew exactly where I was going, even though I was still getting to know the city. I at least knew where the library was, and really, what else do you need to know if you know the location of the library?

It wasn’t until I was standing in front of the library that I remembered I was wearing stolen merchandise. I double-checked the zipper on my hoodie to make sure the t-shirt was hidden. The last thing I needed was to be arrested for theft, and even though the librarian I'd met was nice, I didn't want to test the limits of his mercy. Stealing from a library is like taking money from the collection plate at church—I was pretty sure there was a special place in hell for people who stole from those places. Climbing the steps of the library, I muttered a prayer asking for forgiveness and ducked inside.

This was a reconnaissance mission: get the information I needed and get out. Blend in and hope my face wasn't on the security footage. I needn't have worried. A group of teens, similarly dressed in dark hoodies and jackets, were hanging out in the media area. I slipped into an empty station and opened the browser on the computer. Ten minutes later, I had a printed list of nearby hotels and I was on my way. I was anonymous. Nobody even noticed me.

I had to walk a while, because the first three hotels had no vacancies. The fourth did, and it looked clean enough. Certainly a safer place to stay than on the streets. After getting my room key, I left. I'd noticed a Walgreens nearby, and I needed supplies: shampoo, a brush, lotion...the works. All the toiletries I'd lost when my backpack had been stolen. New clothes too. Next to the pharmacy was a small boutique where I found an inexpensive tunic far nicer than my t-shirts, a pair of leggings, and thank the Lord, new underwear. I'd been wearing the same pair for days, and even though no one else seemed to notice, I knew.

My worst fear in interacting with people was they would think I smelled. I'd taken pains to clean myself up, but restaurant bathrooms were no substitute for an actual shower. With that luxury in mind, I took my purchases to the check-out counter, eager to get back to the hotel. At the last minute, I added two pairs of new socks. With all the rain, the ones I was wearing felt continually damp.

I picked up take-out from the Chinese restaurant next to the hotel and settled in for the night, calling Peter from the phone in my room, leaving him a message about my location. Would he show up the next morning? I thought there was a good chance he would, given his interest in the pearls. If not, I could still sell to Gatsby's. As I showered, I thought about the two-hour drive to Seaside. It was a long drive—what would we talk about all that time? Mom would be horrified at the idea of me getting in a car with a strange man. I could see her shaking a finger at me. *He'll take the pearls and leave you for dead by the side of the road.* He might, but I didn't think so.

I didn't have much—okay, *any*—experience with men, but I felt safe with Peter. He was warm and charming, and he seemed genuinely interested in a business partnership. Plus, he didn't know *where* the pearls came from. How could he even guess at the truth? No one would—the reality of my situation was too weird, too much like a fairy tale to be anything a normal person would imagine. He thought I had a supplier because that was the most logical explanation, and he had been considerate enough to respect my boundary in keeping that source secret—probably because he suspected my source was illegal, but so what? He was willing to play it cool, and pay good money for the pearls. As long I kept the truth from him, nothing bad would happen. I was sure of it. With that thought, I slipped into a deep, dreamless sleep, making up for days of deprivation.

14

Peter was true to his word, picking me up at ten. His car was nice, a black sedan with leather seats. It made him seem older, more sophisticated. I'm not sure what I expected—something sporty, I guess—but the car suited him. Neat, elegant, and smooth as it glided down Highway 26. At the hotel, he'd made a point of opening my door for me and had even complimented me on my new clothes, though he seemed careful not to overdo it.

I think he must have been as nervous as I was, because before he started the engine, he handed me an envelope filled with cash. "For pearls," he said. "I gave it some thought and went to an ATM last night. I'd like to buy ten more, if that's all right. I can only afford that much right now, but I'll have my dad write you a check for the rest when we get to Seaside. We're going to need a bunch, and your pearls are worth it."

I held the envelope gingerly, as though it might vanish in front of my eyes. Four grand, counting the money he'd given me the day before, stashed safely in my backpack. I'd never held that much cash before—Mother always kept what I'd earned locked away, out of reach. And now, I had the opportunity to earn more when we arrived in Seaside. I couldn't believe my good luck.

"You can count it if you want," he said, watching me. His hand rested on the gearshift, the car still in park.

I smiled. "It's okay—I trust you."

"You sure?" he asked, shifting into drive. He checked his mirrors and pulled into traffic. "I could be trying to kidnap you."

I burst out laughing. "That's exactly what my mother would say. She'd say you were going to murder me and leave me in a ditch."

He gave me a sly smile. "She sounds like a smart lady. It's a terrible idea to get in a car with a strange man. Except for me, of course. I have no plans for murder." He chuckled. "Today."

I laughed. "That sounds ominous."

After that, we both seemed to relax, and settled into an easy conversation, the kind where you're getting to know someone you really like. He told me about all the places he'd lived, traveling up and down the coast with his parents, and the museum he was creating with his father. "He was inspired by the freak shows of the Victorian era, like P.T. Barnum's museum in New York. Over the top, but magical—something to stir the imagination. Barnum had his Tom Thumb—we've got our own wonders. We're showcasing all kinds of unusual people."

I froze. I wasn't sure I liked the sound of that, being a freak myself.

Peter noticed my discomfort. "You wonder if we're exploiting people?"

"I, uh…I didn't say that."

"It's a valid concern—one I'm sure we'll encounter from people visiting the museum. But my father is unusual himself—he knows what it's like to be different. He would never force anyone to do something they're not comfortable with, and he pays fair wages. With benefits."

"Dental too?"

Peter grinned. "Best dental plan in the state."

"Dang. Maybe I *will* come work for you and your dad." It had been ages since Mom had taken me to a dentist or a doctor. She'd been so paranoid someone would find out about me, she had refused to make an appointment. One of my left molars had ached so long, I'd forgotten what it was like to be pain-free. The pain was minor compared to what I experienced each month with the pearls, but it hurt enough that I'd compensated by chewing on the right side of my mouth. I made a mental note to see a dentist as soon as I got settled. Maybe working for Peter's dad could be a good thing for me—having health benefits would be a relief. I could still sell the pearls, even if I had a role at the museum. "Not as a mermaid though," I clarified.

"You don't like mermaids?" Peter asked.

"I like them—well, the idea of them. I just don't want to be one." I looked out the window, watching pine trees whip by as we sped past.

"Because you can't swim?"

I turned to look at him. How could I explain my situation without telling him too much? I took a deep breath and released it slowly. "I *can* swim, but I'm a modest person. My mother is… super conservative—she always insisted on staying covered up." I frowned. "Sorry—this is awkward. I'm not really used to people. I was home-schooled."

"Recently? I thought you were older. You look like you're in your early twenties."

I sighed, wishing I could curl into a ball and disappear. "I am. I got my GED years ago, but Mom was...hesitant to let me be independent. I haven't been on my own long." I covered my face with my hands. Oh, why did I tell him that? I peeked through my fingers. We weren't going *that* fast. I could make a break for it—leap out the car door, tuck and roll to the side of the road. That had to be better than dying of embarrassment.

Peter reached over and placed his hand on my knee. "Hey, it's okay. You don't have to tell me anything you don't want to." I lowered my hands from my face and looked at his hand on my knee. He removed his hand and gripped the steering wheel, eyes on the road. "I'm sorry—I didn't mean to overstep."

"You didn't," I assured him. "It's just—I had a weird childhood. That's all."

He nodded, but didn't say anything.

"How old are you?" I asked.

"Twenty-seven," he answered. Okay, six years older than me. Older, with more life experience, but not too much older. He glanced over at me as he slowed to take a curve in the road. "You know, I was home-schooled too."

"You were?"

"Yeah. I mean, we traveled so much. Before my parents came up with the idea for the museum—a permanent home to showcase our exhibits—they had a traveling show. Only it was a collection of exotic animals, rather than people. There was even a small petting zoo."

I leaned back in my seat. "That sounds nice, actually."

"It was—Dad put a lot of trust in me in caring for our animals. But it was hard to make friends—I spent a lot of time on my own. Then, when I got older and mom got sick, they decided to settle in Seaside. Dad put the show on hold, sold the animals to a wildlife park in Bandon." He cleared his throat, avoiding my eyes. "After she died, he started reaching out to contacts to find people who'd be interested in being part of the museum. You'd be surprised at the number of people who auditioned—a lot of people see themselves as unusual. Misfits who want to belong to something, maybe even become a little famous."

I wasn't sure what to say to that. I'd spent my entire life trying to be invisible.

"In the end though, we only picked a handful of people for the show—people who were truly rare," he said.

"Such as?"

"Such as my friend, Siddhartha Gupta, who has Lamellar Ichthyosis—fish scale disease. It's a genetic disorder. It can cause the skin to thicken into jagged scales, opening painful cracks between them. Not so for Sid though—the disease isn't that common, but his is especially rare because his scales are symmetrical and a different color than the rest of his skin. They're greenish-blue, and they have this soft, fluorescent glow under a black light. We'd never seen anything like it." Peter seemed more excited about their find than sympathetic to Sid's plight.

"No offense, but that sounds kind of awful. There's no cure?"

"No cure, but humidity helps. That's why Sid likes living near the ocean," Peter said. He didn't seem insulted by my negativity. Instead he gave me a small smile. "He's become a surfer. A pretty good one too."

"Isn't it weird for him? Being at the beach in his swim trunks with everyone staring at him?" I couldn't fathom being in public with so much skin exposed.

Peter grinned. "No. One, because he works for the museum, and in the show, he'll be displaying his scales as part of his act. He said he wanted to join our little troupe because he wants to educate people about his condition. He's one of those gregarious people who doesn't care too much about what other people think. Maybe because he's literally thick-skinned." He laughed at his own joke. I wasn't sure what to think—I was still trying to picture glow-in-the dark fish scales on a human being. "Two, he wears a full wetsuit when he's surfing. Nobody even knows he's different." He stopped talking and looked at me. "Wait—did you say swim trunks? You know the ocean is freezing, right? Only a crazy person would go out there without a wetsuit. A crazy person or a tourist."

I frowned. I had no idea how cold the water was. I'd always

pictured people in swim trunks and bikinis, soaking up the sun. That's what I'd seen in movies. "I've never been to the beach."

"Really?" He asked, staring at me like I was an alien who'd suddenly beamed in to his car from a flying saucer. "Well, we're going to have to rectify that."

Ah—that was a terrible idea. "I don't know. If it's as cold as you say it is…"

"It's not bad at all with a wetsuit," he promised. "We wear gloves and booties. Of course, it will be nicer when the sun comes out again. The wind can be brutal during the winter, and it's a bad idea to go out during storms. The surf gets pretty rough. Too rough."

Well, if I had a wetsuit covering my scars, it might be okay. "Maybe—if I stay, and it's summer…maybe then."

He nodded. "I'm sure Sid wouldn't mind teaching you to surf. But we won't wait until summer to see the ocean—we can walk on the beach, even if it's cold."

"I'd like that," I said.

"So, you've lived in Oregon your *whole* life, and you've never seen the ocean."

Here we go again, I thought. Time to explain my weird life. No, time to *lie* about my life—but I'd tell as much of the truth as I could. Too many lies and I'd lose track of what I said. "I grew up in Roseburg—not that far from the ocean, but landlocked." I gave him a small smile, even though I didn't feel like smiling. "My mom worked at a convenience store, and we didn't have a lot of money when I was little. I went to regular school for a while, but then, well, then things changed. My mom decided to homeschool me. She went into the jewelry business and made more money so she could stay home with me. But it wasn't enough for us to take trips or anything."

"And your dad?"

"Never met him." I laughed bitterly. "I don't even know his

last name. He and my mom broke up when she was pregnant. She didn't like to talk about him." I straightened up in my seat, remembering the photo I'd found in the attic. "I did see a picture of him once. I look like him. I kind of wish I'd met him, but at the same time I don't, because it's not like he ever made an effort to be part of my life."

"Did he know about you?" Peter asked softly.

I had never thought about that. "It's possible he didn't. The break up was brutal, according to my mom. He left her for another girl." I looked at him. "She won't talk about it, but I don't think she's ever gotten over him."

Peter nodded. "That's rough. I'm sorry."

I shrugged. "It's just the way things were. But now I'm moving on. I knew I'd never have my own life if I stayed with my mother."

"Maybe that's how your dad felt too."

"Maybe." We fell into an uneasy silence, until I spotted a billboard advertising an attraction in Seaside. "The Inverted Experience? What the heck is that?"

He laughed at my outburst. "It's this thing where they have vignettes set up to look like the world's been turned upside down and you can take silly photos. It's fun. Won't be long before we have our own billboards along the Sunset Highway."

He went around a curve and the beginnings of a town materialized. A hardware store, a gardening center, restaurants, houses…then a beachy, lighted sign announcing that we'd crossed the threshold into Seaside. I could see why tourists flocked here. The cedar shake houses were charming and there were plenty of places to dine out.

"How far away is the beach?"

He nodded his head left. "'Bout half a mile, that way. I'll take you down Broadway, to the Prom, so you can see it." A few minutes later, he turned down the main drag of the town, headed west. The street was lined with lights in the shape of sea stars and colorful restaurants and shops sure to attract visitors. It looked like a fun place to vacation, with candy shops, ice cream parlors, even a place with bumper cars. I saw a sign for an aquarium. "Feed the seals?"

Peter grinned at me. "Oh, yeah. We're definitely going there. You haven't lived until you've gotten soaked by seals after throwing them a handful of slimy fish."

I laughed. "Sounds enchanting."

"It is, actually. The whole town is." He gestured out the window to a large storefront lit up in neon, even though it was the middle of the day. "And there she is. Fortunato's Museum of the Extraordinary." I could hear the pride in his voice.

Through one of the windows I glimpsed an enormous salt-water tank. As we drove past, I could see it was encrusted with barnacles and shells inside. "Is that the mermaid tank?"

"Yes. We put it at the front of the museum to catch people's attention. Now that we have pearls, we'll add signage to draw people in."

From what I could see, I liked the look of the museum. It had a fantastic, over the top feel—Victorian steampunk mixed with neon and glittering lights. I could see the influence P.T. Barnum had in designing the vintage circus look. It also seemed to be a nod to Jules Verne, inspired by *Twenty-Thousand Leagues Under the Sea* and *Around the World in Eighty Days*. Whatever the inspiration, it felt like a place where I could be transported to new worlds, much like the books I loved. It felt magical. "It definitely makes an impression. Much different from the rest of the shops on the street."

Peter beamed at me. "That's the idea *exactly*. Can't wait to show it to you. But first, madam, the Pacific Ocean." We entered a roundabout, and I sat up in my seat to look out over a concrete railing that lined the street. Beyond it was water—more water than I'd ever seen, vast and emerald, sparkling where the sun peeked through heavy clouds. It took my breath away. At that moment, I knew: whatever happened with the museum and the pearls, I was staying in this town. I'd spent my entire life without the ocean, and there was no way I'd live without it again.

15

Peter found a place to park on Broadway and we walked along the Promenade—the Prom, as the locals called it. It was a sidewalk that ran along the beach nearly the entire length of the town, from the estuary to the Cove, a popular surfer's beach. Even though it was a cold spring day, I could picture a carnival-like atmosphere to the place in the warmer months—people riding bicycles, walking dogs, playing volleyball on the beach. I wanted to be part of it all.

The wind had a chill that cut straight to my bones, and I made sure my jacket was zipped tight as Peter led me down a set of stairs to the sand. I didn't tell him I'd never walked on sand before. The feel of it squishing under my feet delighted me, though I was later annoyed at the amount of sand that got inside my sneakers. I had to take them off and dump out the sand before I got back in his immaculately clean car. Peter didn't seem to mind that despite my best efforts, sand still got on the car's floor mats.

We walked down to the water, and the sound of the waves filled my ears. Peter laughed as a wave rushed onto shore and I had to skitter back to avoid getting soaked. Giggling, I scooped up a bit of sea foam and flicked it in his direction. When the wave receded, he pointed out a clear blob of jelly it left behind.

"It's a moon jelly," he told me, and bent down to run his fingers over it. "You can touch it. It won't sting you."

I crouched down and poked it with my finger, and then, feeling braver, stroked the smooth surface. "Is it dead?"

"Yeah, but sometimes they have live ones at the aquarium. I'll show you sometime." He straightened up and looked out at the waves. "There are also sea nettles out there, but don't touch those. They do sting."

I stared at the moon jelly. "Do they look like that?"

He shook his head. "No, they're brown, and look kind of like an upside-down cupcake wrapper. They have long tentacles. That's where the stinging cells are."

I surveyed the sand at my feet, and spotted something that looked like a large, armored bug. "What's that?"

Peter looked at where I was pointing. "Isopod. We call them mole crabs because they burrow into the sand." He nudged it with his toe, turning it over so I could see the underside. The creature had a segmented abdomen and lots of legs. Kind of creepy, but I was fascinated to see an animal I'd never seen before. "They're a kind of arthropod. Like crabs or lobsters."

"How do you know so much about this stuff?" I asked him as we strolled along the sand.

"Living at the beach, you tend to pick up information about wildlife," he said. "But I also researched tide pools for my designs for the museum. I wanted it to be as authentic as possible." He stopped, stared at a spot fifteen feet in front of us, and hurried over to it. He crouched down and retrieved something round and white, and then walked back to me, holding it out like a gift. "It's not broken—that's a good omen."

"What is it?" I asked, taking it from him. It was a shell about the size of my palm, and had a symmetrical design radiating out to five points from the center.

He grinned. "It's a sand dollar. Everyone around here has collections of these in their homes, so it's fitting you get your first one on the day you arrive in town."

"Is it supposed to be good luck?"

He laughed. "I think we make our own luck, but sure. I'd say it's lucky we met, and I'm glad you're here, Amelia. I hope you decide to stay."

I gave him a smile. "I'm tempted. It's a nice town." I carefully tucked the sand dollar into my jacket pocket. "Thanks for bringing me here, and for the sand dollar."

"Of course. Ready to see the museum?" he asked.

I nodded, and we made our way back across the sand to the Prom. The early afternoon sun became shrouded in clouds and the wind picked up. "Probably a good time to head in, anyway," I said, shivering.

We retrieved the car and drove the short distance to the museum, where he parked out front. I stepped out, shifting my backpack onto my shoulders, and got my first real look at the museum. "It really is like something out of a Jules Verne novel," I whispered. Within the design of the sign over the entrance was a submarine that looked just like how I'd imagined the Nautilus when I'd read *Twenty Thousand Leagues Under the Sea.* It had been one of my favorite books, though it was hard to choose my absolute favorite. Given my shut-in lifestyle, books had sustained me, helping me escape when I couldn't. They'd given me the courage to dream my life could be more than it was.

Peter noticed me gazing at the submarine. "It's from one of my favorite books," he said, as though he'd read my mind. I stared at him, and he gave me a shy smile. "What do you think?"

"It's beautiful," I said, staring up in awe at the glittering metal sign. I loved the way the submarine stood out from the letters announcing the museum's name, complimenting them without upstaging them. It was eye-catching, yet tasteful, something I was starting to recognize as Peter's signature style. "It looks like something out of a movie."

He laughed. "Then my stage design and special effects classes paid off. I went to school at an art institute in California for a while, right near Universal Studios. We got to work on a few sets there. Not for any big movies, just on the back lot—but still, it was an amazing experience. Dad was skeptical about it. He didn't want to pay my tuition at first, but I think he gets it now."

"I do," a man said.

I turned to see a man sporting a neatly-trimmed beard and a warm smile. He was dressed in an old-fashioned style, with a waistcoat and pocket watch. He was a perfect fit for the museum, just how I imagined a curator of the extraordinary would look.

"This is my father," Peter said, "Vincent Fortunato. Dad, this is Amelia Weaver, the woman I mentioned. She's the one with the pearls."

He had no idea how true that was. I felt bad for hiding an important part of my life when Peter had been so open with me. Covering my awkwardness with a smile, I held out my hand to Vincent. "It's so nice to meet you."

He shook my hand, firmly but gently. "The pleasure is mine, Miss Weaver. What do you think of our museum so far?"

"It's wonderful. I can't wait to see what's inside."

"Well then, we mustn't delay." He held out his arm to escort me. I took it, feeling warmth radiate through me. Vincent had an aura of kindness about him, and I felt instantly at home with him, in spite of having so little experience with men. I wondered if meeting my own father would feel like this.

Peter held open the museum's front door, and we stepped inside. It took a moment for my eyes to adjust. The lights were low, as though the room were lit by gas lanterns rather than by electricity. I spotted Victorian sconces on the walls, and there was a brass chandelier overhead. It had a celestial design—rotating planets made of blown glass, revolving on brass arms around a sun. The sun pulsed with inner light, giving the amber-colored glass a warm glow. I just stood there, stunned, staring up at that magnificent chandelier. "Wow."

Vincent chuckled. "Thank you, young lady. I'm glad you like it."

"I've never seen anything like this," I breathed, tearing my eyes away from the light fixture to look at him.

"Then we've done our job," Vincent said. "That's the whole idea behind this place—to give people an experience they've never had before." He pointed to the glass orbs. "That was my idea, one of the few design ideas I contributed. But Peter is the one who brought it to fruition, hiring local glass artists. He also designed the ceiling."

I looked up again, taking in an indigo sky painted with silver constellations. "It's magical."

"That's the word for it," Vincent agreed. "I'm quite proud of Peter's vision. This was all a figment of my imagination. He made it a reality."

"Thanks, Dad," Peter said, placing his hand on his father's shoulder and giving it an affectionate squeeze. "I like to think Mom can see this place, and it makes her happy."

"She would be ecstatic," Vincent said, beaming at his son. "I only hope our patrons will be as thrilled as Miss Weaver is, when we open next week."

"They will be," Peter assured him. "The pearls will draw them in, and the museum will keep them captivated." He turned to me. "Would you like to see the rest of the museum?"

"Absolutely." I turned to the large aquarium on the left side of the room. It looked as though it were fashioned out of iron, with large bolts and tarnished metal, almost as though it had once belonged on a ship. Upon closer inspection, I saw that the walls of the tank weren't metal at all, just sculpted plaster painted to look that way. It was a convincing deception. The glass looked thick and strong—I imagined it had to be to hold so much water. The tank had to be at least ten feet deep, and took up the entire side of the room. "This is where the pearls will be?"

Peter nodded, pulling me up on a small stage in front of the tank. "See those numbered shelves on the wall there?"

I looked through the glass and could see five rows of shelves, each with a small brass placard engraved with a number. "Yes."

"We'll put fake oysters on each shelf, and the barker—the showman in charge of this exhibit—will ask a museum guest to come on stage and call out a number. The barker will write it on a slate." Peter pointed to a chalkboard on an easel, next to the tank. "And then the mermaid will swim over to retrieve the correct oyster. She'll place it in a net, and the barker will hoist it over the side of the tank. Then he'll open it. If there's a pearl inside, the guest will get to keep it."

I stared inside the aquarium. Barnacle-covered boulders and fronds of kelp decorated the bottom, and orange and purple sea stars clung to the rocks and the sides of the tank. There seemed to be a hidden area behind the oyster wall—probably where the mermaid slipped into the water and made her grand entrance for the public. It seemed like a long swim to the oysters. "The mermaid will have to be good at holding her breath."

"She will," Peter agreed. "But as a safety precaution, we've got an air hose behind that rock there, so she can dive down and take a breath when she needs to."

"Speaking of mermaids," Vincent said. "I've found one."

I must have looked at him like he was crazy, because Peter laughed. In my defense, talking about mermaids in such a casual manner was new to me. "About time," Peter said. "Can she do it?"

"She can. She's quite adept at holding her breath, and she moves beautifully," Vincent said. "She knows just how to move the tail so it undulates through the water. She even swam up to the glass and gave me a wave. Enchanting."

"The suit fit okay?" Peter asked.

"Like a glove," Vincent assured him. "She looks like the real thing." He turned to me, confiding, "Peter is obsessed with authenticity."

"So I've gathered."

"It's important," Peter said, sounding slightly wounded. "You can't expect people to suspend their disbelief if there are obvious flaws in what you present." He gave his father a hard look. "When can I see her?"

"She'll come by tomorrow afternoon for a second fitting, and you can put your fears to rest then." He patted Peter on the arm. "It will be fine, son."

"I know," Peter said. "It's just that we've invested everything in this place. It's got to be perfect."

"It will be," Vincent said. "Now, Miss Weaver. Allow me to introduce you to the rest of our troupe."

16

Vincent led me down a short hallway with a series of doors on either side. The hallway was papered in a velvety green damask, and lit by more Victorian sconces. Vincent stopped in front of one of the doors, which had a large poster in a mahogany frame hung on the wall beside it. The poster looked as though it had been printed on parchment, using a vintage press. *She sings with the voice of an angel,* it read, without any other explanation of what waited within.

"I must warn you, Miss Weaver, those we are about to meet may look unconventional, but they *are* human," Vincent said, his voice taking on a theatrical tone. "Though the artists in our museum are quite used to being stared at, and have come to expect it, I hope you will see beyond appearances. That is the point of this entire exercise, you see. To showcase our humanity, in all its wondrous forms."

"I understand," I said, and swore to myself that whatever I saw in that room, I would not stare.

Vincent opened the door and we entered. This room was more dimly lit than the foyer, and had theater style seating with chairs upholstered in red velvet. There was a stage at the front. On the stage was a glossy black grand piano, and seated at the instrument was a thin woman wearing glasses. Her hair was blond and streaked with violet, cut short in a bob.

"Good afternoon, Charlie," Vincent said. "Is she available for visitors?"

"We were just about to rehearse," the woman replied. She had a British accent, and like Vincent, was dressed in a Victorian suit. "Fancy a song?"

"Always," Vincent said, and gestured for Peter and I to take our seats in the front row. We settled in and the woman at the piano played a series of notes.

"And now," Charlie announced, "the lovely Elena Vangelis."

A woman walked out on stage and took her place in front of the piano, head bowed, hands clasped in front of her. She raised her head as she began to sing.

I admit, at first, I focused solely on her appearance. She wore a glamorous scarlet evening gown that hugged her voluptuous figure. But what struck me most was she had a full beard. It looked long and silky—a match for her dark, curly tresses.

I couldn't help but stare, but then her voice mesmerized me, and I stopped thinking about how she looked. Her voice was high and clear, and the song was hauntingly sad. I couldn't understand the words because they were in a language unfamiliar to me, but I guessed the ballad was Celtic. Her song transported me, making me think of verdant forests and rugged cliffs, and a young woman mourning her love. She held the last note and the acoustics in the room made it echo, like a ghost of the past.

As the echoes faded, Elena caught my eye and smiled. "Perhaps something more upbeat, no? Charlie, do you mind?"

"Not at all," the woman at the piano replied, and launched into a show toon from the musical, *Damn Yankees*.

"Whatever Lola wants…" Elena began, swinging her hips as she moved toward the lip of the stage. "Lola gets…" She made her way down the steps to the front row, her movements slow and sensual. When she got to Peter, she stopped and stroked his cheek seductively with her satin gloved hand. "And little man, if Lola wants you…" She held out her hand to him.

Peter grinned. He took her hand and stood, sweeping her into his arms. They began to tango, Elena singing the entire time. She gave me a wink and I giggled. Here was a woman who was brash and brave and completely comfortable with herself. She made no apologies. It looked like she was having the time of her life. I couldn't help but envy her. She was free to be exactly who she was.

Peter spun her away from him and back, and then, as she finished the song, he dipped her gently. Then they both burst into laughter. Peter set her upright and she gave him a peck on the cheek.

Vincent stood and clapped. "Bravo! Bravo!" He walked over to Elena and took her hand, kissing it in a chivalrous gesture. "Wonderful, wonderful. Elena, you are bewitching. Our patrons don't stand a chance against your charms." He called over to the woman at the piano, "Charlie, are you sure you're all right with everyone falling in love with your betrothed?"

"Do I have a choice?" Charlie asked. She stood and joined Elena in front of the stage, slipping her arm around Elena's waist. "I am powerless in her presence. I can deny her nothing."

Elena kissed Charlie's cheek tenderly. "The feeling is mutual, love."

Vincent turned to me to make introductions. "Elena was the first to join us, all the way from Bellingham. She has perfect pitch and a voice to rival the angels. Charlie was next. She followed Elena home from a bookstore one day, and never left."

Charlie laughed. "Bit of a cliché, falling in love over a book, but here we are."

Vincent raised his eyebrows. "It was a horror novel, if I recall correctly."

Elena chuckled. "It was *The Haunting of Hill House*, and it's a classic, Mr. Fortunato."

"I beg your pardon, Miss Vangelis," Vincent said, smiling, holding his hand to his heart. "This is Amelia Weaver. She will be supplying us with pearls for the mermaid exhibit."

Elena took my hand in hers. "A pleasure to meet you. Amelia…I once had a dear friend named Amelia. She went by Mia."

"Mia," I said, trying out the name. "I like that. Does she live in town?"

"No," Elena said, shaking her head. "Someone I knew long ago. But I hope you and I will be great friends."

I smiled. "I hope so too." It had been a long time since I'd had a friend.

"Well," Peter said. "There will be plenty of time for you girls to chat later. We haven't introduced her to Sid or Gabriel yet. If you'll excuse us."

"Of course," Charlie said. "We should focus on rehearsing. Not much time until opening day."

"No, and I want to make sure our act is perfect," Elena said. She released my hand. "See you soon, Amelia."

17

It's a weird feeling, having an instant connection with someone, but that's how I felt about Elena. She was kind, witty, and charming. I could see why Charlie had fallen so hard for her. I almost wanted to *be* her. I imagined Elena had struggled to come to terms with her plight, like me. Unlike me, she had found a way to be fully herself, to present herself to the world without fear or shame. I wasn't at that point in my life yet. I wasn't sure if I'd ever be in that place. The need to hide one of the most integral parts of me was strong—it had become second nature to lie, to keep my scars covered.

But maybe I could change. Maybe I could be brave. I looked forward to talking with Elena again, maybe just the two of us. I thought she could show me how to reinvent myself, to begin my life again.

I was thinking about that as Vincent and Peter led me to the next room. This one was even darker than the first. On the walls were undersea murals of aquatic creatures and seaweed. They glowed under a black light. This room had a stage as well, and a spotlight was focused center stage.

"Sid?" Peter called. "You here?"

The spotlight suddenly went out, and a glowing figure appeared on stage. He had the shape of a tall, thin man with a swimmer's build, but his body was covered in fish scales, exuding soft greenish-blue light. Even though Peter had told me about Siddhartha's condition, I found myself staring, mouth gaping. It had to be an illusion, didn't it? No one actually looked like that, like the creature from the Black Lagoon. Ironic, I know, coming from a human oyster.

The spotlight came back on, and Sid shielded his eyes against the harsh light. The glow from his skin disappeared, and he looked almost normal, if you ignored the scale pattern that appeared tattooed into his dark skin. The colors were still there, though not as prominent under a bright light. His face was not as scaly, just a few marks at his temples and the sides of his neck. If he were wearing more than swim trunks, you'd hardly notice. He could have covered the markings with makeup and passed as a regular surfer dude, with shaggy black hair.

"Hi, Peter, Vincent," Sid said, stepping down from the stage. "And who is this?"

"This is Amelia," Peter said. "She'll be helping us with the mermaid exhibit. How's the comedy act coming along?"

"Good," Sid said. "I've been writing the act around my sister's wedding and her fiancé's uptight parents meeting my crazy family. I'd tell you a few jokes, but they need a little work before I'm ready to do this in front of an audience."

"That's all right," Vincent told him. "We *will* want to see the act though, in the next week."

"Give me a day," Sid said, "and I'll be good to go." He gave me a conspiratorial smile. "It's scary, putting yourself out there in front of people. Scariest thing I've ever done, to tell the truth."

"That ten-foot wave we surfed was pretty scary," Peter said.

"Yeah, nothing like flirting with death, is there?" Sid said. "I get your point—tourists can't be scarier than that."

"That sounds insane," I chimed in. "A ten-foot wave?"

"Don't worry—we'll start out a lot smaller," Peter said.

I gave him a friendly shove. "We better." I still wasn't entirely convinced I wanted to surf, but I was sold on spending time in the ocean.

Sid looked from Peter to me and grinned. "New recruit?"

"I'm working on her," Peter said. "She'll be in the water before we know it."

"I don't know about that," I said.

"Don't worry," Sid said. "He can ride the crazy waves and you can stick with me in the shallows. It'll be fun."

"Can't wait," I said, and I was surprised to realize I was telling the truth.

18

Peter led me down the hallway to the next room. "Last artist in residence, and I have to warn you, he's a beast."

"Peter," Vincent chided. "He's your brother."

"Kidding," Peter said, holding up his hands in surrender to his father. "Just a little sibling rivalry."

"You never said anything about a brother," I said to Peter.

"He's my adopted brother. We haven't always gotten along," Peter said, and then, to his father, "But we're *trying*."

"I know," Vincent said, "and I'm glad of it. You know things have not been easy for Gabriel."

"What do you mean?" I asked.

"You'll see soon enough," Peter said, opening the door. This room also had a stage, and on it were an easel and an oversized canvas, large enough that I couldn't see the person sitting behind it, just a pair of legs clad in jeans and large, tan work boots.

"Good afternoon, Gabriel," Vincent called. "What are you working on?"

"Another landscape," a deep, gravelly voice said.

"Lovely," Vincent said. "Though I do wish you'd practice portraits, since that will be what patrons desire."

"I haven't had anyone to inspire me," the man said, rising from his seat and coming around the canvas. He stopped short when he saw me.

I realized my mouth was gaping again, and I quickly shut it. The giant man standing in front of me was covered in hair—fur, really. He reminded me of the wolfman from the old black and white movie—the one with Lon Chaney Jr. I'd seen all the old monster movies as a kid, and loved them. But seeing the wolfman come to life was a different story. At nearly seven-feet-tall, Gabriel looked terrifying. "Hello," I managed, my voice small.

Gabriel stepped down from the stage and strode toward us. His flannel shirt had splotches of paint in multiple colors, as well as long streaks of green paint. It looked like he'd wiped his hands down the front of his shirt. "Who's this?" Gabriel's canines were longer than normal, and reminded me of fangs.

Peter put an arm around me—protectively, I think. That didn't give me confidence about my safety. "This is Amelia. She's here to help us with the museum."

"I see," Gabriel said. I couldn't tell if that was good or bad in his opinion. He stuck out a large, paw-like hand, and I shook it gingerly. He held my gaze as if appraising my features. I stared back. His face was completely covered in hair—even his eyelids were furry. His eyes were strangely captivating—a warm brown that was almost golden, and sharply observant, like a hawk's. "Am I supposed to paint her?"

"No, she's here to help with—" Peter began.

"Would you *like* to paint her?" Vincent asked, cutting Peter off.

Gabriel scanned my features once more and stepped back, dismissing me. "I guess."

"It wouldn't hurt to practice," Vincent said quietly.

"I suppose," Gabriel said sullenly. He went back to his easel.

"We should go," Peter whispered to me. I nodded, and let him guide me to the door.

Vincent hesitated, as if he wanted to say one last thing to Gabriel, and then shook his head as if he'd changed his mind. He followed us out without another word, closing the door gently behind him. "I don't know how to help him," he confessed.

"You've given him as much help as you can," Peter said, finally letting his arm drop from my shoulders. I guess the immediate danger was over. "At some point he's going to have to help himself."

"Living here has been difficult for him," Vincent said. "I thought it would be an improvement over his prior living conditions, but I fear I was wrong. I'm afraid he's exchanged one cage for another."

That piqued my interest. I knew a thing or two about being caged.

"It's a cage of his own making," Peter said. "Gabe's free to go wherever he wants. There are no iron bars here. It's his choice to be a recluse." This seemed to be an argument they'd had before. There was a familiarity in the way they bantered back and forth.

"But Peter," Vincent said. "We must be patient with him. Gabriel going out in public is different than it is for you or me. He sticks out like a sore thumb. He can't hide who he is."

"I'm about out of patience, Dad," Peter said. His jaw tightened. "Everybody here pulls their own weight, no excuses. We don't give anyone else a pass. You think it's easy for Elena? Or Sid? Or any of the others?"

Vincent looked hurt at that. "Of course not."

"He doesn't like people staring at him? Well, he's going to have to suck it up. It's not like he has a lot of other opportunities for employment," Peter said. This was a side of him I hadn't seen before. It frightened me. I made a mental note to tread carefully and not get on Peter's bad side. "Look, I've got a ton of work to do before opening day. And I promised Amelia—" He gave me a conciliatory smile, as though he felt embarrassed to have pulled the curtain back on his family's problems. "I promised her that you'd have a check for the rest of the pearls. I've paid for twenty, but we're going to need more."

I tried on a winning smile, as though I had not just been witness to the argument between them. "Half of which I've not yet given you. Do you have a secure place to put them?" I adjusted my backpack on my shoulders.

"We've got a safe in the office," Peter said. "My apologies, Amelia, but I'd better get going on my projects. Dad, could you show her the rest of the museum and make sure she gets her check?"

Vincent gave me a warm smile. "I'd be happy to."

"Oh, and she'll need a place to stay," Peter said. He looked at me, concerned. "If you're still interested in staying in Seaside, that is. I hope we haven't scared you off."

"Not at all," I assured him.

"Good. Okay then, I'm off." Peter hurried back down the hallway.

I turned to find Vincent offering his arm to me. "Come with me, young lady. I'll show you wonders great and small."

19

Vincent led me out into the main corridor and then down a second passage. "We've got three main acts, and then the rest of the museum is dedicated to exhibits," he explained.

"Just three? Peter said something about others."

"Ah, he was talking about the rest of the staff." Vincent smiled and nodded to an older man who was sweeping the floor. Large, splotchy birthmarks covered his face, neck, and arms. The man gave him a friendly wave before returning to his task. "Everyone here has something that makes them special—it might not be so extraordinary as it is with Gabriel, Sid, or Elena, but there's something that makes them stand out. We made that a priority in our hiring. We wanted to provide opportunities for people who might not have employment otherwise, because of a physical oddity."

"Like a disability?"

Vincent shook his head. "Not necessarily. Many of our staff are able-bodied, but there might be something that would lead an employer not to hire them. Take Beth, for example." He waved at a woman who was adjusting the wigs on a wax statue of conjoined twins. She gave him a broad smile, which seemed to take some effort since she had a growth covering the right side of her face. "Beth has tumors on much of her body—all benign, so they're not causing her harm, physically, at least. But she's had trouble getting work, especially in positions where she'd be face to face with the public. I intend to change that. She'll be managing our gift shop. She's very bright, and has proven herself to be invaluable as we've set up the museum. She's good with details and numbers."

"I thought it was illegal to discriminate against people," I said.

"Oh, it is," Vincent said. "If you have a documented disability. The folks we hire often don't, but they face a great deal of bias. It's not always blatant, but it's still harmful. Our mission is to bring awareness to that, and change people's minds. Representation matters—it normalizes those of us who are different and over time, people become more accepting. At least, that's my hope."

"That's admirable," I said.

"Thank you," Vincent said. "It's a bit of a selfish cause, I'll admit, given my own history with such things."

"Peter mentioned that," I said, hoping I hadn't overstepped my bounds.

"Yes," Vincent said. "I imagine he did. It's no secret—it's part of the story of our museum. That's what we're doing here. Telling stories." He pointed to a wax figure of a tiny man. "Tom Thumb, from P.T. Barnum's museum. People may have seen his image, but do they know his story? Do they see him as something other than a figure in a freak show?"

"I doubt it."

"As do I. We must reveal our humanity. Otherwise, we have failed in our mission," Vincent said gravely. "That's why I hope Elena, Sid, and Gabriel will be received well. They are more than acts in a sideshow—they have extraordinary talents that should be shared with the world. I want them to be seen for their humanity."

"But why only three acts, when you have other staff?" I asked.

Vincent hesitated, and I worried I really had crossed a line.

"I'm sorry. That was a rude question," I said.

Vincent shook his head. "No. No, it's a perfectly reasonable question. Each of our staff has different talents." He turned and we started back toward the front of the museum. "Not all of them are suited to entertain an audience. And being in front of an audience isn't for everyone. There's a great deal of pressure and scrutiny. It takes a toll."

"Like with Gabriel?"

Vincent stopped in front of the gift shop and stroked his beard. "Indeed. Gabriel is struggling, but given his history, he'll be fine. He's strong. He can take any insult hurled at him from would-be hecklers."

"What *is* his history?"

"I think it would be better if you heard that story from him," Vincent said, staring at me.

I couldn't see that conversation happening. It didn't seem like Gabriel liked visitors. "I…I don't know if that would be a good idea."

Vincent chuckled. "You might be surprised. He liked you."

I scoffed, brushing him off. "I don't think he did." If anything, he saw me as an intruder.

"Oh, he did," Vincent said with a knowing smile. He tapped his temple. "I know Gabriel, maybe better than he knows himself. He needs to be inspired. No, more than that—he needs a friend. And I can see that you have already earned Peter's trust, and so you've earned mine."

"Well…thank you." Vincent's words made me feel both flattered and off-balance. It's not like I'd done anything special to earn anyone's trust.

"I'd like to ask you for a favor, young lady."

Uh-oh. That sounded bad.

"I'd like you to sit for a portrait with Gabriel," Vincent said.

"Are you sure he won't devour me?" I didn't mean to voice that thought, but the words slipped out. I admit, my encounter with Gabriel had left me rattled. He was intimidating.

Vincent burst out laughing. "Quite sure, though he does come across as gruff, doesn't he?" He pointed to a painting hanging in the gift shop. "But look, a person who can do that can't really be a monster, can he?"

It was a landscape featuring the beach I'd been on, not two hours before. There was Tillamook Head, with the faint image of the lighthouse far offshore. Golden beams of light shown down, piercing dark clouds, and frothy waves crashed onto shore. The piece was moody, but stunningly beautiful with deep greens and blues. It was the kind of painting I'd always dreamed of hanging in a place of my own.

"That's gorgeous," I breathed. "No, I don't think a person with that kind of gift could be a monster."

Vincent took my hand and gave it a squeeze. "Then you'll sit for him?"

"I'll think about it."

"Fair enough," he said. "Now, I owe you money, and I believe you need a place to stay?"

"I do. Thank you."

"You can stay in our guest room for tonight, if you don't mind rooming with three unruly bachelors," Vincent said. "We're good cooks though, so perhaps that will make up for our lack of house-keeping."

"I'd be honored," I said.

"Would you be interested in renting a guest house?" he asked. "I have a friend in town who's been looking for a renter, but the apartment is a bit small. Too small for a family, but perhaps for a single person…"

"I'd love to take a look. Do you know how much the rent is?"

"I'm sure we could negotiate a reasonable price," he said. "I'll give Barbara a call, see what we can work out." He ushered me into his office and made the call, and then wrote out a check for twenty more pearls.

Forty-five pearls sold in two days? Not too shabby.

"I didn't even think to ask—you do have a checking account?" he asked as I stared at the check.

I looked up at him. "Not locally. I'll have to set one up."

"We'll stop at the bank after we check out the apartment tomorrow," he said.

"I can't thank you enough, Mr. Fortunato," I said.

"Please, call me Vincent," he said. "You've joined our troupe, so you're family."

I smiled at that. My independence from my mother had been hard fought, but I felt like I was finally winning. I'd found a place where I could belong.

20

I saw Gabriel again that night. Vincent drove me to their house, a neat, butter-yellow bungalow near the beach, which was clean in spite of what he'd said before. Gabriel was in the kitchen, and I got the feeling he might have tidied up before we arrived. Maybe he wasn't so bad after all.

The smells coming from the kitchen made my mouth water. "Wow, what is that?" I asked Vincent.

"I hope you're okay with spicy food—Gabriel is making mole poblano."

"What's that?"

"It's a sauce made from chili and chocolate, among other ingredients," Vincent said. "He likes to serve it over chicken and rice."

"I've never had it, but it smells amazing," I said. My stomach growled, and I realized I'd skipped lunch. It wasn't like me to forget to eat—especially since my resources had been stretched thin lately and food had been a luxury—but it'd been a busy day between the beach and the museum. "Where's Peter?"

Vincent gave a frustrated sigh. "He'll be working late tonight. That boy—he's such a perfectionist. Everything has to be flawless before he'll be satisfied. I suppose it won't surprise you to know he made the Dean's List in college?"

I laughed. "No. He's ambitious, isn't he?"

"He's exhausting," Gabriel called from the kitchen.

"Ambition is a virtue," Vincent called back. To me he said, "Peter studied architecture for a time in college, but his true love has always been the movies. That's why he left the University of Oregon and moved to Los Angeles."

"He mentioned he studied stage craft and special effects," I said.

"Yes," Vincent said. "All the magic you saw at the museum is because of him. He's put his heart and soul into it. But he works too hard. I hope he'll take some time off, once we open."

"Sounds like it's deserved."

"Supper's ready," Gabriel called, and he surfaced from the kitchen, carrying a steaming dish, which he placed on the dining room table. Three places had already been set for us—nothing fancy, but I was impressed nonetheless. Dinner at my house had always been casual. When Mom worked for the Stop and Go, I'd often been left to fend for myself, microwaving ramen or mac and cheese. When she stopped and was with me full time, things didn't change much. We made our meals and sat in front of the TV. I can't recall us ever sitting at the kitchen table together.

Vincent pulled my chair out for me, a gesture that felt a little awkward since it was something I'd only ever seen in movies, never experienced firsthand. I was charmed though—he was old-fashioned, but a true gentleman, and seemed genuinely kind. Based on how he treated the museum staff, he seemed to pride himself on seeing the best in people.

Gabriel brought out a few other dishes and a plate of warm tortillas, and then took the seat across from me. He avoided my gaze, instead busying himself by loading his plate with food.

I decided to try and pull him out of his shell. "This all looks wonderful, Gabriel."

He muttered his thanks, and drizzled sauce over his chicken and rice before passing the dish of mole to me. Stomach growling, I took a generous scoop of chicken and mole sauce, a side of rice, and two tortillas. Then I placed my hands in my lap as I waited for Vincent to fill his plate. I was hesitant to start eating—I wasn't sure if they were the kind of family that said grace or just dug in, but I didn't want to commit a faux paux.

I wasn't sure how I felt about Gabriel, but I liked Vincent, and I was scared he'd think I was uncultured if I said or did the wrong thing. I *was* uncultured, truth be told. Most of my knowledge of the world came from my mom, books, and the old movies we'd borrowed from the library. The more I was exposed to the real world, the less I trusted what my mother had told me about it. I began to understand that the outside world frightened her, and that was why she'd projected her fears onto me—to scare me into obedience. Maybe she wasn't a bad person. Maybe she really had wanted to keep me safe, but her methods had kept me in a chokehold to her will. Watching Vincent and Gabriel, I could see my limited experience with people put me at a disadvantage. I tried to compensate by making the kind of small talk I'd seen in movies. "Your home is beautiful, Vincent. Thank you for hosting me."

"You're quite welcome, my dear," Vincent said, taking a bite of his dinner. "We so rarely have guests, and I fear the three of us get into a rut, sometimes."

"We *never* have guests," Gabriel said.

"True," Vincent said to him, "and it would do us good to be more social." There seemed to be more to that statement than was spoken, but Gabriel didn't take the bait. He just ate quietly.

I tucked into my own plate, tasting the mole. It was spicy—much spicier than I was used to—but delectable. The sauce had a rich, multi-layered taste. "This is really good. There's chocolate in this?"

Gabriel lifted his head to meet my gaze. "It's unsweetened."

"Delicious," I said, and took another bite to show my appreciation. "I've never had anything like it."

"Thank you," he said quietly. "It was my mother's recipe."

"She opened her own restaurant, didn't she?" Vincent asked him.

"Yeah, after I left," Gabriel said. "She still had three kids to feed."

Vincent placed his hand on Gabriel's arm. "She did the best she could, son."

Gabriel huffed and moved his arm away.

Vincent seemed hurt but unsurprised. He gave me an apologetic look. "Gabriel had a difficult childhood," he said.

"Vincent," Gabriel warned.

"I won't go into the details," Vincent said to him, "but I think our guest should know a little about your history. I've asked her to sit for you so you can practice doing portraits."

Gabriel's brows furrowed as he looked from me to Vincent. "I don't *need* practice. And I *really* don't need you talking about my family to a stranger." He got up from the table and left his plate, his meal only half finished. Then he disappeared, tromping up the stairs. Vincent and I didn't speak as we listened to his footsteps fade. There was the distant sound of a door closing hard. Not slamming shut, but a clear message that we were not to intrude.

"I'm sorry," I said. "I didn't mean to invade his space."

"You have nothing to apologize for, but I do," Vincent told me. "He's not wrong—I overstepped my bounds, and I should have been more sensitive about his family. Gabriel's had so many of his boundaries violated, he's built a hedge of protection around himself. I've been trying to trim it down, branch by branch, but I'm afraid I trample through sometimes." He sighed. "But it *is* a hedge, not a wall, and I believe we can break through to him. It would do him good to have a friend. Still, I'm sorry. I enlisted you in my mission and I've put you in an awkward position. Please, don't feel obligated to sit for him."

"I'd like to though," I said, surprising myself. In spite of his moodiness, Gabriel intrigued me. He was a brilliant artist and a damn fine cook. His prickly demeanor was obviously armor, and I thought we might have some things in common—it's not like I had a stellar childhood either. I imagined our circumstances were vastly different, but maybe much the same too. Different cages, same baggage. We were both damaged. I just hid it better. Gabriel told the unvarnished truth; I told so many lies it was hard to keep them straight. I guess I'd built my own hedge of protection.

"That's kind of you," Vincent said, studying me. "Perhaps we'll see how he is in the morning."

"Yeah," I said. I sopped up the last of the sauce with a piece of tortilla and then stood, stacking Gabriel's plate on top of mine. "Thanks for the meal. Can I take your plate to the kitchen?"

"That's quite all right," Vincent said. "I can clean up."

"No, I insist," I told him, holding out my hand for his plate. "You've been so nice to me—the least I can do is take care of the dishes."

"All right, young lady," Vincent said, chuckling as he stacked his silverware on top of the plate and relinquished it to me. "I can see you won't take no for an answer. But I can't let you do all the work. You wash, I'll dry."

"Deal," I said. We got to work, and I asked him about his own history. He was surprisingly open about his reasons for opening the museum—what it was like being bullied because of his webbed feet, and the love and support he'd received from his wife. It was clear he had adored her and missed her terribly.

"I think Frida would have liked you," he said. "You've got

spirit. She did too. She was never afraid to stand up for others. She was fearless."

"Thank you," I said. "Though I would never claim to be fearless."

"I think you're quite courageous, striking out on your own." He dabbed at the serving dish the mole had been in, wiping it dry before putting it away on a high shelf.

"I had to," I said, scrubbing one of the plates. I rinsed it off under the tap. "My mother is…" I hesitated, unsure of how much to reveal. "She means well, but she's controlling. I knew I'd never have my own life if I stayed."

"How did you get into the pearl business?" he asked.

"It was a venture my mom and I started together." This was a lie I'd practiced. "She wanted to home school me, and being in the jewelry business let her work from home. When I left, I decided to branch out on my own." A simple lie based in truth. If you have to lie, that's the best kind to tell, so you're sure to stick to your story. I felt bad telling it, but even though I liked Vincent, I wasn't sure I could trust him. Not just yet, anyway.

"Does she know where you are?" he asked. He had been drying a drinking glass, but now held it in one hand, his dishtowel in the other as he leaned against the kitchen counter, studying me.

I swallowed, caught off guard by the intensity of his gaze. "I, uh, I haven't been in touch lately."

"Do you think she's worried about you?"

Probably. I imagine she was frantic, though I wasn't sure if it was out of concern for my well-being or if it was because her golden goose was gone. "She might be."

"Will you call her? At least let her know you're all right?" he asked.

I straightened my shoulders. "I don't think that's a good idea."

He stared at me for a moment and then nodded. "I understand. I won't pry, but may I say just one thing? As a parent, I would want to know my boys were safe, even if they didn't want me in their lives. I would respect their wishes, but I would want to know they were okay."

I frowned. "That's the problem though. I don't think she *would* respect my wishes."

"I see. Well, whatever you decide, I support you. But if you do decide to make that call, I'll be right there with you."

Tears pricked my eyes. I blinked, forcing them back. His sincerity was disarming. Having unconditional support wasn't something I was used to, and the certainty with which he'd spoken, even though he barely knew me, made me want to cry. I'd never had someone support me like that. "Thank you," I whispered. I could have hugged him, but I didn't trust myself not to burst into tears. Instead, I gave him a small smile and focused on scrubbing a spot of sauce that clung stubbornly to the copper pan.

Vincent put his hand on my shoulder and squeezed gently. "Of course," he said softly, and then went back to drying dishes.

We worked in silence, finishing the dishes, wiping down the table and countertops. Then he tossed the dish towels into the laundry and offered to show me my room for the night.

"The guest bath is just down the hall, and there are fresh towels in the linen closet," he said.

"Thank you, Vincent," I said. Focusing on cleaning up, I'd managed to stuff my emotions back down, so I was able to speak with a steady voice and offer a genuine smile. "I really appreciate you letting me stay here."

"Well, with any luck, you'll have your own place tomorrow," he said. "I think you'll like the guest house, and I'm sure Barb will enjoy your company. She's been anxious to find a good renter. Good night, Amelia."

"Good night."

21

I didn't see Gabriel until that afternoon. He was still in his room at breakfast, and didn't come out when it was time for Vincent and me to visit Barbara Putnam. Her studio guest house, built over her garage, was tiny but clean. It held a queen bed, a small dining table with two chairs, and a worn loveseat. There was a kitchenette and a bathroom. Best of all, it looked out onto a grove of trees to the west. I envisioned warm light filling the room in the evening as the sun set.

The estuary was a few streets down—not the beach exactly, but a nice place to walk at low tide, Barbara told me. I didn't care that the apartment wasn't on prime real estate. It looked like a wonderful place to live, and if I wanted the beach, I could easily walk to the Prom from Barbara's neighborhood. The studio was small by anyone else's standards, but I'd never had a place of my own before, and I fell in love with it instantly.

Vincent seemed pleased that Barbara and I hit it off, and politely excused himself once we'd made a deal. I told him I'd stop by the museum later, once I'd gotten settled. Barbara and I talked for a while—she was a widow, and was glad to have a renter at last. Her last tenant had left in the middle of the night without paying that month's rent, so she'd been hesitant about taking a chance on me. It sounded like Vincent had put in a good word. I felt grateful—I barely knew him and he'd done me more than one kindness. And, thanks to Vincent and Peter buying the pearls, I could afford both first and last month's rent. I made a mental note to thank them later.

After getting the key from Barbara, I locked up the apartment and walked down to the bank to open checking and savings accounts and rent a safety deposit box to store the pearls. That was a lesson I could thank my mother for. If she taught me anything, it was the importance of keeping valuables in a safe place. That lesson had come to mind after I was mugged. Better late than never to change course.

My next stops were the Blue Heron Boutique and the Beach Cottage, two stores Barbara had recommended, where I purchased clothing, toiletries, towels, bed linens, and other essentials for my new home. Nothing extravagant. Realizing I had a number of bags to carry, I also bought a vintage, aqua-colored bike that had a woven rattan basket on the front and wire baskets on the back. That would come in handy for groceries too, since I didn't drive. I could see myself taking the bike for a spin on the Prom to watch the sun go down. I never imagined I could fall in love with a town, but I was smitten with Seaside.

I rode back to the apartment, wind in my hair. The day was surprisingly warm and sunny, and by the time I parked my bike, I was in a hurry to take off my jacket. Barbara waved at me from the kitchen window, and came out the back door to help me carry my bags to the apartment.

"Someone got a new bicycle, I see," she said, smiling warmly.

I gave her a goofy grin. "I always wanted a bike like this. It's perfect for getting around town."

She laughed. "You might not think so when the winter wind

and rain get wild, but at least you've got fenders for the puddles. I'm glad to see you're settling in."

"Thanks. I think I'll ride down to the museum—see if they need any help."

"I'm sure Vincent will appreciate it. He's getting antsy about opening day," Barbara said, giving me a pat on the shoulder and leaving me to finish putting away my purchases.

Vincent was in a meeting when I arrived at the museum, and Peter was nowhere to be found. I loitered in the gift shop, admiring Gabriel's paintings. My eyes were drawn to the landscape I'd seen before, the one with the stormy waves and Tillamook Head. I knew I should save my money and not make any frivolous purchases—another life lesson Mom had drilled into me—but I kept thinking about my little apartment and the blank wall behind the loveseat. The painting was the perfect size, and would bring color to an otherwise blank canvas.

Beth, the woman Vincent said he was putting in charge of the gift shop, was standing by the cash register. I ventured closer to the painting, aware that Beth was watching me, and checked out the price. It was costly for my budget, especially since I'd just spent money setting up house. But I had to have it.

I now had several thousand in the bank, plus pearls I hadn't yet sold, and I could already feel a new crop forming under my skin. It wouldn't be long before they'd be ready to shed, and then I could sell those too, if not to the museum, then perhaps to Gatsby's or some other shop. I promised myself I'd be careful with my money, after this one indulgence.

"Do you like it?" Beth asked me.

I turned to her, grinning. "I *really* do."

"I'm still setting up the shop," Beth said, "so the credit card machine isn't up and running. I hope that's okay."

"No problem. I've got cash."

Beth bubble-wrapped the painting and slipped it in a paper

bag. It wasn't so large I couldn't carry it in one of the baskets on the back of my bike. I'd have to take it home while the weather held out. I headed out of the gift shop, intending to make a quick trip back to the apartment, when I saw Gabriel heading down the hall to the room where he painted. I didn't think about it—I just followed him.

When I entered the room, he was on stage, placing a blank canvas on his easel. He looked up at the sound of the door closing behind me.

"Hi," I said, tucking the paper bag under my arm.

"Hello." He held my gaze for a moment and then busied himself with tubes of paint, squeezing out colors onto the palette that was sitting on a small table next to the easel.

He didn't seem to mind me being there, so I approached the stage. "Thank you for dinner last night. It was amazing."

He didn't raise his head, but muttered, "You're welcome."

"I think we got off on the wrong foot," I said. "I didn't mean to intrude."

He looked up from the palette, screwing the cap onto a tube of paint, and sighed. "It wasn't you. Vincent can be…" He hesitated, as though trying to find the right word. "He can be *pushy*. But he means well."

"He really does care about you."

Gabriel scratched his nose with a paw-like hand. "I know. He's trying to help me, but he doesn't understand what it's like, being like this." He gestured to his face. "He thinks he understands, but he doesn't."

"It's easier for him to hide how he's different," I said. The irony of that statement and my own condition was not lost on me.

"Yeah," Gabriel said. He plucked an elastic hair band from his shirt pocket and pulled his shoulder-length, jet black hair back into a pony tail. He nodded at the package I was holding. "What's in the bag?"

"Oh." My face flushed with heat. "I, uh, bought something. For my new place." I kept the painting tucked tight under my arm, embarrassed to show him what I'd bought.

He raised a shaggy eyebrow. "Something? From *our* gift shop?"

I glanced down at the museum's steampunk submarine logo, stamped on the bag. I glared at the logo, annoyed to have been found out so easily. The last thing I wanted was for him to think I was in love with his work. Even though I was. Which wasn't the point. Dammit.

He gave me a sly smile. "Let me see."

I groaned and peeled back the bubble wrap a tiny bit so he could see a corner of the canvas.

His smile widened into a toothy grin. "As I suspected."

I tried to be nonchalant. "I had a blank wall in my apartment. I needed something to fill the space."

Gabriel laughed, clearly pleased with himself. "Sure. And my painting happened to be the right size for that space."

"Actually, yes."

He pulled a stool out from under the table, and set it in front of me on stage. "Here. Sit."

I looked from him to the blank canvas, and frowned. Fine. Why not? I leaned my new painting against the lip of the stage and then mounted the steps and took a seat on the stool.

He gave me an encouraging smile and picked up a paintbrush. It looked thin and fragile in his large hands.

"Wait," I said. I stood up and shrugged off my coat, and then smoothed down my long dark hair, arranging it to cascade down one shoulder. I was wearing one of my new tops—a plain, cream-colored sweater.

"Good," he said. "Okay." He screwed up his face in concentration, looking from me to the easel, and then got to work.

I watched him in silence for a while, and then asked, "So, is this how it works? Your show?"

He paused, brush hovering over the canvas. "Oh. Well, I'm supposed to talk while I paint, but it's hard to do both at the same time."

"What are you supposed to talk about?"

He dipped his brush in dark blue paint and quickly made a series of broad strokes on the canvas. "My life. About how I like to paint, but also my, you know, situation."

"Oh. Okay. Talk to me then."

He looked at me, uncertain, and dipped his brush in a teal color from his palette.

"Vincent wants you to practice, right?" I asked.

"Yeah." He sighed. "I hate this part."

"Which part?"

He brushed on paint in quick, short strokes. "Talking about myself."

"I get that." And I did. "But it's not much of a show if you're painting in silence. You're an interesting person. People want to know about you."

"I know. But it feels like I'm selling a little bit of my soul every time I tell my story." There was a strained look on his face.

I thought I could understand what it felt like to share something so intimate, to feel like I was selling part of myself. I rose from my chair and stepped closer to him.

He held up his hands to stop me. "No! Don't look yet. It's not done."

I took one more step forward, careful to look at him and not the painting. He lowered his hands to rest on his knees. There was a look of confusion on his face, like he was wondering what, exactly, I was doing. Honestly, I didn't know either.

I reached out and placed my hand on his hand. He froze, staring into my eyes and then down at my hand on his. I don't think he was used to being touched. He probably avoided it. I know I did. Even so, I squeezed his hand gently. It was furrier than most people's, but definitely human. "You don't have to share anything you don't want to. But maybe if you can help people understand what it's like to be you, they'll have more empathy for other people."

"That's exactly what Vincent says. He's got more faith in people than I do."

I slid my hand off his and stepped back to perch on the stool. "I can understand that. I haven't exactly had the best experiences with people either." I shifted in my seat. "But you're the one on stage. You control your story. You get to decide what parts to tell and what to leave out." That I could definitely relate to. I was an expert at leaving out details in my own story.

He dipped his brush in a dark brown color and began painting again. "Okay," he said softly. "Okay." He took a cloth and blotted the canvas, and then dipped his brush in a warmer brown. "I was ten when my mother sold me to a traveling circus."

His words jolted me. My own mother wouldn't have won the mother-of-the-year award, but I couldn't imagine her selling me to somebody.

"She wasn't a bad mother," he said, reading my expression of shock. "It's just that we were very poor, and I was the oldest, and she had three other children to care for. We lived in a little town in Arizona called Los Lobos, near the border of New Mexico." He looked back at the canvas, drawing the brush down in long strokes. "It wasn't even a town—just a truck stop with a diner and a tiny trailer park in the middle of the desert, next to the highway. We lived in a two-bedroom single-wide—mom and dad and my little sister in one bedroom, and me and my brothers crammed into the other. There was this chili farm about 20 miles away, and every morning, the farmer would send a pickup truck around to pick up the men from the trailer park. They would all pile in the back to go pick chilis. When I was seven, there was an accident—one of those freak dust storms that would sometimes blow over the highway and make it impossible to see. The truck my dad was in got side-swiped by a semi and rolled. The driver was okay, but the guys in the back didn't make it. After that, my mom scraped by, cooking at the diner to keep food in our bellies. She was always a good cook—making magic out of simple recipes and ingredients, but her dream was to open a restaurant where she could cook Italian food and Mexican food, recipes she'd learned from her mom and my father's grandma. Sometimes I'd walk over with my siblings and we'd get to eat what was left at the end of the day—the food that would have gone to waste. It was still good, the diner just hadn't had enough travelers come through for the day. The tough part was being out in public—people tended to notice me and stare. Word got around about me, I guess, because one day a man came by our trailer. He said his name was Javier Ramos. He claimed he was my dad's uncle, and he wanted me to join his traveling show. He offered my mother five thousand dollars—a fortune for my family—if she'd let me go with him."

I sat still on my chair, transfixed by his story.

He cleaned his brush and picked up a smaller one. His eyebrows narrowed as he concentrated on adding details to his artwork. "Things were okay for a while—he treated me well, fed me as much as I wanted. But as I got older, he worried I would run away, so he built a cage, and locked me inside. It was a trailer with wheels and sides that opened up so people could look inside when we had a show. He called me El Lobo—the Wolf—because of the way I looked and because of the town I grew up in. Funny thing is, we didn't have wolves in Los Lobos, we had coyotes. But Javier was interested in showmanship, not authenticity." Gabriel put down his brush and picked up a palette knife. "I never even tried to run away, but he was scared his main attraction would escape. He only let me out of the trailer to wash and use the toilet, and he had a man—a big man—that he hired as a guard to keep me in line. I only ever knew him by his last name, Jones. Javier called him Jones the Bones, because he'd been in prison for aggravated assault after breaking a man's legs. He'd been in a biker gang and had tattoos on his neck and arms. He scared the hell out of me, but Javier would joke around with him like they were best buddies. For all I know, they met in prison. Jones followed me in when I washed up, and he refused to leave my side, to give me any privacy. Not that I was so used to privacy—growing up in our tiny trailer, but still. It was different with my brothers and sister."

I shifted in my seat, uncomfortable. Gabriel and I had more in common than I'd realized. Privacy was a luxury.

Gabriel didn't seem to notice my reaction. "Jones made sure I knew about his time in the gang—he would tell me about the people he'd hurt. He hit me if I was too slow in following his orders, and my great-uncle wouldn't listen when I complained. But I got bigger—I grew taller and at night, when everyone else in the circus was asleep in their own trailers, I climbed the bars of the cage so I got stronger. I hung upside-down and did sit-ups." He smiled to himself. "I even did push-ups. I couldn't run around much because the cage wasn't big enough, but I could do that."

A dark shadow passed over Gabriel's features. "It was a good thing I did get stronger, because one night, Jones came to my trailer. That man hated me. He started hitting me. He was drunk, and he yelled that I was the son of the devil, and my mother was a witch, and that's why I was born a monster. He was going to kill me."

Gabriel cleaned his brush and set it aside. "I was only thirteen, and he was bigger than me, but I was wiry. All that climbing built up my muscles, made me quick on my feet. He lunged for me, and I leapt out of the way. I pushed him, and he hit his head on the bars of the cage. Hard enough that I heard something crack, and his head started bleeding. He'd locked the door behind him, but I grabbed his keys. Then I just ran. I ran as fast as I could into the night."

Gabriel looked at me. My hands were cramped from holding onto the stool, mesmerized as I listened to his story. I nodded my head for him to continue.

"They caught me pretty quick. I didn't know where I was. We were in Blythe, a town in California I'd never been to, so I ran to get as far away as I could, but somebody like me is easy to find." He laughed bitterly. "I tried to disguise myself. When I ran down an alley, I found a dirty ball cap someone had lost, and I shoved it on my head to hide my face. But people tend to notice a boy covered in hair, and the police found me the next day, hiding behind a couple of trashcans, outside a restaurant. They took me to jail. Jones had a family, and they showed up, demanding justice. My great-uncle came by, but he didn't help me, even though I told him I killed the guard in self-defense. He just shook his head and left. He planned to leave me there to rot. I guess I wasn't worth the bad publicity, even though I'd brought in lots of cash before."

"How did you get out?"

"Vincent." Gabriel stepped back from the painting, inspecting it. "Vincent was in California on vacation with his wife and son, and they saw my story in the papers. Kind of hard to miss with a sensational headline like, *Werewolf Boy Slaughters Circus Guard.* My photo was on the front page. Vincent could see I was just a skinny kid, and he felt bad for me, so he came to see me in jail. I was scared of him at first, but I was also desperate for help. After I told him my story, he promised he would get me out. He hired an attorney, and somehow—to this day, I don't know how—convinced the sheriff that since I was a minor, and since I'd been caged and abused, I couldn't be held responsible for my actions. He offered to adopt me, give me a decent home. The sheriff agreed. The charges were dropped and the sheriff turned me over to Vincent's custody. He brought me to Oregon." Gabriel looked at me. "This part I wouldn't share with an audience, but I'm sure there were bribes involved. I think Vincent bought off the sheriff and bought off that man's family. He didn't buy off my great-uncle though. I know, because just before I was released, Javier Ramos came back to the jail, angry. He and Vincent had an argument, and I'll never forget what Vincent told him. He said Javier wasn't really my great-uncle, and I'd never be his slave again. That was the last time I saw him."

I stared at Gabriel, trying to wrap my mind around his story, to understand how he'd survived so much. "Did you ever see your family again?"

He shook his head. "No, but Vincent wrote to my mother, to let her know what had happened, and that I was okay. She did write back, to say that she'd been tricked into giving me up. She didn't know that Javier Ramos wasn't really related to us, and she was sorry for what had happened to me. She said she prayed I could someday forgive her."

"Did you?"

He shrugged. "I don't know if I'd call it forgiveness, but I've come to peace. It's been almost fourteen years. I barely remember her. As far as I know, she still lives in Los Lobos. My brothers would be grown by now, and my sister would be a teenager. I wish them well, but I don't want to see them." He looked at me. "I'm better off where I am."

I nodded. "I know the feeling. Things weren't so great with my mom. I don't wish her harm. I just want to be on my own."

"Yeah." He rolled his shoulders, as if shaking off a weight he'd been carrying. "Okay, then. Ready to see the painting?"

I nodded, and he turned the easel around. It pivoted easily on wheels, and as it swung around, I was first struck by the brilliant colors he'd incorporated. My portrait was done in an impressionist style, as though a filter had been cast over my features, softening them. My cream-colored sweater almost seemed to glow against brilliant blues and greens in the background, a technique I'd seen him use in landscapes. My hair—a deep brown—had golden highlights as though I were standing in a shaft of sunlight. That wasn't a stretch from reality, but there's a difference between looking at yourself in a mirror and seeing a version of yourself rendered through someone else's perspective. My pale gray eyes were large and luminous, almost otherworldly. It was a portrait of me, but an improved version. "You made me beautiful," I whispered.

Gabriel looked down, suddenly shy. "I paint what I see." He avoided my gaze, cleaning his brushes, which was good because heat had creeped into my cheeks. "I've been inspired by Jose Royo, a modern impressionist from Spain," he said. "I like his style—the way he uses color, how he captures a person's expression. It's all about the emotional connection to another human being."

Hearing his story, I'd begun to view him in a different light. Now I was just floored by his talent and his ability to create a portrait so quickly. "It's *really* good." An understatement, but I was at a loss for words.

"Thanks," Gabriel said. He dared to meet my eyes, and I gave him a smile.

"How did you learn how to do this?"

"Self-taught." He straightened his shoulders, looking more confident. "The worst thing about Javier Ramos putting me in that cage wasn't the physical abuse. It was the lack of mental stimulation. I had limited schooling, but I could read and write. He didn't care about that. He expected me to sit there, day in and day out, so people could look at me. But I was looking back. That's why portraits are hard for me—painting someone is intimate. It's about seeing and being seen, and I'd rather be the one doing the observing. I don't like being watched."

He liked to hide behind the canvas. That was something I'd noticed as he painted my portrait. He hunched, to make himself smaller. Not an easy task, considering he had to be at least six foot nine—maybe taller. But I didn't share all that—I simply nodded to show I understood.

"There was a girl who worked at the circus. Julieta. She was a few years older than me, and I never knew her last name, but it doesn't really matter. What matters is she liked to read. She was stationed at the food booth, selling sopapillas—a deep-fried pastry her mother made as Julieta served customers. She'd put the warm sopapillas on a paper plate and dust them with powdered sugar." Gabriel frowned. "They smelled delicious—I always wanted to try them, but never dared to ask. I was afraid Jones would slap me if I did. Anyway…between customers, Julieta would read. She always had a book with her." He smiled at the memory. "She caught me watching her once, and she gave me a kind smile. She waved her book at me, and I smiled back. Just before closing time, she snuck over, put her finger to her lips to warn me to be quiet, and stuck the book between the bars of my trailer. I hid it under my mattress, instinctively, knowing Jones would take it from me if he found it. I read it as quickly as I could in secret. My mind was starved for knowledge of the world outside my cage."

"What was the book?" I asked.

"It was a worn copy of *The Alchemist*, by Paulo Coelho. Changed my life."

"I've read it," I said. I'd found a copy of that book in the attic. I don't think it was my mother's. I think it was one of a handful of things she'd kept that belonged to my father. Maybe she forgot it was up there. It was in the same box where I'd found the photo of my dad, and that alone was enough to make me want to read it. It was one of the books that gave me the courage to think about leaving. One of the tenants of the book was that if you wanted something with all your heart, the universe would conspire to help you achieve it. I didn't know if that was true, but I was starting to believe it. I'd wanted to escape, and things were finally going my way. "It's an inspiring book."

"Yeah. It is," he said. "After I finished that book, she snuck me more. Then she gave me a journal and a pen. I guess she thought I'd use it to write, but I've never been good at getting my ideas on paper. Not with words, anyway. I started sketching. The first portrait I ever did was of Julieta. It was crudely done, but I caught her eye across the midway. I tore the page from the journal, crumpled it up, and dropped it outside my cage. She casually left her station and picked it up. Then she smiled. Her smile was what kept me going. I started drawing the people who came to the circus, and the more I practiced, the better I got."

"What happened to your journal? I'd love to see those drawings."

He frowned. "I lost it. I remembered to grab it when I ran away—it was the only thing I had of any importance, but the police took it away from me when I went to jail."

I remembered what it had felt like to lose my backpack with everything I owned when I arrived in Portland. It was devastating. "I'm sorry."

He shook off my concern. "It's all right. Vincent and Frida got me out soon after that, and when Frida discovered I could draw, she encouraged me to practice. She bought me my first set of paints. She used to sit for me, even after she got sick. It was hard to watch her grow weaker—she lost so much weight because of the cancer. I threw out those paintings, but Vincent kept one of the first ones I did. He hung it in his room."

"He really does admire your talent," I said. "He's worried about you."

"I know." Gabriel pulled on the elastic band holding his hair in a ponytail, and let his hair fall to his shoulders. He stuffed the elastic band in his shirt pocket. "He thinks if I tell my story it will help me."

I brushed my own hair out of my eyes. "Can I be honest with you about that?"

He looked confused. "About my story? Sure, I guess."

"I don't think you should tell it."

He raised his eyebrows. "What?"

"It's just..." I struggled to organize my thoughts. "What happened at the circus—that man attacking you—that was the worst night of your life, am I right?"

He nodded.

"You went through something horrible." I ticked off a list on my fingers. "Physical abuse, emotional abuse...and you lost your family."

"Yes."

"So...if you tell your story to an audience—to strangers who don't know anything about you—day after day, won't that take a toll on you? I mean, I watched you when you were telling me that story, and it looked like you were reliving a traumatic experience. It was a compelling story, and it definitely made me feel more empathy for you, so I get what Vincent is trying to do here. I have no doubt it would engage an audience and make them think about how they treat other people. But how will telling that story help *you*? I don't think it will."

"I hadn't thought about that," he said quietly. "But I have to say something—I have to show people I'm relatable. I can't just paint in silence."

"Okay, but do Elena or Sid tell a story like that? Do they make themselves that vulnerable?"

He shook his head. "Not really. I mean, Elena talks briefly about what it was like to be bullied for her appearance, but most of her act focuses on her singing. And Sid—well, heckling runs off him like water off a duck. He's a comedian. He just laughs everything off."

"They don't let people in—not like you do." Which was funny, considering how thick his armor had been when I'd met him.

"No."

"I don't see how you can tell that story every day and not let it consume you. I don't know how you can move past what happened if you do that." I put my hand on his arm, and he froze at first, and then relaxed. "It's not my place to tell you—or Vincent—what to do. I just got here. But if it were me, I'd talk more about what you love about painting and less about the terrible things that happened to you." I looked into his eyes. "It's your life. You get to decide how much of it to share, and who's allowed to be part of that."

Gabriel put his hand over mine and squeezed gently. "Thank you," he said softly. "After everything that's happened, everything Vincent's done for me, I didn't know how to tell him no."

"That's why you've been so angry."

He nodded. "Yeah. I felt like I owed him—like I had to give up my privacy to pull my weight around here."

I winced, remembering what Peter had said the day before. Gabriel didn't seem to notice. "Maybe you should talk to Vincent. Peter too. They might not like it, but they should respect it." I slipped my hand out from under his.

"I will."

I gave him a smile. "Good."

22

I left Gabriel with the intention of taking my painting home, but as I headed toward the museum doors, I saw Peter and Vincent standing in front of the aquatic exhibit. Peter turned at my approach and waved me over with a grin. "Ever seen a mermaid?"

I smiled. "Nope. Never."

"You're about to." He pointed to the tank and I heard a splash.

I stared through the viewing window, catching a flicker of movement as something emerged from behind the oyster wall. An otherworldly being came into view—long, blond hair streaming behind her, tail undulating as she swam. She dove down, toward the bottom of the tank, disappearing behind a curtain of kelp, and then appeared closer to the window, waving at us. Closer up, I could see her face was narrow with high cheekbones, almost elfin, which made her look even less human and more like a creature from the deep. Her blond hair had streaks of green and blue, which matched the iridescent scales on her tail. She wore a bikini top encrusted with shells and pearls. She flicked her tail and glided over to the oyster wall.

Vincent smiled at me. "Well? Pick one."

I stared at the numbered shelves. "Number 17, please."

Vincent picked up the slate next to the window and wrote down my number. The mermaid nodded and selected the correct oyster. Then she swam back to the window and placed the oyster in a net, which Vincent pulled over the side. He retrieved the oyster and opened it. Inside, one of my pearls sat nestled on a bed of pink latex. "Lucky guess," Vincent said, and I shot him a grin.

"Oh, I've got more where that came from. Let someone else keep it," I said.

"She's beautiful, isn't she?" Vincent asked, closing up the hinged shell. "And she really can move in the water."

"Oh, she's beautiful all right," Peter said, "but you didn't tell me she had tattoos."

Startled by his tone, I jerked my head to look at him. He was visibly angry, his hands clenched at his sides.

Vincent waved him off as he put the oyster back in the net so the mermaid could return it to the shelf. "A minor detail. It's not a big deal."

"It *is* a big deal, Dad," Peter said. "I keep telling you—the magic is in the *details*." He gestured at the other displays in the room. "That's what makes all this work. Details make or break the illusion." He stormed over to the tank, jerking his thumb at the woman swimming inside. I followed his gaze—the mermaid had a tattoo of a hibiscus just below her collarbone, a sleeve of similar flowers on her left forearm, and a series of stars trailing down her right side to her navel. "You think a real mermaid strolls on shore and frequents a tattoo parlor?"

Vincent looked unsure. "Well, no, but…"

"We've got two days before we open, and I don't have time to find another mermaid," Peter said. He groaned, venting his frustration. "You said you'd handled this, Dad."

"I did handle it, son. She swims beautifully, and she hardly needs to use the air hose at all," Vincent said. "She looks real to me." He looked at me, as if he hoped I'd chime in with support. I just looked from him to Peter, eyes wide. In spite of my "expert" advice to Gabriel on how to talk to Vincent about his discomfort with his show, I'm terrible with conflict. I freeze, feeling awkward and useless.

Peter threw his hands in the air. "You know what—never mind. I'll fix it." He took off, toward the back of the museum where he kept his office.

I gave Vincent an apologetic look and hurried after Peter. "Peter! Wait."

Peter whirled, his eyes narrowed in anger. "What?"

"Can I help in some way?" I asked.

"I'm going to have to rework the suit—pour new latex to cover her up. Then I have to make adjustments to make sure it actually fits her, and attach the original top to the latex. And try, somehow, to make it look like she's *not* wearing latex. So, no, not unless you know how to sew," he said.

"I do," I said quietly. Sewing was one of the things that had kept me sane as a shut-in. I taught myself and designed costumes for my dolls, inspired by the dresses I saw in old movies.

His jaw unclenched and he sighed. "Okay. Good. Come with me." He turned back to his father. "Send the mermaid to me when she dries off. I need both her and the suit," he called. Then he led me down the hall to his workshop.

It was part business office, part laboratory, with a high ceiling and industrial ductwork. On one side of the room, there was a minimalist-style stainless steel desk, with a laptop and printer, a coffee mug stuffed with pencils and pens, and a set of file folders. Nothing fancy—a practical place to work, with no décor or photographs. The other side of the room was filled with equipment and colorful things I didn't have words for. Some, like power tools, I recognized. Others, which appeared to be molds and materials in various shapes and textures, I'd never seen. A rack of metal shelves held neatly labeled art supplies.

And then there were other objects, which seemed out of this world. Hanging over Peter's oversized wooden work table was a giant, bronze angler fish with eyes like lanterns, glowing with amber light. The fish had sharp, curved teeth like four-foot-long needles. The creature could have been at home in a deep-sea movie. There was a replica of the Man in the Moon from Georges Méliés film, *A Trip to the Moon.* A rocket ship was buried in the moon's eye, just like in the movie. In the corner of the room, a life-sized zombie stood, arms raised menacingly like it was about to grab its next victim. It looked so realistic, with rotting skin and bloody wounds, it startled me. For a second, I thought there was an actual person standing there, dressed up to trick or treat. Peter's workshop looked like a place where Hollywood magic happened.

I longed to ask him about his creations, but I could see he was in no mood for chit-chat. Later, I learned these objects, as amazing as they were to me, were cast-offs from various film school projects. Peter told me he'd created the zombie for a friend's indie horror flick, and was considering using it when we decorated the museum for Halloween. He had an idea to do an after dark tour, complete with a haunted house.

Peter led me to the work table and gestured for me to take a seat on an industrial-style metal stool. "What we've got to do is create a mold to fit her body, and then pour latex that will look like her natural skin. Then, I'll have to attach it to the tail and make it fasten from the back. If you could adhere and sew on the bikini top, that would help. Problem is, I'm not sure how to make the transition from the top of the latex to the real skin of her neck, so it looks seamless. Same thing for her wrists. I want the latex to blend in."

I thought about the design of the bikini top, how it was

encrusted with shells, pale green sea glass beads, and tiny fresh-water pearls. "We could make her a decorative collar and cuff bracelets—something to hide the edges of the latex shirt."

He nodded. "That could work. Do you think you could help me sew that on?"

"I'll give it my best shot," I promised.

"Fair enough," he said, and started selecting materials from a series of shelves and galvanized steel bins, placing them on the table. "I'm sorry about before."

"It's okay. You were upset."

He frowned as he opened up a can labeled *Alginate*. "I shouldn't have lost my temper though. I'm stressed, but so is everybody else. Thing is, I think the mermaid will be a huge draw for this place, and we need to get it right. She's got to be perfect."

I nodded. "You don't want anything to break the illusion."

He gave me a smile and pointed a finger in my direction. "*Exactly*. You get it. I just wish Dad did."

"It'll be okay," I assured him. "We'll make it work."

There was a knock on the office door. "Come in," Peter called.

Vincent entered, a sheepish look on his face. He carried the mermaid costume over one arm. The woman who was playing the mermaid was a few steps behind him. "This is Chandra," Vincent said. "Chandra, this is Peter, my son, and Amelia, who is new to our museum."

I waved a hello, and watched as Peter shook Chandra's hand. He seemed much calmer. If he was embarrassed by his anger, he hid it well. Maybe he was just trying to move forward, to focus on solving the problem. "Nice to meet you, Chandra. Thank you for coming in. We'll need to make some adjustments to your costume."

She nodded. "Mr. Fortunato mentioned that on the way over. He said you needed to make a mold or something?"

"Yes," Peter said. "We'll need to create a mold of your torso, and then I can pour latex to build the top of the costume." He paused. "Are you okay with removing your shirt so we can wrap your body?" He looked at me. "Amelia, if I tell you how to do it, could you help her? That way she'll have a bit more privacy."

"Of course." I was happy to be included, and curious to see how the process would work.

"Yes, that's fine," Chandra said. "I'm wearing my swim suit under my t-shirt, anyway."

Peter frowned. "Unfortunately, we've got to apply the paste directly to your skin. If you're wearing any kind of fabric, it will pick up those textures. But my father and I will leave the room, and Amelia can help you."

Chandra looked unsure. "Okay. I guess."

I gave her what I hoped was a comforting smile. I felt awkward about all this myself, but it wouldn't help to share that. Peter talked me through the procedure, how to apply the paste and what he called "bandages," which would wrap around her torso. He looked at Chandra. "It will dry quickly and it might feel itchy, but it will make a cast of your torso that we can then peel off. Amelia, once you've got her wrapped, could you grab me to see if everything looks okay? We'll have to work quickly because if it doesn't work, we'll need to start over, but we can make some adjustments before it dries."

"Sounds good," I said.

"Okay. Dad and I will be right outside," Peter said. He and Vincent exited the room, leaving me and Chandra to stare at each other.

"All right," I said. "We should get started."

She nodded and pulled off her shirt and bikini top while I prepared the mixture. I tried to keep a steady hand as I wrapped her body. I was nervous, not just from worry I'd make a mistake, but also because I wasn't used to touching someone so intimately.

I think Chandra sensed my anxiety, because she talked a lot as I worked, using humor to make light of the situation. Maybe she was nervous too.

"Well," she said. "I've never done *this* before."

I forced a laugh. "Me neither. I guess there's a first for everything." I crouched and laid a long strip of cloth on her stomach and smoothed it out. The process was similar to creating the paper mâché mask I'd made in elementary school.

"Never been a mermaid before either," she said.

"Are you local to Seaside?" I asked, dipping another strip of cloth in the molding mixture.

"No, just passing through. I was hitchhiking the 101, but I came downtown to see the beach, and saw the ad for the job in the museum window. I thought, that looks fun. Why the hell not?"

"You swim really well."

She smiled. "Thanks. I grew up surfing in California. Thought I'd check out the Pacific Northwest for a while."

"Do you like it?" I asked, patting down a bandage.

"Yeah. Rains more than I'm used to, but it's all right. I could see myself staying here a while, if this works out."

I added a strip of cloth to her neckline. Before we started, she had pulled her long, wavy hair into a quick bun to get it out of the way, and now tucked a stray lock behind her ear. I caught a glimpse of a tattoo there, another hibiscus. "You must really like hibiscus flowers."

"Sorry?"

"Your tattoos." I gestured to her ear and collarbone.

"Oh, those." She laughed. "Got my tats after a bad breakup. He was a control freak. The tattoos were my way of reclaiming power."

I thought about my mom trying to control my life. "I hear that. Good for you for leaving."

"I had to get away, get lost. Start over. You know?"

"Yeah. I do." I placed one last strip of cloth on her shoulder, and inspected my work. The bandages looked smooth, clinging to the angles and curves of her torso. "I think we're done. I'll get Peter to make sure I did it right." I went to the office door and opened it. Peter and Vincent were talking quietly in the hall. They stopped and looked over at me. "We're ready," I said.

"I need to finish ordering supplies," Vincent told Peter. He placed his hand on his son's shoulder. "But let's talk later, yes?"

"Sure," Peter said. I tried to read his expression, but it was guarded. He walked into the room, all business, inspecting my work on Chandra. "Hmm." He smoothed the edges at her neckline and wrists. I'd left the back open, as he'd instructed. We'd need a second mold to complete the project, fusing the two parts together. "Looks good. Nice work, Amelia."

I breathed a sigh of relief. "Thanks." Part of me wanted to impress Peter, the other part was worried I'd set him off, the way Vincent had. I basked in his attention, but after witnessing his anger, I felt intimidated by him too. But he was an artist and a professional, and I understood that his reputation as both were at stake. It wasn't personal.

"All right, Chandra," Peter said, walking a slow circle around her. "Let's give this ten minutes to dry, and then we'll peel it off and do the other side. Then you should be done for today, but we'll need you back at nine tomorrow morning for a fitting. How's that sound?"

"Sounds good, Peter." She gave him a winning smile, which he returned with a warm smile of his own.

I tensed up. I'm not sure if I was jealous of the attention he was paying her, or the easy familiarity in her tone. Maybe both, but it was a reminder of how little experience I'd had with men, how much of a disadvantage I had in navigating the world after growing up so sheltered. Maybe someday I'd possess that kind of casual confidence too. I decided to befriend Chandra, to learn what I could from her. That was how I became the barker for the mermaid exhibit.

23

Peter and I worked late into the night on the costume, to get it ready for the fitting. As he crafted the latex shell and painted it to match Chandra's skin tone, airbrushing it to add subtle shading, I created a collar and cuffs that would sit at her neckline and wrists. I imagined her as a mermaid queen, arrayed in shells and pearls befitting her station. Nothing cheesy—I kept the look organic, with materials a sea-dweller could find in her habitat. I felt a rush of warmth when Peter praised my work.

"Looks fantastic, Amelia. Let's tack the pieces to the costume, temporarily, in case we need to adjust it after the fitting. Fingers crossed, this thing will fit like a glove, and the way I've fastened it in the back will make it easy for her to get into. It's going to be snug, but she'll still be able to slip out during breaks." He focused his attention on a zipper he'd hidden. It had a long leash so she could zip it herself, and then tuck the leash into the costume, exactly as if she were wearing a wetsuit. "On the bright side, this should keep her warm when she's in the water. She'll have to do the show a few times a day, and that salt water tank is chilly."

"I'll be around to help if she needs me," I told him. He'd shown me the dressing room he'd built on top of the tank. Above the glass viewing windows on the first floor of the museum, the hull of the tank, which resembled a ship, continued upward to disguise a second, hidden floor. There was a space behind the tank and filter system with a ladder so Chandra could climb up to the platform over the tank. Beside the platform was a room shielded from public view where Chandra would be able to get changed, get a snack, shower off, even use the restroom—all the things she'd need to do throughout the day. It made sense to have a space where she could take a break without having to climb up and down the ladder, since she was sporting fins. The tail for the costume was heavy and cumbersome on land. She had a phone up there to call us if she needed help, and her secret room had port-hole windows so she could peek out and view the museum's lobby. Peter had thought of everything.

"I had to weight the tail," he'd explained as I'd picked it up, trying to get a sense of how it worked. "Otherwise, she'd just float to the surface."

"Well, that would ruin the effect," I said.

"Yep. The weights I used give her neutral buoyancy, so she's able to dive to the bottom of the tank. They help her control her body to make her look more natural as she's swimming."

I have to admit, I wanted to try it myself. I bit my lip to keep from volunteering. Playing a mermaid looked more fun than I'd originally thought it would be, but I couldn't risk the exposure.

The fitting the next morning went well. The costume fit Chandra perfectly, which allowed me to finish sewing on the embellishments while Peter got the museum ready for opening day.

There was so much to do—cleaning, hanging banners, making reminder calls to the media. I tried to stay out of Peter's way as he directed the museum staff in completing tasks, focusing instead on my new job as a carnival barker. The idea of speaking in front of a crowd was terrifying, but I forced myself to take up the challenge. Vincent helped me come up with lines, to get the crowd's attention and keep them engaged. After rehearsing extensively, I got comfortable with it. I stopped being scared and started feeling excited. After a lifetime of being hidden away, I'd never dreamed of performing. Then again, I was doing all kinds of things I'd been too scared to do before. It felt liberating.

The best part was when Vincent took me to the dressing room at the back of the museum, and let me pick out my own costume for dress rehearsal. I chose an outfit that made me look as though I'd emerged from an underwater steampunk adventure, starting with an olive green, fitted jacket with brass buttons that fastened down one side. I paired that with dark trousers and knee-high leather boots. I enlisted Chandra in helping me fix my hair, a braided updo that looked complicated, but was easy enough for me to do myself. She did my makeup too—something I'd never worn before. Looking in the mirror at the smoky eye and dark, burgundy lips Chandra had given me, I hardly recognized myself, which was perfect for somebody on the run, trying to build a new life.

As I stared at my reflection, I heard a rustle of fabric. "Oh, sweetie, you look amazing!" I turned to see Elena, taking an evening dress from a rack of clothes.

"Thank you," I said. "Chandra's good, isn't she?"

Elena beamed at Chandra. "You come visit me next, honey." She glanced at her own reflection and smoothed her dark curls. "That smoky eye is killer, and I desperately need your help."

"You got it," Chandra said. "But you already look beautiful, you know." I agreed—Elena looked elegant as always, her makeup flawless.

"Oh, thank you, hon. But it never hurts to have that something extra." She gave us a wink and waltzed off, dress in hand.

"You do look nice, Amelia."

I turned to see Gabriel, coming out of a changing stall. He

wore a white button-down shirt and black slacks. Nothing as fancy as Elena with the gowns she wore for her act, but a leap above his usual paint-covered flannel shirts and jeans.

"You look nice, yourself," I told him.

Chandra gave me a knowing smile and excused herself. "I'll go help Elena. See you later, Mia."

"Mia?" Gabriel asked.

"I'm trying on a nickname," I explained. "Since I'm in the process of reinventing myself. Moved to a new town, might as well change my name."

He chuckled. "Might as well. So, Vincent roped you into performing?"

I shook my head. "I volunteered. Like I said, I'm trying new things."

"Good for you."

"Did you talk to him?" I asked.

"Ah." He hesitated. "I tried. Vincent wasn't entirely happy—he didn't feel like me talking about painting was nearly as compelling as my story of growing up in a cage."

"But if you feel uncomfortable about telling your story—"

Gabriel held up his hand, stopping me. "He didn't like it, but he understood. He said, 'It's your act. Just make sure you keep people engaged.'"

"Oh. That's good, right?"

He nodded. "Yeah. I feel better about it. So, uh…thanks."

"You're welcome. I love your painting, by the way." I smiled, remembering the way the morning light brought out the colors and made it glow against the stark white walls of my apartment.

"Which one?" he asked.

"The seascape," I said, confused. Did he not remember our conversation the day before, the one where I'd embarrassed myself admiring his work?

"Oh," he said. "*Oh.*"

"What?"

"I thought you meant your portrait," he said. "You don't know?"

"Know what?"

"Vincent hung it in the lobby next to the ticket booth. To entice people to come to my show," he said.

"Oh."

"Is that weird? I told him he should ask you first," he said.

"No…I'm just surprised." I peeked at myself in the mirror. It was a little weird, considering I was so new and had somehow endeared myself to these people, and now had a role in an act located close to the entrance of the museum. But I looked different in costume, so maybe that was okay. People might not recognize me. I hoped not, because if my mom ever found out where I was…well, that would definitely be a problem.

"He said the painting was so beautiful, he had to hang it up. You know Vincent—once he gets an idea in his head…" He stared at his feet. "Sorry. I feel like a stalker now."

I slugged him in the arm playfully. "Yeah, knock that off. Next thing I know, you'll be parking outside my house."

He smiled, looking uncertain. I'm not sure he knew I was joking.

"Ready for tomorrow?" I asked.

"Opening day? Oh, hell no. But it will happen whether I want it to or not, won't it?"

I laughed. "Yep. If it's any consolation, I'm nervous too. But ready or not, here we come."

24

I woke up feeling nauseated. I wasn't kidding when I told Gabriel I was anxious about opening day. I got dressed anyway, mounted my bicycle, and rode down to the museum well before it opened. Beth, the gift shop manager, let me in, and I got to work, making sure signs were in place, helping Chandra get ready for her act, and then slipping into my own costume. It wasn't just me who had the jitters—I felt a nervous energy in the air. Everybody was worried. What if we opened the doors and nobody showed?

Luckily, our fears were unfounded. Thirty minutes to opening, a crowd amassed in front of the door. The press showed too. I spotted a reporter from the *Seaside Signal* interviewing attendees and taking photos. The doors opened and the crowd poured inside, filling the lobby. Vincent had tapped Beth, me, and others to direct people, to encourage them to visit the different shows and hall of exhibits so no single area became overwhelmed with people. Our visitors behaved themselves for the most part, aside from a snide comment here and there about the new freak show. The reporter approached me, but I declined an interview, taking her to Peter instead. I had no intention of becoming a spokesperson for everyone. I didn't need that kind of attention.

Chandra the Mermaid was a big hit, and in spite of my pre-show jitters, I did okay, remembering my lines and speaking loudly enough for the crowd to hear me. That was a huge accomplishment for somebody who had spent most of her life as a shut-in. There was no one to appreciate that but me, since I hadn't shared that particular tidbit about my life, but I was proud of myself. In the short time since I'd left home, I'd made significant strides toward my independence, to become a functioning adult.

As we closed down the museum that day, our collective anxiety changed to joy. We'd done it. We'd had a successful opening, and with spring break the next week and tourist season starting soon after, we'd keep our momentum going.

As the weeks came and went, I fell into a familiar pattern of coming to work, getting to know my new friends, and going home to a comfortable apartment. I was happy. For the first time in as long as I could remember, I was truly happy.

Even my monthly shedding of pearls didn't feel so bad. There was still pain and swelling leading up to the release of the pearls, but the exercise from biking to work lifted my spirits, and I could come home to my own place, where I could take a warm bath to ease the swelling. It was nice to have a steady income between my role at the museum and selling the pearls. Having financial stability reduced my stress, and that made growing the pearls easier to bear.

On the night of that first month in my apartment, when the pearls burst from my skin, I was able to care for myself in privacy. No mother standing over me, murmuring superficial words of comfort while she waited impatiently for me to finish so she could get the pearls cleaned up and packaged, to take to the jeweler's. I remembered how it had felt when I'd been homeless, shedding the pearls in a dirty restroom, biting my lip to keep from crying out because I was scared someone would discover my secret. Now I could grit my teeth and cry with no one to hear me. Now, if I made a mess, no one yelled at me about the blood on the floor or the bathroom towels. I cleaned up the mess myself and threw the dirty towels in my own washer in the garage downstairs. Mom always made such a big deal out of having to clean up the blood. It surprised me to learn that all it took was a little laundry detergent, bleach, and water. Looking back, I don't know what all the fuss was about.

No one at the museum had a clue about my secret, and I planned to keep it that way, making sure I left early on the day when I felt the pearls coming, claiming illness. If someone had asked, I would have attributed my aches to menstrual cramps.

I've observed that when the word *menstrual* is used, people react in one of two ways. Women nod in sympathy and offer their own stories of suffering. Men suddenly have someplace important to be, avoiding the conversation altogether. In any case, people didn't ask questions about my sudden bout of illness, and neither Peter nor Vincent pressured me to reveal my source for the pearls.

I got along well with my co-workers at the museum. There was comradery in dealing with the occasional heckler, and shared joy over happy news. In early May, Elena and Charlie got married. We gathered at the Cove at low tide to watch their nuptials, and then headed to the museum for the reception. Vincent, kind and generous as always, had transformed the lobby of the museum into a banquet hall for the evening. Tables sat under the celestial ceiling, where constellations sparkled with white light and glass planets orbited the glowing sun. Each table had a silver-plated lantern for a centerpiece, which cast soft light. Sea green glass floats and white flowers encircled the lanterns.

It was the first wedding I'd ever attended, aside from one when I was seven where I served as flower girl for my mother's cousin in Idaho. I relished the excuse to dress up, and bought a long-sleeved, sequined dress with a miniskirt. It covered my scars and showed off my legs. I'd come a long way from being a shy, homeschooled kid. When I showed up at the wedding, Chandra gave me a whistle of approval, and Peter gave me a smile that made me feel warm all over.

Now I sat with them and Gabriel at one of the tables, finishing dinner. We watched as the best man, Charlie's brother, and the maid of honor, one of Elena's best friends, gave their toasts. We smiled as Elena and Charlie had their first dance as a married couple. When the DJ invited the rest of us to the dance floor, Peter asked Chandra to dance, and she accepted with a smile. I felt a sting of jealousy, but wasn't surprised. They'd been spending a lot of time together, when Peter wasn't busy with the museum or on a trip. He took a lot of trips once the museum opened—meeting with potential partners he hoped would invest in our project, picking up supplies for the gift shop, and every now and then, taking a break at a cabin he'd bought several years before.

I watched the dancers, longing to be among them. Elena and Charlie glided past our table, wrapped in each other's arms. I was thrilled they were so happy together. Charlie looked dapper in a cream-colored vintage suit, the purple highlights in her hair now teal and aqua blue. Elena looked radiant in her long white gown, her dark curls cascading down her back. A crown of flowers had been woven into her hair. "She looks beautiful," I said.

"She's brave," Gabriel said, admiration in his voice.

I turned to him. "What do you mean?"

"The way she embraces how she looks. Elena could hide the beard and pass as normal. She could shave, get laser hair removal…but she doesn't," he said. "She puts herself out there and doesn't apologize. She's brave."

I hadn't thought of it that way, that Elena had the option to hide who she was. "What about you?"

"Me? No, I'm not brave."

"But you put yourself out there too."

He let out a bittersweet laugh. "I don't have a choice."

That couldn't be true. "You couldn't shave, or…?"

He laughed again, this time with more humor. "I have hair growing out of my *eyelids*. You ever tried to shave your eyelids? I have, and it's not pretty. No, no chance of passing for normal here." He straightened his tie. "This is as good as it gets."

"So there's no cure for…for what you have?"

"Hypertrichosis? No. It's genetic and it's rare. Far as I know, there are less than a hundred people on the planet dealing with this. Which means it's not much of a priority for medical research, when you think about more pressing concerns like heart disease and cancer. It's not like I'm dying. I'm just ugly." His tone was angry but resigned.

I put my hand on his arm. "You're not ugly."

He gave me a weak smile and patted my hand. "Thanks, but I have no illusions about what I look like. I've got to live with myself as I am. Even if there was a cure, that would require altering my DNA, and that's not possible, yet."

"If it *were* possible, would you do it?" I'd asked myself a similar question hundreds of times. If I could get rid of the pearls, would I? I didn't have an answer.

He sighed. "I don't know. I've lived like this for so long, I can't imagine anything different." He looked out at the people on the dance floor, having a great time, oblivious to his pain. "But it would be nice to be able to go someplace and not have anyone act like I'm a monster. To simply do the things everyone else does, and not have to think about the way I look."

I nodded. I knew more about that than I dared to say. "So what if we did?"

He looked at me, puzzled. "Did what?"

I stood up. "What if we went out there and joined them?"

His eyes widened. He looked terrified. "Oh. Oh, no. I don't dance."

"Come on." I smiled and offered him my hand. "Let's be brave together."

He shook his head. "I told you. I'm not brave."

"Then you'll lose your chance," Peter said. He was escorting Chandra back to the table. Her cheeks looked flushed from the exertion of dancing. "If you won't dance with Mia, I will."

Gabriel's look of terror twisted into a scowl. I hesitated in accepting Peter's outstretched hand, waiting for Gabriel to change his mind. But he didn't. "Do what you want," he said to his brother. "You always do."

I felt hurt at being dismissed so easily, but brushed the feeling aside. Fine. I'd been trying to be kind. If Gabriel didn't want to put himself out there and take a chance, that was his choice. But I'd been waiting my whole life to dance with someone, and I was done waiting. I gave Peter a warm smile and took his hand. "I'd love to dance with you."

As we stepped out onto the dance floor, I heard Gabriel huff behind us. I made a point to ignore him. Instead, I gave Peter a sheepish smile. "Confession time. I don't actually know how to dance."

Peter chuckled. "Well, lucky for you, I *do*. And it's a slow song, so we can buy time while I teach you." He led me to the edge of the dance floor, taking one of my hands and placing his other hand at my waist. "A waltz is pretty easy to learn, and it works for this song. You just take a big step and then two little steps, making a box with your feet. You step backward, I step forward. Just watch my feet and you'll pick it up quickly." He gave me a reassuring smile.

"Okay." I wasn't sure I understood, but I'd give it a try.

"All right. Here we go. ONE, two, three, ONE, two, three…"

I stepped backward, staring at Peter's feet. I mirrored his

movements, awkwardly at first, but then I got the hang of it. I looked up at him, my face beaming.

He grinned. "There you go! You've got it."

As the song ended, he spun me around, and I giggled. "Oh, that was fun. Thank you." I let go of his hand, meaning to head back to our table.

He grabbed my hand and pulled me back to him, chuckling. "Oh, we're not done." The new song was upbeat, and people started forming rows on the dance floor.

"What's this?"

"It's a line dance called the *Electric Slide*. Kinda dated, but popular at weddings." He guided me to his side and gestured to the line of people in front of us. "Just watch what they do and follow along."

I grinned. "Okay." I watched a girl in front of me as she crossed one foot behind the other, stepping forward and back and then side to side, moving her arms in tight circles as she punctuated her steps. Peter cracked up as I failed miserably in mimicking her, but I didn't mind. I laughed too. I was having the time of my life. I got the hang of it eventually, and wasn't too shabby either.

"Not bad for your first time," Peter said.

We danced together for two more songs, and then he led me back to our table. When we got there, Gabriel was gone.

25

I didn't see Gabriel for the rest of the weekend. I think he was avoiding me. It didn't really matter though, because I had bigger things to worry about once the week started. On Monday morning, Chandra didn't show for work. I tried calling her, texting her, and nothing. I asked around, and none of the other staff had seen her either.

Problem was, the museum had been reserved by North Coast Tours, a travel agency that catered to tourists who came in on the cruise ships that docked in Astoria, a city northeast of Seaside, on the Columbia River. Our beachside town was a popular spot for those kinds of tours, and we'd been lucky to land a contract with North Coast Tours. People on cruises brought in a ton of money to the museum in entry fees alone, and the mermaid exhibit was a big hit, especially with retirees. Almost everyone loved the mermaid, and the few who didn't liked the opportunity to gamble, slapping down ten bucks for a chance to win a pearl. We averaged giving away one pearl a day, and as long as we got twenty people to play the game, the pearl paid for itself. On cruise days, we'd have at least a hundred people vying for a chance at the pearl. The exhibit more than paid for itself.

To have to shutter the exhibit on a cruise day would be a disaster. I didn't know what to do. I rushed to Peter's office, to let him know we had a problem.

"We'll have to close the show for the day," he said.

I was surprised at how calm he seemed. I certainly didn't feel calm. "But we'll lose so much money! We've got one hundred and sixty people coming on this tour—can we really afford to miss this opportunity?"

He shrugged. "We don't have a choice. I can't fit in the mermaid costume." He gave me a pointed look. "Can you?"

I didn't want to admit it, but I could. At least, I *thought* I could. Chandra and I were the same size—we'd borrowed clothes from each other. I'd let her borrow a dress when Peter took her to dinner, and she'd lent me a pair of shorts when we went down to the beach after work. "Maybe, but I've never tried to swim with the tail."

He looked at the clock. "We've got an hour until opening, when the guests get here. It's a whole lot easier to find someone to fill in for your role than hers, and we're low on options. I suggest you try on the costume."

I clenched my hands in frustration. I couldn't say I hadn't thought about playing the mermaid. I'd been against it at first, but after watching Chandra play the role, the idea grew on me. She made it look so fun, and people loved her for it.

Children adored her, saying she looked like a mermaid princess. They'd stand in front of the glass of the tank and she'd swim by, giving them high fives.

A little girl recognized her one day when she was visiting the museum and Chandra was there dressed in street clothes, picking up her paycheck. "Where'd your tail go?" the girl had asked.

Without missing a beat, Chandra crouched down and said, "A sea witch granted me a wish, so today I have legs." She gave the girl a wink, stood, and tucked her check into the pocket of her jeans.

The little girl nodded solemnly. "Magic," she said, as if that were a perfectly logical explanation. She hugged Chandra's legs and then skipped off happily, back to her waiting parents.

The idea of bringing that level of joy into someone's life was appealing, I admit. I was annoyed at Chandra for being irresponsible and angry at Peter for putting me on the spot, but he was right. If we wanted to keep the exhibit open, I was our sole hope for making that happen. I sighed. "All right. I will *try*. No promises."

He surprised me again, this time with a hug. "Thank you, Mia. You're the best, you know." He was warm and his hair smelled like the ocean. He must have gone surfing earlier that morning. Flustered, I gave him a smile and hurried to try on the costume.

I climbed the ladder to the top of the tank and opened the door to the small dressing room next to the platform. The suit was there, draped over a towel rack. I'd helped Chandra enough times to know how it slipped on and fastened in the back. That wasn't the hard part, assuming it would fit. I closed the door and peeled off my clothes.

The costume did fit, and thankfully, I was able to get dressed by myself. I was midway through my pearl cycle, so while my wounds had healed, the new bumps on my back were starting to swell enough that anyone who saw my bare skin would have a whole lot of questions.

The hard part was it was impossible to walk or even stand with a tail, so once I had the suit on, I had to scoot on my butt, reach up to open the dressing room door, and then scoot some more until I was sitting on the edge of the platform. Once there, I had a moment of panic.

I wasn't afraid of the water. I knew how to swim, and I'd watched Chandra navigate the tank so many times I'd memorized the way she moved her body, holding her arms out in front of her and swishing her tail up and down. I knew exactly where the air hose was if I needed a quick hit, and I knew how to turn on a screen of bubbles in front of the glass, if I needed a curtain to shield my movements so I could make a quick escape or move the oysters around on the shelves without being seen.

In theory, I knew exactly what I needed to do to make this work. I also knew that once I slipped into the water, there would be no turning back. Maybe Chandra would come to work the next day, and this one would be a one-time thing, but I didn't think so. Somehow, I knew she wouldn't be back.

I took a deep breath and let it out slowly, expelling carbon dioxide from my lungs. Then I took another deep breath and slipped beneath the water. Without goggles, things were blurry, but I could see well enough to make my way toward the front of the tank.

I moved awkwardly at first, forgetting to use my arms as a counterbalance. Once I did that, I had more control and my body slipped smoothly through the water. I dove down behind the boulders and kelp that hid the air hose and tested it, slipping the regulator in my mouth and pressing the purge button. At first, it only shot water into my mouth, which would have frightened me if I'd been deeper underwater. As it was, the tank was only ten feet deep, so I could easily surface in an emergency. I pressed the purge button again, harder, and cleared it. This time the air came easily, and I breathed it in for a moment, steadying myself.

My heartbeat slowed. I took one last breath of air and put the regulator back on a hook hidden behind a rock below the kelp. Then I made my way to the glass.

Peter was there, standing on the small stage. He grinned at me and waved, and I waved back. I was still annoyed, but most of my anger had been replaced with wonder. It felt magical to be able to swim so effortlessly. The weight in the tail both propelled me forward, more forcefully than if I were kicking with my own legs, and provided me with the neutral buoyancy I needed to control my body. I could swim up and down without floating to the top or sinking out of control to the bottom. The tail was perfect, but of course, I would expect nothing less from a device Peter had created. He was meticulous in his work.

Peter picked up the slate and pointed to the shelves of oysters. Ah, time to test the game. Using chalk, he wrote the number 43 in large letters on the slate, and held it up to the glass. I swam to the wall to find the correct oyster. Since my vision was blurry, it was difficult to see the numbers on the placards, but that didn't matter. After working as a barker for weeks, I had the layout memorized. All I had to do was count four shelves from the top, and pick the third oyster. I grabbed it, swam back to the front of the tank, and placed it in the waiting net. Then, as Peter pulled the net up and over the side of the tank, I slipped behind the kelp for another hit of air.

I popped back up to see him wrenching open the shell—it wasn't that hard to open, but when you're a barker you exaggerate your movements, adding to the suspense. He plucked a pearl from the pink bed inside and held it up. A cheer erupted from the staff who had gathered around to watch me practice. I guess I'd saved the day.

26

When I broke the surface of the water, Peter was waiting for me on the platform. I leaned my elbows on the edge. "Guess I'm the mermaid now, aren't I?"

He knelt down and grinned at me. "I guess you are. You're *perfect* for the role. Better than Chandra was."

I wasn't so sure about that. "I don't know…"

He laughed. "I *knew* you wouldn't believe me, so I took the liberty of filming you practicing." He held out his phone and played a video.

I felt disoriented for a moment, because the person in the video did not look like me, or at least, not how I envisioned myself. I saw myself as a petite brunette. In the time I'd been living on my own, I'd received enough attention from men to know I was pretty. The mermaid in the video wasn't just pretty.

She was lithe and graceful, long dark hair streaming behind her, scales flashing. She looked like the kind of otherworldly creature who could make a sailor fall in love with her, or drown the man who crossed her. She looked beautiful and powerful. I wanted to be her again.

I resisted the urge to smile because I didn't want Peter to win too easily. "I mean, it was okay. I guess I could do this for today. But if Chandra comes back..."

He frowned. "She's not."

"What?"

He held up his phone, scrolling through his messages. "I got a text from her. She said her ex stopped in town, on his way to Seattle. She decided to leave with him."

That couldn't be right. I remembered what she had said about her breakup, and why she'd gotten her hibiscus tattoos. "That doesn't make sense. She said he was a jerk. Why would she go with him?"

"I don't know, but here it is." He showed me the text. "Maybe it was a different boyfriend."

I frowned, skeptical. She never mentioned another boyfriend, but it was possible. We'd gotten close working together, but not close enough for her to divulge her entire history.

Peter sighed. "I don't know, Mia. People do crazy things for love. Sometimes they do things that don't make a lot of sense, that end up being self-destructive."

I looked up at him, wondering how he felt about Chandra leaving. They'd gotten close as well, in a different way. At the wedding, they'd looked comfortable with each other. I would have thought they had a future together—maybe he had too. He seemed hurt that she'd left without saying goodbye in person. Maybe he'd cared for her more than I realized. I reached up and touched his cheek. "I'm sorry."

He gave me a weak smile, trying to put on a brave face. "It's okay. Life goes on."

"So does the show. Okay, I'm in. I'm the mermaid."

His smile widened into a grin. "You really are the best, you know." He slipped his hand behind my neck and kissed my forehead tenderly.

The relative quiet of the museum erupted in a cacophony of

voices as the doors opened for the day and the tourists from the cruise ship filed in.

"Show time," he whispered, and stood to go. He started down the ladder, leaving me with a goofy smile on my face.

27

My days as a mermaid came and went quickly that May. I did at least two shows a day, sometimes four if we had a cruise ship come in. We had more difficulty finding a replacement barker than Peter thought we would, so he and Vincent traded off, scheduling my shows between the ones for Elena, Sid, and Gabriel. During breaks, I'd hang out on the platform to read or eat lunch, not bothering to change out of the suit if we had two shows scheduled close together. If there was time, I'd get changed and head over to the gift shop to help Beth. There was always something to do at the museum, and as it gained notoriety, we needed all the help we could get. We were closer than ever—a family sharing in the excitement of our success.

The only dark cloud in my life was the pearls. As my skin began to swell, the mermaid costume fit tighter and it became more difficult to swim. My muscles ached. I never complained—I couldn't risk questions that might expose my secret—but I knew I needed a plan for the day the pearls came. In the past, I'd been able to map out cycles almost to the day. As that day got closer, I began to drop hints to Vincent that I was going to call in sick. "I think I might be coming down with something," I told him on Tuesday. "I hope it's not the flu."

"Are you feverish?" he asked.

I placed my hand on my forehead, which did feel a bit warm, but not nearly as warm as the skin on my back, which was red and covered with welts. "I am. I may have to stay home if it gets worse."

Vincent gave me a worried look, and checked the museum's calendar on his phone. "I understand. Although…the tour company booked another day with us tomorrow. Do you think you could hold out until then?"

I thought about it. I figured the pearls weren't due until Thursday, so I had two days before I reached the danger zone, when the pearls were apt to shed. The harvest usually happened at night, so even if I pushed it to Thursday, I'd probably be okay. But I wouldn't risk it—I'd call in sick that morning. I could do with a day of rest anyway.

In spite of my plans, the pearls came a day early.

On Wednesday morning, I stretched and suited up just before our visitors from the cruise ship gathered in front of the tank for the show. Peter was acting as barker, and I noticed Gabriel on the edge of the crowd, wearing a dark hoodie so he could keep a low profile before his own show. He didn't usually come to see my act, but we'd been on better terms lately, so I was glad to have spotted him through the porthole window in the wall that hid my dressing room. I slipped into the water and swam toward the front of the tank, showing off a bit for the crowd, ducking behind kelp and then reappearing, swimming up and then diving back down again so they could get a good look at my shimmering scales. I disappeared behind the rock to get a hit of air and then came out and waved.

It was difficult to hear when I was under water, but I could tell by Peter's gestures that he had picked a volunteer from the crowd and was asking the man to pick a number between one and fifty. Peter wrote the number on the slate—37—and I selected the correct oyster. I placed it in the net and Peter hoisted it over the side of the tank.

I watched as Peter opened it, and the crowd went wild. There was a pearl inside. The man grinned and plucked the pearl from the oyster. Then he pulled a woman on stage. She seemed confused at first, until the man knelt down and held out the pearl to her. A proposal of marriage. She burst into tears and nodded her head. He leapt up and gave her a kiss.

People in the crowd applauded the couple, congratulating them on their engagement. Then a woman in the crowd put her hand over her mouth and pointed at me. The lady standing next to her seemed to be screaming, her mouth open in a wide O. Peter whirled toward me, a look of shock on his face. I stared at him, puzzled, until I realized the water around me was scarlet. Tendrils of blood snaked from my body.

No, no, no! It was too soon for the pearls to come. This couldn't be happening.

Horrified at being discovered, I flicked my tail and fled for the surface, grasping for the platform. As I pulled myself up, my body convulsed with pain, causing me to lose my grip and slip back in the tank. I gasped and got a mouthful of salt water. I managed to pull myself back up, onto the platform, and lay there a moment, choking on the water I'd just inhaled. I coughed, trying to expel it from my lungs. Once I could breathe again, I scooted toward the dressing room and unzipped the back of the costume. A pearl, covered in blood, burst free from my back and rolled down the length of the platform, hitting the water with a delicate splash.

I rolled on my stomach and braced myself on my elbows, hit with another wave of pain. I thought I'd developed a tolerance for this. It always hurt, but this time, the pain was excruciating. All I could do was lay on my stomach and breathe, half inside the dressing room, fins splayed out on the platform behind me. The skin of my back ripped open. More pearls burst free, hitting the floor with a clink as blood pooled beside me.

"Amelia!" The speaker had a deep voice, and suddenly he was beside me, turning me on my side as I barfed up water I'd swallowed and part of my breakfast. I looked up to see Gabriel, his warm brown eyes filled with concern. He was kneeling in blood and vomit, but didn't seem to notice. He grasped my hands gently, looking into my eyes. "Amelia, what's happening to you?"

I gritted my teeth against another wave of agony, gripping his hands tightly. "Surprise," I said, when the cramp passed and I could speak again. "I'm a human oyster." I would have been mortified by the mess I was making if my entire body wasn't throbbing with pain. I guess I thought if I made a joke, even an awful one, I could improve the situation.

"The pearls come from *you*?" he asked. He let go of my hands and picked up a pearl, still streaked with blood. He looked at the pearl and then at my shredded back, his eyes wide with alarm.

This was a guy who'd experienced a lot of terrible things in his life. Seeing that reaction from Gabriel was not helpful in alleviating my own horror at having my darkest secret revealed. I knew what he'd do next. He'd leave me there, on the floor, sick to his stomach with disgust.

He didn't. He stood up and grabbed a couple of washcloths from the shelf next to the dressing room sink. He ran them under warm water, and then helped me into sitting position. He handed me one of the cloths. "For your face," he said, and I gratefully wiped the vomit from my lips. Then he kneeled behind me and gently began dabbing at my wounds, wiping my back clean of blood.

"You can't tell *anyone*," I told him.

"I won't," he promised.

"What the hell happened here?"

Gabriel and I looked up to see Peter standing on the platform outside the dressing room, staring down at the bloody floor. He toed a pearl with his foot, as though he couldn't make sense of it being there. Then he spotted my raw back and gasped as the last pearl worked its way out of my skin and fell to the floor. He dropped to his knees in front of me. "Oh, Mia." He shook his head in disbelief. "Mia, why didn't you tell us?"

"I couldn't," I said, looking up at him. "I was too scared."

"Scared of what?" Peter asked.

I started coughing again, and Peter grabbed my water bottle from my bag. I took a long drink and wiped my mouth. "Thanks."

Gabriel pulled my long hair back, to get it out of my face, and as he did, his fingers brushed my forehead. "You've got a fever. Here, this will help." He grabbed another washcloth and ran it under the tap, this time in cool water. He took a towel and rolled it into a pillow and then helped me lay on my side again. He placed the cool washcloth on my forehead. "Better?"

I nodded, and closed my eyes. Now I felt embarrassed, for being on the floor with the bare skin of my back exposed, for the mess I'd made, for lying to them after they'd trusted me. I could almost hear my mother's voice, chiding me. I wanted to curl into a ball and disappear.

"What were you scared of?" Peter asked again, softly.

"You," I said.

"Me?" he asked, incredulous.

I opened my eyes to catch Peter giving Gabriel a look of disbelief. "I never wanted you to see me like this," I told him. "Either of you."

"But why?" Gabriel asked.

I sat up again and gestured to the blood and vomit on the floor. "Because of this. It's disgusting. And look at my back—it's hideous. My scars are hideous."

Gabriel took my hand. "No, they're not." I could see he was trying to be kind, but I knew the truth about my scars—they *were* ugly. Still, I appreciated the sentiment. "Are you in pain?" he asked softly.

I shook my head. "It's always better once I shed the pearls. The wounds are a little sore for a while, but the swelling before they come is worse."

"*Always* better? How often does this happen?" Peter asked.

"Every month," I said. "Now you know why I've been so cagey about where the pearls come from. You wouldn't have believed me if I'd told you the truth."

"I guess you're right," Peter said. He looked dazed, as though he still didn't believe it, even though he was seeing it with his own eyes."

"My mother always said if I told people what I could do, they'd lock me up," I said.

Gabriel looked startled. "Why?"

"Greed." I held his gaze. If anyone could understand, he would. "If people knew they could get rich off my so-called gift, they'd hold me captive, force me to hand over the pearls. Funny thing is, that's exactly what she did to me. That's another reason I was afraid to tell you."

"I would never do that to you," Gabriel assured me. "I know what it's like to be caged."

I nodded. "I know you do. But I haven't known either of you all that long. I didn't know if I could trust you."

"You can trust us," Peter said firmly. "But your mother wasn't completely wrong. It's smart to keep this a secret. I'm sure everyone at the museum would protect you—you're part of our family—but I can't vouch for the rest of the world. There are bad people out there."

"So we make a pact," Gabriel said, giving his brother a hard look. "We keep this between the three of us. We don't even tell Vincent."

"Are you worried he'd hurt Mia?" Peter asked.

"Not intentionally," Gabriel said. "But you know how he is. He trusts people too much. He wants to believe the best about everyone's intentions."

Peter nodded. "Wouldn't be the first time he's been a bad judge of character." He rubbed his chin thoughtfully. "Okay. This stays between us. I'll tell the staff you bumped your head and that's where the blood came from. Then I'm driving you home to recover. And in the future, you tell us if you need help, Mia. You don't have to carry this alone. You know that, right?"

"Yes." My emotions felt jumbled—shame over having revealed my secret in such a grotesque way, gratitude for their acceptance of who I really was. I felt foolish for doubting that they cared for me, for believing I had to hide an essential part of my existence.

"No more lies," Peter said. "If you're in that much pain and the pearls are about to come, we keep you out of the tank. The money we make on this show is not worth your health, and it's not worth the risk of exposing your secret. Agreed?"

I nodded. I didn't trust myself to speak. Between my embarrassment about my scars and the relief that we were still friends, I worried I would cry.

"Gabe?" Peter asked. "You agree?"

Gabriel looked up at him. "Yeah, of course." He seemed lost in his own thoughts, as though something we'd said bothered him. It wasn't until later that I found out how much my lies had cost me.

28

In the weeks that followed, Peter and I grew closer than ever. He offered to teach me how to surf, and invited me to join him and Sid early one morning at the Cove. I'm not going to lie—I was terrible at it. But Peter was a patient teacher, and Sid kept me laughing. That was enough to keep me going even though my arms felt like limp spaghetti from carrying the surfboard and trying to maneuver it through the waves. They kept me in shallow water at first, so I got the hang of getting my board into position and then paddling like mad to catch a wave. I felt elated when I was able to get up on my knees. Most of the time I rode the wave on my stomach, when I was lucky enough not to fall off altogether.

"Admit it," I said to them. "I suck."

"Everybody sucks on their first day," Sid said. "You should have seen Peter when we started a few years ago. Total horror show."

"Thanks, buddy," Peter said, flicking water at his friend. "You'll get it, Mia. Just keep working at it."

"And have fun," Sid said. "Don't take everything so seriously."

I nodded soberly. "I'll try."

Sid laughed and paddled out to catch the next wave.

Peter stayed with me, sitting on his board, watching the waves. "Okay, here comes a good one. Get in position. Now paddle, paddle, paddle, PADDLE!"

I followed his instructions, and paddled until I felt like my arms were going to fall off. It was a strong wave—it felt like a solid mass under my board. As it lifted me, I pushed myself up and got to my knees. Then I managed to get one foot underneath me, and the other, crouching. I stood up.

Gliding beside me, Peter let out a whoop and pumped both his fists in the air. "Yeah! You did it!"

I shot him a maniacal grin…and promptly fell off my board, rolling in the surf. I was still grinning when I got to my feet, wrangling my board.

I slept well that night, from sheer exhaustion. I was sore the next day, but in spite of that, I felt amazing. I'd done something I never dreamed I could do, and I couldn't wait to try it again. I promised myself I'd go surfing with the guys as often as I could. Even if I sucked, it was great exercise and I could use the work-out. It would distract me from the pain of the next crop of pearls, and the salt water helped my skin heal faster, even though it stung as it washed over my open wounds.

Surfing was also a good distraction from Gabriel. He seemed distant after discovering my secret, and I didn't know why. He'd been kind to me when he found me on the floor, but now seemed to be avoiding me. Something between us had changed. I hoped it could be mended.

Since he wouldn't come to me, I went to him. One day, after performing as the mermaid, I got changed and sat in on his show. He'd come a long way from the quiet, sullen guy I'd first met. He wasn't a comedian, like Sid, but he had a self-deprecating sense of humor, and he used that to charm the audience.

He'd invited a young woman to the stage, a pretty blond who looked flattered to be chosen and terrified to suddenly be on stage in front of everyone. As Gabriel talked, she calmed, focusing on him instead of all the eyes watching her. She seemed fascinated by him rather than afraid, and when he revealed her portrait, she visibly gasped, covering her mouth with her hand. A bit dramatic, if you ask me, but the audience loved her reaction and the painting. They applauded, and Gabriel took the girl's hand as they both took a bow. Then she retreated from the stage to rejoin her friends in the audience, giving Gabriel a shy smile.

He'd once told me he was ugly, but girls in the audience certainly didn't seem to think so. They probably imagined him as the beast from the fairy tale, picturing themselves as the heroines in the story. One kiss to break the spell and he could be a prince. It was a nice thought, but there was no more a cure for Gabriel's condition than there was for mine. We had that in common.

I waited in the back row until the museum guests left, and then quietly walked toward the stage as Gabriel cleaned up, getting ready for his next show. He looked up at my approach, quickly returning to his task when he saw it was me.

"Hey," I said. "How are you?"

"I'm good." Non-committal. And wow, it's amazing how much concentration it takes to clean paint brushes. He seemed entranced by them, avoiding eye contact with me.

"I haven't seen you around lately," I said. "Everything okay?"

"Sure. Everything's peachy."

I walked up on stage and stood in front of him. "Gabriel." When he didn't respond, I put my hands on my hips. "Come on, Gabe. Tell me what's wrong."

He shrugged. "Nothing's wrong."

"Really? Then how come you won't look me in the eye?"

At that, he sighed. He tapped the last brush on the edge of the cup he used for cleaning, shaking out the moisture. He placed it on a towel to dry and looked at me. "I can't believe you lied to me."

"Okay…"

His eyes narrowed. "No, *not* okay. After I opened up to you, told you my whole life story, you said nothing. And then, at the wedding, when I talked about how Elena was brave for not hiding who she was…I mean, wouldn't that have been a good time to say, oh, by the way, I have my own deep, dark secret? I told you *everything*—I bared my soul to you—but you couldn't trust me?"

I didn't know what to say. He was right. "I'm sorry."

He scoffed. "You outright lied to me, Amelia."

I pleaded with him. "You don't understand. I've been hiding my whole life. It was drilled into me. It's how I've survived."

He shook his head, disgust etched on his face. "Well, some of us don't have that option. Some of us don't get to hide." He took the still wet portrait and stormed off the stage, leaving me standing there.

29

I had suspected Gabriel was avoiding me before, but now I had no doubt. I didn't see him for days, and it bothered me more than I thought it would. I'd never had a friend like him before. There had been a connection between us, a kind of kinship, even though he hadn't known the truth about me. Now, I feared our bond was irreparably broken.

I threw myself into performing and surfing. I got better at both. Things got better with Peter too. He invited me to dinner at Norma's, a seafood restaurant near the Prom, and afterward, we went for a walk along the beach. We watched the sun go down, and then, as the first stars came out, he kissed me. Afterward, I couldn't stop smiling at him. His attention made me giddy. I'd never had a boyfriend before, so I guess I was making up for lost time. He was handsome and charming, and he made me want to do stupid things.

We started spending all of our time together when we weren't busy at work. I lost myself in him completely. I stopped thinking about Gabriel at all.

Then one day, in the middle of my show, I saw a woman leap up on the stage in front of the tank, gesturing angrily at Peter. I thought perhaps there was a problem with the pearls—maybe he'd picked a different guest and she was mad. It was difficult to make out her features from underwater, but then she got close to the glass and I realized who she was. My mother. She'd found me.

Startled, I flicked my tail and swam away, even though the show wasn't over. As I surfaced, I gripped the edge of the platform, trying to slow my panicked breathing. A rush of cold fear washed over me. *She found me. She'll make me go home. I'll never be free again.*

But I was an adult. I was independent. She couldn't force me to do anything.

It's funny how easy it is to fall back into rigid patterns of thinking developed during an abusive childhood—how fear and instinct can overpower logic. I took a deep breath in and let it out slowly. Then I hoisted myself onto the platform.

As I did, I heard a voice—Peter's. "You can't go in there! Guests aren't allowed backstage."

I heard the clang of footsteps on the rungs of the metal ladder, and then my mother was there, standing in front of me. She looked older than I remembered—maybe worrying about me had taken a toll. Her eyes narrowed in rage as she stared down at me. "What the *hell* do you think you're doing?"

I sucked in a breath, too stunned to answer at first. My heart raced like a frightened rabbit within the cage of my chest.

She put her hands on her hips. "Well? You just up and leave without a word, and I don't know if you're dead or alive, only to find out you've joined some circus to—what? Live out your childhood fantasy?"

Childhood fantasy? Is that what she thought this was? I glanced down at my fins. I mean, I'd loved mermaids as a kid—what girl didn't? But I wasn't living out a fantasy. I was building a *life*. Not that it mattered to her—she wouldn't have listened if I told her this was how I'd won my independence. She never listened. "How did you find me?"

Her lips twisted into a sneer. "It wasn't hard, sweetheart. I called all the jewelers in the state, asking about pearls. Nobody knew anything. Except one lady in Portland, who bought pearls like the kind I was looking for. Her supplier lived in Seaside, she said. Then, I find out there's this—" She gestured angrily around her. "This *freak* show selling pearls, so I decide to check it out. And lo and behold, I find out my daughter is the *biggest* freak of all. Your little mermaid act is plastered on a billboard, honey."

"What?"

"Dad," Peter said. He'd climbed the ladder while my mother ranted. "He used your image for one of the advertisements we posted on the 26. I should have told you." He turned to my mother, fists clenched. I'd never seen him so angry. His voice shook with rage. "She's *not* a freak. And this is not a freak show."

I heard heavy footsteps on the rungs of the ladder, and watched Gabriel climb out onto the platform to stand beside Peter. Mom's eyes widened when she saw him.

"Not a freak show?" she said with a haughty laugh. She jerked her thumb at Gabriel. "Then how do you explain this guy?"

Gabriel towered over her five-and-a-half-foot frame, but she didn't look intimidated at all. Instead, she actually took a step toward Gabriel, menacing him. To his credit, he stood there stoically, refusing to be baited.

She whirled back to me. "Do they even know what you are?"

"We know," Gabriel said.

"Then you're more of a fool than I thought you were," she said to me. "You think you can trust these people?"

"I trust them more than I trust you," I said. "They've never locked me in an attic."

"I did that to *protect* you," she insisted. "You think they won't lock you up once they get tired of this charade? They'll take the pearls and whore you out. Mark my words, girl. They *will*. And after they break you, you'll come crawling home." She gave me a cruel smile. "And I'll be there waiting. Why? Because I'm your *mother*. That's what mothers do."

"You need to leave now," Gabriel said. His voice was calm, but I could see the tension in his jaw. There was a storm brewing in his eyes. Would he hurt her? He could, easily. I honestly wasn't sure if I wanted him to or not. In that moment, I hated her. For locking me away for so many years, for shaming me now.

"I never want to see you again," I said, teeth gritted. It was all I could do to not scream at her. I wanted to lose myself in a blind rage and hurt her like she'd hurt me.

"Leave, or we call the police," Peter said, taking a step toward her. "Never come back."

"Fine," she said, waving him off. "Come home when you're done playing mermaid, Amelia. I'll be waiting."

She climbed back down the ladder and Peter followed her to make sure she left the museum.

Gabriel and I stayed frozen in place, listening to footsteps fade.

He knelt down next to me. "Are you okay?"

I shook my head, blinking back tears. "No. But I will be."

He took my hand and squeezed it firmly. His warm touch steadied me. "Yes. You will."

30

I'd been waiting for that moment, for my mother to reappear in my life. It was something I'd dreaded, but felt was inevitable. I couldn't hide from her forever. Now that I'd seen her again, and confronted her for what she'd done, I felt a weight lift from my shoulders. I thought I'd been independent before. Now I truly was.

The incident with Mom was a catalyst for me, but it also healed my relationship with Gabriel. I guess it gave him insight into why I'd lied. After work, Gabriel sometimes gave me rides home on his motorcycle. I'd invite him into my apartment for coffee, and we'd sit in front of my picture window and enjoy the sunset, or take a walk down by the estuary to watch deer graze and cormorants sun themselves on driftwood logs.

We didn't talk about what had happened with my mom, but there was a shared understanding about what we'd experienced in our lives, things we understood that most people couldn't. We didn't *need* to say anything. We could just look into each other's eyes and know. I'd never connected with anyone like that, not even Peter.

That's not to say I wasn't happy with Peter. I was. It was my first time falling in love with somebody, and it felt like a dream. That June I drifted in a state of ecstasy, blissfully naïve. It was a summer full of firsts for a girl who had spent most of her life locked away. There was so much I didn't know, so much my sheltered childhood never prepared me for.

I felt like I was living in a fairy tale, showered with Peter's affection. Being with him made me feel warm, like walking on the beach on a sunny day. I didn't care how cheesy or reckless it was. I realize now I wasn't using my best judgement. But how could I have known what the future would hold?

I was nervous about him seeing my scars, but he'd already had a good look at them. Still, as we sat on my loveseat and he slipped his hand under the back of my shirt and ran his fingers over my skin for the first time, I flinched.

He looked at me with concern in his eyes. "Does that hurt?"

It did, a little—but I was used to pain. My skin always felt swollen and tender, but it was still early in the cycle, so I wasn't worried about open wounds. I wouldn't have let him touch me if there had been. That would have been mortifying, and I couldn't bear the thought of Peter looking at me with disgust.

I wasn't used to being touched. I avoided it. But I didn't want to avoid Peter. Despite the shame I felt over my scars, I craved his touch. I gave him a small smile. "It's all right. It's just that I've never been touched like this before."

He withdrew his hand. "We can go slow." He placed his hands on his knees and looked down at them. "I keep forgetting you're not like other girls. The way you grew up was so different than everybody else."

I didn't want to be different. More than anything, I wanted to be a regular girl. I took his hands in mine. "I want this. I do. It's just...my scars. I know they're ugly." I sighed. "I wish I was normal and didn't have to think about stuff like this."

"No," he said. "Don't say that. Don't ever wish you were

normal." He leaned around me, gently lifted the edge of my shirt, and kissed one of the scars nestled in the small of my back. He sat up and looked into my eyes. "And don't ever be ashamed of your scars. They're proof of what you've survived. Proof of your strength."

My breath caught. "I love you," I whispered.

Peter leaned forward and kissed me on the lips. "I love you too." He sat back and grinned. "Don't you ever forget that."

Peter was far more experienced than I was. He'd been out in the world, living in different places, going to college, dating people. I'd never been with anyone, and in early July, the first time he suggested he spend the night at my apartment, I nearly had a panic attack. I'm embarrassed to admit it, but my first thought was of my mother. What would she think of a man staying over? Then I thought of my landlord. My mother would never know what I was up to, but Mrs. Putnam certainly would. What would she think?

Peter caught me blushing and asked me what was wrong. I confessed, reluctantly, and he laughed. "You're worried about what Barbara thinks?" There was a derisive tone to his voice. "You know Dad stays with her all the time, right?"

"Vincent and Barbara are together?"

"They have been for years. She was a *big* comfort after Mom passed, if you catch my meaning," he said, pressing me against the wall next to my front door. He tucked a strand of hair behind my ear. He leaned in, his breath on my neck. "So, I hardly think you need to worry about what they think. We're both adults here, right?"

I still felt uneasy, but I forced a smile. "Right. Of course." I was almost 22. I didn't need anyone's permission.

His lips brushed my neck and I stopped thinking about anything but his touch. I led him to my bed and he showed me everything I'd missed.

31

Weeks flew by, and Peter became my whole world. He practically moved in with me. I lost myself in him, which made it hard when he had to leave. He had a business trip in Seattle, and as I watched him pack, I told him I wished I could go.

He gave me a consoling smile. "Not this time, babe. But one of these days we'll go on a trip together. I never showed you my cabin, did I?"

I shook my head. "You talked about it, how beautiful it was. But no, I've never seen it."

He nodded. "It's been too long since I was there. We'll find time when I get back. Promise."

I wrapped my arms around his neck. "I'll miss you."

Peter laughed. "I'm gone for two days, Mia."

I rested my head against his chest. "I know. But still."

He grinned down at me. "Still." He leaned down and pecked my cheek. "Be good."

With that, he left my apartment. I felt hollowed out as I watched him drive away. Looking back, I feel dumb for falling so hard for him. I would have done anything for him. Reflecting on what happened afterward, that's not the only thing I feel dumb about.

When he got back from Seattle, we had our first fight. I had just gotten out of the tank after playing the mermaid, and I happened to look out the porthole window of my dressing room, taking in the lobby. The crowd was dispersing, going from my show to view the other shows and exhibits in the museum. I spotted Peter, and felt my breath catch. He was back, but he hadn't called me to let me know. Or maybe he had, but I'd been in the water. My new cell phone was in my bag and I wasn't used to checking messages.

He looked handsome, refreshed from his trip. Apparently, I wasn't the only one who thought so, because he was chatting with a pretty redhead. She laughed like he'd just said something charming, and he leaned over and brushed a lock of hair behind her ear. I froze, watching them flirt, my blood boiling at the thought of him using the signature move he'd used on me. Suddenly, I regretted ever proclaiming my love for him. I felt like an idiot.

I avoided him the rest of the day, accepting a ride home from Gabe. Peter showed up at my place an hour later. I'd given him a key, so he came in without knocking. I avoided eye contact, focusing my attention on the ramen noodles boiling on the stove. Some habits never die. I'd been a ramen junkie as a kid, because it was cheap and we didn't have a lot of money for a long time, and because my mom worked so much it was one of the few meals I could prepare for myself. I still liked it, but at least now I tried for a level of sophistication to my meals, adding ingredients I never would have tried as a child.

"Looks tasty," Peter said.

"It is," I answered, scooping a bowl for myself, not offering him any. I sat down at my kitchen table and started eating.

Peter sat down across from me. "What's wrong?"

I set my spoon down. "I saw you today. With the redhead."

"What?" He raised his eyebrows in surprise, and then leaned back in his chair when he realized what I meant. "Oh. That." He reached across the table and took my hand. "That was *nothing*, Mia."

I wrenched my hand from his grasp and pretended to tuck a strand of his hair behind his ear. "That? That was *not* nothing."

He stared at me for a moment and then gave in. "Okay. You're right. She asked me a question about the museum and we started talking, and I guess we hit it off." He took my hand again. "But it didn't mean anything, Mia. I *promise*. I adore you."

I huffed, pulling my hand away. I shoveled noodles into my mouth.

He rose from his chair and came around the table to kneel in front of me. "You have to believe me. I love you."

I looked down at him, spoon hovering midair. He did look repentant.

"Forgive me, Mia. Please."

I put down the spoon. "You hurt me."

He nodded. "I see that now. I'm sorry. I was an idiot, and I'll never hurt you again. I promise." He took my hands. "Say you believe me."

I sighed and closed my eyes. "I believe you."

He squeezed my hands and kissed both of them. "I'll make it up to you. As soon as I get back from Portland, I'll take you to the cabin. We'll have a romantic weekend. It'll be great. You'll see."

I opened my eyes. "Wait—what? You're leaving again?"

"Just for a few days."

I stared at him. "But you just got back." I hated that he sounded grown up and I sounded like a petulant child.

He gave me a sheepish look. "I know. I've got to meet with this wealthy couple who invested in the museum when we first came up with the concept. They've got questions. I have to reassure them they made the right decision and they'll get a good return on their investment. And maybe, if I'm lucky, convince them to put more money into this."

"But I thought the museum was doing really well."

"It is. But we're close to the Prom and our overhead is high. Buying a commercial property isn't cheap in a beach town, you know?"

I did know, because he liked to tell me about the inner workings of the museum. He was proud of it, and wanted me to be proud of him. I couldn't begrudge him for taking care of his business. Especially when my own livelihood depended on it. "Of course. It's just—I miss you when you're gone. That's all."

He rose to his feet and kissed me. "I know. I miss you like crazy. So, I'll get this done and come back as soon as I can."

I believed him. I believed him completely.

32

Peter kept his promise. He got back on Friday morning and told me to pack a bag for a weekend at his cabin. Vincent was annoyed about us leaving, since weekends were one of the busiest times for guests at the museum, and we brought in a lot of money from my show. He brightened when Peter presented him with a check from the investors. I only caught a glimpse of the check—I didn't see how much it was for, but it looked like there were a lot of zeroes on it.

"Have a fun trip, you two," Vincent said, clapping Peter on the back. "You deserve it."

Peter whisked me off for lunch at Angelina's, my favorite pizza place. Then we left the droves of tourists for the Sunset Highway. It was August, and tourist traffic in Seaside was still steady. It would be, until the rains started up again in October.

It felt like we drove forever down the 26. As we got close to the North Fork of the Necanicum River, Peter took a left onto what appeared to be an old logging road. There were no signs to mark it, and it was obscured on either side by trees and overgrowth. I never would have noticed it if Peter hadn't pointed it out.

From there, we crawled along a curving dirt road for three miles. Under the canopy of the trees, it was shaded from the bright summer sun. I cracked my window, listening to the crunch of the tires on the gravel road and stellar jays calling to each other in the woods. The earth smelled rich and damp. "It's beautiful here," I said. "Peaceful."

"Glad you like it," Peter said. He looked down at my feet. "Oh, good. You wore sneakers."

"Why?"

"We have to walk a bit, once we get to the end of the road. I guess I should have told you that," he said.

I brushed him off. "I don't mind. How far?"

"Two miles or so," he said. "And…there's no electricity. Or running water. But there's the creek." He ran his hand over the stubble on his jaw as though he were nervous. "Guess I should have told you that too."

I thought about my days on the streets of Portland and laughed to myself. It couldn't be worse than that. "I'm good with roughing it."

He grinned. "That's my girl."

The road ended abruptly. He put the car in park, and we got out. I couldn't see the creek, but it was close. I could hear water trickling. It was chilly under the trees. I grabbed my sweatshirt and tugged it on, and then retrieved my backpack from the back seat of Peter's car. Peter popped the trunk and pulled out his own pack, as well as a cooler.

He held it up and gave me a wry smile. "No fridge, so we have to pack in food. But the cupboards are stocked with non-perishables. We won't go hungry."

"How do you cook?" I asked. I truly didn't know—Mom had never taken me camping.

"Got a grill." He shifted the cooler to his other hand, and took mine. "Come on. We'll want to get settled before it gets too dark."

I looked around. The sun set later in the summer, but under the trees, the light was already dim.

The hike to the cabin wasn't bad, but there was no trail to speak of. Peter knew where he was going, picking his way through ferns and over fallen logs. I didn't spot any landmarks—all the trees looked the same to me. But I could hear the creek, burbling to my left—a constant companion. It sounded inviting. I looked forward to slipping off my shoes and soaking my feet in the cool water.

When we finally arrived, I did just that. Peter watched me balance on mossy rocks, and then laughed when I slipped and squealed with surprise, getting soaked up to my knees. "Crazy girl," he called, picking up my discarded backpack and sweatshirt and placing them on the steps of the cabin. "You're going to fall in and I'm going to have to come in after you."

"Why don't you?" I teased. I wriggled out of my t-shirt and wet jeans and tossed them on a large flat rock on the bank of the creek. Then I waded out to a deep spot where the roots of a tree had dammed the creek and created a still pool. The water was cold, but I treaded water and gave him an expectant smile.

He chuckled. "Why don't I?" He stripped down and joined me.

It was a nice start to the weekend. Afterward, we grabbed our clothes and scurried inside the cabin, freezing from our soak in the chilly water. We shoved our bags inside the front door and Peter hurried to find towels so we could dry off. He lit a fire in the stone fireplace so we could warm up. We curled up together on an old sofa and he rubbed warmth back into my hands.

"Hungry?" he asked.

I nodded, brushing his wet hair off his forehead.

"You get dressed and warm up. I'll heat up some soup."

"I love you," I told him.

He smiled and brushed his lips against my cheek. "You better."

He got up and pulled on his jeans, and I took my backpack into the small bedroom off the main room. The cabin was tiny—the main room held a small living room and the kitchen. A round dining table in the middle of the room separated the spaces. There were windows on either side of the front door, and one in the bedroom as well. There wasn't a bathroom, so much as a composting toilet and a stainless steel bowl that served as a sink, set into an old nightstand. A pitcher of water stood by so I could wash my hands. The set up was rough, but homey. I could see why Peter liked it here.

As we sipped soup and warmed up our insides, I took in the rest of the cabin. The kitchen was sparsely furnished—cupboards, a butcher block counter top, a sink that must have drained to the outside since there was no plumbing. No faucet either, just the basin. No modern conveniences like a microwave or stove. A large, red cooler was positioned under the window in the kitchen. Peter noticed me looking at it.

"If I'm here for longer trips, I fill that thing with ice. Keeps the food cold."

"I guess it'd be hard to live here long-term," I said.

"Nah. It just requires a change in thinking—living off the land."

I could barely imagine sleeping in a tent—Mom hadn't been into that sort of thing. "How would you do that? Go fishing?"

He nodded. "Fishing, hunting, gathering berries and edible plants."

"And you know how to do that. Did your dad teach you?"

He shook his head. "My father is not an outdoorsman. I taught myself." He frowned. "I taught myself a lot of things." He looked up at me. "The things I'm interested in are different from what my dad enjoys. It's like with college—I wanted to go work for a movie studio and learn how to do special effects. So I did, but then Dad wanted me to come back and help him with the museum. I told him I would, but I wanted to do it on my own terms, with what I'd learned—to make it into something bigger than he had envisioned. When I get interested in something, I tend to...*obsess* over it. I learn everything I can about the topic and I get focused on details, because details are what makes something work. That's where the magic is. That's where Dad and I have butted heads sometimes—he throws things together and assumes they'll work. But they don't—you have to pay attention to detail." He gestured to the window, to the view of the woods outside. "It's like surviving here. You gather edible plants, you have to pay attention to the details. Eat the wrong thing, and you'll die."

"That's a scary thought."

He nodded. "Yeah. Nature can be brutal. Foxglove will give you a heart attack. Amanita muscaria—that's a type of mushroom —is toxic. At best you'll hallucinate, but you could get really sick. Giant hogweed can give you nasty blisters."

I stared at him. "You know a lot about this stuff."

He laughed. "Well, like I said. I tend to obsess."

I couldn't argue there. Even though the cabin was Spartan, he had attended to all the details. The tiny cabin held everything he needed, and was immaculately clean. How long had it taken him to transform this place into what he'd envisioned? I gazed at the river rock fireplace. Beside it, I spotted a narrow door I hadn't noticed before. It blended into the cabin's wood paneling and was secured with a padlock. "What's that room? A second bedroom?"

Peter stiffened. "No, that's just an old root cellar. I keep my tools in there. You'd be surprised at how much maintenance this place needs."

I wasn't—it was clear he was meticulous about keeping the

cabin in good shape, even though it was old. I would have thought the forest would have reclaimed the place decades ago. Maybe it had, but it was obvious Peter—or the previous owner—had kept brush trimmed back, and the roof seemed to be in good repair. There was no moss on the cedar shingles. That was no easy task given the amount of rain we got in the Pacific Northwest. And once blackberries took root, they could easily overrun a small structure like this. We'd had to pick our way around a mess of them on our hike to the cabin. "But why do you keep the door locked?" I asked him.

Peter gave a light-hearted laugh that contrasted with his earlier reaction to my questions. "Because I have nice tools! I've got a gas-powered chainsaw in there that cost me a small fortune. Totally worth it though, because I can't hike out of here every time I need firewood. I can't afford tools that break on me—I need things I can rely on. I keep them locked up because I don't want them disappearing if somebody breaks into the cabin while I was gone."

"Oh, that makes sense," I said.

He nodded. "Anyway, some of the steps to the cellar are pretty rotten, so it's not safe to go down there. I've been meaning to fix them, but haven't gotten around to it. Keeping it locked helps me remember, so I have to take a second with the door, and think about where I'm going to be putting my feet navigating those steps. My luck, I'd tumble down them, knock myself out, and no one would ever think to look for me here."

"Sounds hazardous. Maybe you should fix them."

"I should," he said. "But in the meantime, promise me you won't go poking around in there. I'd hate for you to get hurt."

"I promise," I said, even though I felt like something was off about his explanation. It wasn't so much that he was lying as he was leaving something out of his story about those stairs and the tools he kept in the root cellar. Maybe it was something private and he was making up excuses because he was embarrassed about it. His evasiveness piqued my curiosity, and made me more interested in the forbidden cellar than if he'd simply told me the truth.

One thing is for sure. I wish I'd never looked in that cellar.

33

That weekend together is one of the best memories I have of Peter. On Saturday, we hiked up to the ridge above the cabin, and he showed me an old cave he'd discovered. He gave me a lesson on which plants were edible. I liked salmonberries the best—they were juicy and tart, though some were tastier than others.

He told me about nurse logs—fallen trees that provide nutrients to new saplings—and showed me how those trees grow up to have hollows as the nurse log rots away. I still have the photo he took of me standing in one of those hollows.

Then, on Sunday, everything changed. I woke up feeling nauseated and barely made it to the composting toilet before emptying the contents of my stomach.

Peter stood in the doorway of the bathroom, looking concerned. "Are you okay?"

I shook my head, kneeling before the toilet. "I think I ate something bad. Can salmonberries give you food poisoning?"

"I don't think so," Peter said. "Those berries were fresh off the bush, and we washed them before we ate them. You can't have food poisoning because I've been eating everything you've been eating and I'm not sick."

I just groaned in response, and curled into a ball on the bathroom floor.

Peter knelt down and placed his palm on my forehead. "You're not feverish. Any other aches or pains?"

I shook my head and closed my eyes. Talking was the last thing I wanted to do. I felt like if I moved at all, I'd start heaving again.

"I'm sorry you feel so bad," Peter said. He rubbed my back for a moment, which would have felt nice, if I hadn't felt so awful. Then he stopped, and said, "Weird."

I opened one eye. "What?"

"I was just thinking. It's been a while since you shed the pearls, right? So you should have a new batch coming in?"

Sure. What did that have to do with anything? "Yeah, I guess so."

"Well, it seems like your back gets pretty swollen when that happens, right?" he asked.

His questions were starting to test my patience. All I wanted to do was curl up in bed and sleep this off. "Yes."

"Your back isn't swollen at all," he said. "How long, exactly, has it been since you had your cycle?"

I tried to think. It wasn't easy to do, since I was fighting off dizziness and nausea. "Six or seven weeks?"

"Okay. And your menstrual cycle is connected to the pearls, right?"

"Mm-hmm." I took in a breath and let it out slowly, trying to keep from vomiting again. Nope, that wasn't going to do it. I pulled myself up into kneeling position and retched into the toilet. I didn't have much left in my stomach after that first round. I felt a little better though, so I moved over to the basin. I poured myself a glass of water and rinsed out my mouth, and then trudged over to our bed and collapsed.

"Here," Peter said, helping me get back under the covers. He smoothed my hair back from my forehead and gave me a soft kiss. "Go back to sleep, Mia. You'll feel better when you wake up."

I was too exhausted to argue. He slipped out of the room, and I closed my eyes.

When I opened them again, the light in the room had changed. I didn't know how long I'd been out, but it must have been hours. Peter had picked wildflowers and placed them in a glass on the small table beside the bed. That made me smile.

I sat up, gingerly, blinking the sleep out of my eyes. No nausea. That was good. I could hear Peter moving around in the kitchen as I stumbled out of bed.

He turned as I entered the room. "How are you feeling?"

"Better."

"I went into town," he said. "Got you some saltine crackers and ginger ale. I thought that might help."

"Thank you." I wrapped my arms around his waist and rested my head on his chest.

"I, uh, got you something else," he said, sounding nervous. He reached over to the kitchen counter and handed me a slender box.

I read the label and looked up at him. "A home pregnancy test? I'm not pregnant."

"I don't want to scare you, but you could be," he said. He gave me a weak smile. "Humor me, at least?"

"Okay." There was no way I could be pregnant, could there? Please let the test be negative, I prayed. I wasn't ready for a baby. I didn't know anything about kids.

I went in the bathroom, peed on the test stick, and waited for what seemed like forever. One line appeared, and then a second one. Panicked, I grabbed the directions for the kit. When I read what the second line meant, I whispered, "Oh no."

Peter must have been standing right outside the door. "What? What does it say?"

I stepped into the bedroom, showing him the test stick. "I'm pregnant."

I figured Peter would be as freaked out as I was, but he wasn't. His face broke into a smile. "Really?"

I froze, unsure of his reaction. "Yeah. Really."

"Oh, Mia," he said, folding me into his arms. "That makes me so happy."

I looked up at him. "Really? You want this?"

He pulled back, staring at me. "Of course, I do. I'm crazy about you. I mean, I know this is a wild situation, to think about having a baby, but there's no one I'd rather do this with. You're going to be a great mother."

I wasn't so sure. "I just—I need to sit down for a second." I sat down on the edge of the bed. "How could this happen?"

Peter sat down beside me, looking at me like I had two heads. "Didn't your mom have the talk with you? I mean, I know you were sheltered…"

"Of course, she did," I snapped. That wasn't exactly true. We had talked about reproduction, briefly, around the time I had my first period. But then the first batch of pearls appeared and everything changed. We *never* talked about sex. Everything was clinical and sanitized with her—the basic mechanics of the menstrual cycle and how women got pregnant. Nothing about the reality of what it was like to be intimate with someone. Nothing about birth control. I don't think she thought I'd need to know. I don't think she ever envisioned me leaving that house.

I sighed and took his hand. "I'm sorry. I'm scared to death right now. I don't think I can do this."

He pulled me close and stroked my hair. “I know. But you *can* do this, Mia. I’ll be right here with you. We’ll do this together.”

34

On the ride back to Seaside, we made a pact to keep the pregnancy secret until we both felt comfortable telling people. I needed time to get used to the idea of having a baby. I still wasn't sure I even wanted one, but Peter seemed thrilled about the idea of being a father.

It surprised me. I wouldn't have thought he'd feel that way. It seemed like he liked kids—he was kind to the children who visited the museum—but it's not like we had ever talked about having kids. We were just having fun being together, being in love. I'd never brought up a future together because I'd never been in the kind of place where I felt secure about the direction my life was headed. I was still trying to figure out how to be an adult, on my own. He'd never brought it up either. I assumed he wasn't certain about a future with me. Maybe he was, after all.

Going back to work felt strange. I thought for sure people would be able to tell I was pregnant, like they could somehow read it on my face. They couldn't. I knew I'd only be able to keep it secret for so long. I wondered how long it would be before I could no longer fit in my mermaid costume. At what point would it become dangerous to hold my breath for long periods of time? Could oxygen deprivation harm the baby?

The next time he came to my apartment, Peter surprised me with a gift.

"I hope I'm not being presumptuous," he said, handing me a copy of *What to Expect When You're Expecting.* He looked vulnerable, like he was afraid I'd push him away. It was weird, feeling like I had this strange new power over him. Before, it felt like he was the powerful one in our relationship. He knew so much more about the world. Now I had something he wanted, something he could lose if I walked away from him.

"Thank you," I said, reading the chapter headings in the table of contents. "This will help."

"Are you okay?" he asked.

I nodded. "I think so. It's becoming more real to me. I'm getting used to the idea."

"Good. I really want this with you, Mia."

He looked so sincere and open, I felt off-kilter. How could I say no to him? How could I deny him something he wanted so badly? I loved him, didn't I? I did. I honestly did. He was happy and he was good to me. That was enough, wasn't it? So why did I feel so unsure? "I love you," I told him, stuffing my doubts deep down inside me, hoping he couldn't see them written on my face.

He knelt down and smiled up at me. "I love you too." Then he pulled me toward him and gently kissed my stomach. "We're going to be ridiculously happy."

Keeping the secret was hard. We started spending time at the cabin on our days off from the museum. I felt free out in the woods, like we could really be ourselves when no one was watching. We played house, sleeping in, sharing meals, taking walks, talking about the baby.

And then, one day, Peter went into the cellar to get the chainsaw so he could cut us more firewood. He closed the door behind him, like he was afraid I'd peek inside. When he came out, carrying the chainsaw, he put the lock back on the door. Then he went into the bedroom to return the key to where he kept it hidden.

I was sitting on the sofa, reading a book, pretending I hadn't been paying attention. It bothered me that we were having a child together but he didn't trust me enough to show me the root cellar. That lack of trust was one of those stupid things that gnawed at the back of my mind from time to time, and as the weeks passed, it bothered me more and more. That day, sitting on the couch, I listened when he put the key back. I heard one of the drawers in the antique dresser slide open and shut. And when he left the cabin with the chainsaw, I got up to find that key.

35

It took me a long time to find the key. At first, it was because I moved slowly and stealthily, scared he'd come back in and hear the floorboards creak, and catch me looking for it. Then it was because I couldn't figure out what he'd done with the key.

I carefully opened all the drawers in the dresser one by one, sifting through them. The key was nowhere to be found. Then I opened the middle drawer in the top row—it was a narrow drawer, more decorative than functional. When I slid it open, I heard the faintest clink of metal hitting wood. I felt along the insides of the drawer, but there was nothing there besides several pairs of Peter's socks. Then I got the idea to slide the drawer all the way out and look at the back. There it was. A tiny key tucked into a small manila envelope, pasted to the back of the drawer. I never would have thought to look there if my curiosity hadn't gotten the best of me.

I heard Peter's boots on the steps of the front porch and quickly slid the drawer back into place. Then I took my book and stretched out on the bed, as though I'd been there the whole time.

Peter poked his head into the bedroom and smiled at me. "Tired?"

"Yeah. I was thinking about taking a nap." I forced a laugh. "This pregnancy is kicking my butt."

"I've read that the first trimester is the hardest, with morning sickness and all," he said. "You rest and I'll rustle us up some dinner."

I didn't use the key that weekend. There wasn't a chance. I don't think Peter suspected anything, but he stuck close by me, doting on me. He cooked a delicious dinner and afterward, gave me a foot rub. Any other woman would have felt incredibly blessed to have such a kind and loving man in their life. But not me. No, the thought of that key was like an itch in my brain. One I was dying to scratch.

It wasn't until two weeks later that I found myself alone in the cabin. It was mid-September, and unseasonably warm. The ice in our cooler melted faster than we expected, leaving our food to float in a cold soup. Peter went back to town for more ice. I asked him to pick up take-out pizza from Angelina's too. He was so accommodating of my every wish, I felt guilty about my intention to betray his trust.

Had I known what was in that cellar, I would have run away from the cabin as fast as I could.

36

After I opened the lock, I carried it with me into the cellar. I'm not sure why—it wasn't a conscious choice. Maybe it was gut instinct, residual fear from spending too much time locked in an attic.

I remembered what Peter had said about some of the steps being rotten, so I was careful. Sure enough, the third step down groaned loudly when I put weight on it, so much so that I quickly moved to the next step, fearful it would break. That fourth step was solid, but the twelfth step, eight from the bottom, was clearly rotted. I'd had the foresight to bring a flashlight with me into the dark cellar, and I could see how weak the wood was. It almost looked like it had been gnawed on by termites. I didn't dare put weight on that one.

I made it down the steps without breaking my neck. The cellar had a dirt floor and no windows. The walls were built from river rock, the same as the foundation of the old cedar shake cabin. Whoever had built the cabin had probably taken the stones directly from the creek. There were thick, wooden pillars set in concrete to brace the ceiling—these seemed to be in good shape and a newer feature of the cellar. Maybe Peter had installed these to make sure the roof wouldn't come crashing down. He'd also brought in racks of metal shelves. These held the tools he'd mentioned, and various jars of chemicals. I didn't know what any of them were used for, but some of them looked similar to those Peter kept in his workshop back at the museum. I wondered if he experimented with special effects here too. Maybe that was why he seemed self-conscious about all this. He was working on projects he wasn't ready to share with anyone.

I almost left then. I should have. But I saw a set of shelves toward the back of the cellar that caught my eye. I walked over for a closer look.

The shelves held four strange, gourd-like ceramic jars. They reminded me of fairy-tale pumpkins, like the kind that had been turned into Cinderella's coach. There was something beautiful about them, like they'd been sculpted with the same love and care as the creations in Peter's workshop. I placed the lock on the shelf and lifted the lid off of one of the jars and set it on the floor. Then I trained the beam of my flashlight on the contents of the jar.

At first, I wasn't sure what I was looking at. I wondered if Peter was working on some kind of display for the museum for Halloween. He already had that zombie he'd created for his friend's movie and he had mentioned doing an after-hours haunted tour. Tourists hadn't been as plentiful after Labor Day, but we could still get a lot of traffic between late September and October 31st.

The thing in the jar resembled a floating human head. Long blond hair drifted in a halo around a shriveled, feminine face. I had to give it to Peter—it was horrifying. If I hadn't known him and seen his work at the museum, I would have thought it was real.

I was curious as to how he'd pulled this off, it was *that* good. There was a set of metal tongs on the shelf above the jars. I used them to gently prod the floating head in its bath of clear liquid. It floated to the side, turning slightly. Then I saw the tattoo.

It was a hibiscus flower, tucked just behind the woman's ear. I'd seen that tattoo before.

I sucked in a breath as I realized who I was looking at.

Chandra.

A snippet from a long-ago nursery rhyme drifted through my mind.

Peter, Peter, pumpkin eater,

had a wife and couldn't keep her.

Put her in a pumpkin shell

and there she lived, very well.

Peter had lied.

He'd lied about Chandra quitting her job to leave town with her boyfriend. He'd lied about the text he'd received. Which meant he was probably the one who'd sent the text from her phone after he'd killed her. I was sure of it.

Panicked, I lifted the lid on one of the other jars. A shock of red hair floated on the surface, obscuring the face. I didn't need to see the face to know it was the girl Peter had flirted with at the museum. The one we'd fought about. I had thought he was cheating on me. I never would have imagined this.

"Well, what do you think?"

I screamed and dropped the flashlight. It winked out, leaving me in darkness.

Peter switched on his own flashlight and directed the beam at my face. I blinked at the bright light as he took a step toward me.

"I warned you not to come down here, Mia. You promised you wouldn't."

I held up my hands to shield my face from the light. I could see his dark silhouette. He looked bigger, menacing, now that I knew what he was.

My heart thundered in my chest. I took a breath to calm

myself. "I know, and I'm sorry I broke my promise. I was just so curious about what you've been working on down here."

"And now that you've seen it?"

My throat felt as dry as dust. I swallowed. "It's good—it's *really* good. That'll scare the heck out of people come Halloween."

Peter clucked his tongue at me. "Oh, Mia. You're a terrible liar, you know that?" He chuckled. "But I find that so endearing. It's one of the things I love most about you."

"Are you going to kill me too, Peter?"

"What?" He sounded genuinely surprised, but I didn't know what to believe anymore. Unlike me, he was an incredible liar.

"I can keep your secret," I told him. "I know I'm not good at lying, but I'm *great* at keeping secrets. And you've kept mine, so I owe you."

He sighed and leaned up against one of the columns. I took the opportunity to move past him, closer to the stairs.

"I'm not going to kill you, Mia." He reached out and gently stroked my stomach. "How could I, when you're the mother of my child?"

I didn't answer. Instead, I leapt up the stairs, taking them two by two. I forgot about that rotten step.

It snapped under my weight. I could have seriously injured my right leg, crashing through the step, but my left knee hit the step above that one, saving me from falling all the way through. I pitched forward, into the steps. I braced myself with my hands, and somehow kept my face from bashing against the wood. But my stomach took the brunt of the fall. It knocked the air out of me. Pain radiated from my belly to my back and thighs. I took a gulping breath into my aching lungs. I was bruised all over, and my right ankle felt twisted and swollen.

I winced when I felt Peter's hands on me. He carefully lifted me off the steps and carried me back down into the cellar. He laid me down by one of the pillars, and then stood up, shining the light over my body, taking in my injuries.

"That had to hurt," he said. I couldn't tell if the compassion in his voice was real or not. "But I didn't do that to you. I told you about those steps and you didn't listen." He sighed again. "You did this to yourself, Mia."

Then he reached down and clasped something cold and metal around my swollen right ankle, sending a sharp pain up my leg. I pushed up on my elbow to see what it was. It was a slender metal cuff attached to a chain, which he then looped around the wooden column. And, adding insult to injury, he used the padlock I'd carried down to the cellar with me to secure the chain.

"Where's that key?" He slipped his fingers into the front pocket of my jeans, grinning when he found the key to the padlock. "Can't have you escaping, now, can we?"

He slipped the key into his own jeans pocket, grabbed his flashlight, stood, and started up the stairs.

"Where are you going?" I asked, gritting my teeth against the pain throbbing in my ankle.

He stopped midway up the stairs and turned, giving me a look of pity. "I need to think. I honestly don't know whether I should marry you or murder you, sweetheart."

With that, he trudged up the stairs and closed the cellar door, leaving me in the dark.

37

I tugged on the chain holding me prisoner. Had Peter used this chain on his other victims? If I had to bet money, I'd say yes, based on the calm way he'd locked me up. He'd had practice.

I had to get out. Peter had acted like he was still deciding my fate, but I didn't believe for one second he'd let me go, and I didn't want to end up as a floating head in a stupid ceramic jar. I was scared and angry, and for the moment, the adrenaline rush from wanting to survive was keeping my head clear. I let my eyes adjust to the dark, searching for the means to escape.

Then I felt a sharp pain that reminded me of a menstrual cramp, and warmth spread across the crotch of my jeans. I took shallow breaths to get through the cramps, scared to move. I reached down between my legs and felt wetness there. It was too dark to see the blood, but I knew that's what it was. I was losing the baby.

That's when the tears came. I curled up in a ball and cried. I wanted this child. I hadn't realized how much I wanted it until I was in danger of losing it. And that brought another worry. Peter wanted the baby too. If I was no longer pregnant, what incentive would he have to keep me alive?

Sobbing, I spread loose dirt from the floor over the front of my jeans, hoping to hide the blood. I was already filthy from sitting on the floor, so I could only hope it would work and buy me time. I couldn't tell how convincing it looked because the only light in the room was at the top of the stairs, coming through the thin crack below the door. I could hear Peter up there, pacing the floorboards. His heavy footfalls beat with the same rhythm as my frightened heart.

After what felt like an hour, he opened the door. The light from upstairs was blinding. He stood there for a moment, watching me, and then came down the stairs, carefully avoiding the step I'd smashed through.

He sat down on the third step from the bottom and stared at me, silent and unmoving. His face was in shadow, but I could feel his eyes on me, studying me. I hoped my tear-stained cheeks made me look contrite.

Finally, he said, "I've made a decision."

I swallowed, willing my voice not to shake. I couldn't stop my hands from shaking though. I placed them in my lap. "Okay. What did you decide?"

"I'm not going to hurt you," he said. "I love you too much."

I wasn't sure what to say. My feelings toward him had changed. Finding out your boyfriend is a cold-blooded killer will do that. "Thank you. Can I come back upstairs?"

"Not yet," he said. He rested his elbows on his knees and tented his hands. "You've betrayed my trust, Mia. We had a sacred bond, and you broke it."

I opened my mouth to reply, but he held up his hand, shushing me.

"I'm not saying that was a deal-breaker for this relationship. I'm committed to making this work," Peter said.

Funny—murdering people was a deal-breaker for me, but it didn't seem prudent to tell him that. Instead, I said, "Go on."

"You're going to have to earn back my trust," Peter told me. "I'm going to go back to town for a few days and—"

"You're leaving me down here?"

"Let me finish." His tone was exasperated. Not angry, just frustrated, as though he were dealing with a disobedient but beloved child. "I'll be gone for two days, at the most. I'm going to leave you here for a short time, and I want you to think about what you want in this relationship, how you're going to win back my trust."

I bit back a haughty response. It would do me no good to make him mad, but he was ticking me off. *I* needed to win *his* trust? After all he'd done? I burned with anger, but luckily, common sense prevailed. Yes, I needed to earn his trust. If I wanted to get out of here, I *had* to do that. Get him to let down his guard, and then get the hell out. "What can I do?"

"We'll figure that out when I get back. I've made you some sandwiches and filled up a jug of water. You'll be fine."

"What if I need to pee?"

He chuckled, not exasperated now, but amused. "I'll leave you a bucket. And a blanket in case you get cold." He leaned forward and slipped my sneakers off my feet. "I'll be holding on to these for a while. Where's your phone?"

I cursed under my breath. If only I'd thought to bring it down with me, and somehow kept it hidden. Not that I could have anticipated my current situation, but still—I was angry at myself for not being smarter. "Upstairs. On the bedside table."

"Okay. Good."

"It's not like I can get a signal anyway," I said. It was an inane thing to say, but I was trying to get him to trust me. Instead, I came off sounding like a kid who'd been grounded rather than a full-grown woman chained in a cellar. Peter knew better than I did that phone service at the cabin was spotty. You'd have to hike up the mountain or get to the highway for reliable service. If I could escape, I planned on using the phone to call for help. But I couldn't do that if he confiscated it.

He stood to leave. "I get that you're unhappy with me right now, Mia. But you need to ask yourself this. Have I ever hurt you? No. I've never laid a hand on you. Have I been good to you? Yes, yes I have." He turned and began to walk up the stairs.

I could think of a few reasons why I disagreed with those statements, but the thought of being left alone, down in the dark for days, terrified me. What if he left me here and never came back? What would happen when my food and water ran out? As frightened of him as I was, I didn't want him to go. "Wait. I just need to know why."

He stopped and turned around. "Why what?"

"Why did you do it? Why did you kill those girls?"

He sighed and came back down the steps. "It's difficult to explain."

"Try. Please."

He crouched down and planted himself on the bottom step, directly in front of me. He was so close I could have touched him, but I didn't dare. His eyes burned into mine. "I have this…need. It's kind of like my art, when I get an idea to create something, and it completely absorbs my thinking. I get lost in the process of sculpting and painting, and that need doesn't ease up until it's done."

I stared at him, speechless. I remembered how focused he'd been when he had altered the mermaid costume. He had worked on it nonstop, late into the night, barely touching the take-out we'd ordered. He had obsessed over every detail. *It has to be perfect,* he'd told me. *It won't work unless it's perfect.* I understood his artistic side. I just didn't get how that translated to murder.

Peter seemed to sense his answer wasn't sufficient, because he shook his head. "No. No, that doesn't quite do it justice, does it? It's more like…well, it's like your pearls."

"What?"

"You told me that shedding the pearls made your whole body ache. Do you remember that? You said the ache was worst right before the pearls came out. That in that moment, you could barely think of anything but getting them out of your body. You said it took everything you had to resist ripping your own skin open, forcing them out. In that moment, you'd give *anything* to be free of the pearls. Then, finally, your skin would split and you'd shed the pearls. And even though that experience left you with wounds, you felt such a sense of relief. You were so grateful for the release." He reached over and took my hand, hesitantly, as though he were frightened of how I'd react. "That's how it is for me. The need to hurt someone gets so strong that I'd do anything to be free of it. And the only way to do that is to kill. If I don't, I'm afraid I'll end up hurting someone I care about. I'm afraid I'll hurt you, Mia, and I don't want to do that. I really don't."

I couldn't believe he was comparing his desire to kill with a disease I'd never wanted and couldn't control. I should have been angered by that. But maybe what he was saying was true in a way. Maybe his need to hurt others was a kind of illness.

I reached up with my other hand and cradled his cheek. "There's *got* to be another way for you to deal with this."

Peter let go of my hand and pulled away from me. "There's not. Believe me, I've tried. The need has only gotten stronger." He stood and walked over to the shelves. He grabbed an empty bucket and placed it at my feet. Then he went back upstairs.

He returned a few minutes later, carrying a large baggie filled with sandwiches, a gallon jug of water, and a blanket. He handed me the baggie and placed the jug and blanket beside me. He knelt down and brushed my hair back from my forehead. "All right.

I'm going to go, but I promise I'll be back. We'll talk more then. Think about what I said."

I tried to fight back tears and failed. "Okay."

"I love you." He kissed me and leaned back, searching my face. "Tell me you love me, Mia."

I forced a smile through my tears. "I love you."

He seemed satisfied, because he returned my smile and gently brushed a tear from my cheek with his knuckle. "That's my girl. Be good while I'm gone." He rose to his feet and turned toward the stairs.

"Can I—can I at least have a flashlight?"

He didn't turn around. "No."

He walked up the stairs and closed the door. The cellar was even darker than it had been before.

38

I needed to think. If he left, I had time to get free and run into the woods. I'd make it to the highway and flag down a ride. But what if he wasn't leaving? What if this was a test to regain his trust? I listened intently. I heard his footsteps grow fainter, and then I heard the front door close. I waited, breathless, to see if he'd return. I heard nothing. Maybe he really had left.

Okay, let's assume he was gone. What did I need to do to escape? I tested the cuff around my ankle. It was solid. I couldn't pull the cuff open or slip my foot out of it. No way that was coming off without a key. But if I made it out, I could find a locksmith. Or a blowtorch. Something. The cuff wasn't my priority. The chain was.

I pulled on the chain, testing its strength. Yeah, no way I was breaking free without a bolt cutter. I thought I'd seen one on a shelf, nestled among other tools, but the wall of shelves was all the way across the room. It might as well have been on another planet because even if I stretched all the way out, as far as the chain would go, there was still a good three feet between my outstretched hand and the shelves. The flashlight I'd dropped was even further away. Useless.

I crawled back to the column and leaned against it. I could reach the stairs, but what good was that? The steel links in the chain were strong. Rubbing the chain against the wooden step would do nothing to break it.

My stomach growled. When was the last time I'd eaten anything? Breakfast, and I had no idea what time it was now. All I knew was I felt bruised and hopeless. My cramps had subsided, but I didn't dare hope the baby was okay. Maybe losing the baby was for the best, considering who the father was. I felt like crying again. I couldn't imagine raising a kid, only to have him turn out to be a monster, just like his dad.

Instead of crying, I ate a sandwich. Food helped, and to Peter's credit, he hadn't skimped on cheese or turkey. He'd even made different kinds of sandwiches—two turkey, two ham, and two with peanut butter and jelly. I hated myself for feeling gratitude over that.

He'd locked me up and left me, and he'd killed at least four people that I knew of, based on the number of ceramic jars I'd seen. I should have hated him. Part of me did. But I hated myself too. What if I had never come down here? Would things still be okay between us if I didn't know about those girls? No. How could I even think that?

Knowing or not knowing didn't change the fact that he had killed people and he didn't show any signs of remorse as far as I could see. Let's say I had never found out. He was going to kill again. He'd said as much. Besides, he probably put rat poison in my sandwiches. Despite what he'd said about us working things out, I couldn't see how he could let me live. Not when I knew what he was.

I heard something skitter in the dark. It sounded like it was on the other side of the room, near the shelves with the ceramic gourds. I tried not to think about all the critters that might live in a dark cellar out in the woods—rodents, spiders, maybe even a garter snake or a bat. But it didn't matter what was down here in the dark with me. If I couldn't get out, I was dead anyway.

You would think I'd be more freaked out about being trapped in a cellar with dead bodies than rodents. I wasn't afraid of ghosts. I'd witnessed too much evil in the world to fear the dead. All I felt for Peter's victims was pity. How horrifying their last moments must have been.

Those girls hadn't deserved to die, and certainly not like that. Chandra might not have been a saint, but she had been my friend —one of the first I'd made starting my new life. She had been kind to me. I decided that if her spirit was still here, we were on the same side. And if she planned to haunt me, she could at least give me a hand breaking the chain.

What did haunt me were thoughts of my mother. If she could see me, what would she say? A simple *I told you so*? I don't think so.

Mother was never one to watch me make mistakes and let it go. No, for years, over and over, she reminded me of incidents where I'd screwed up. She held on to those stories the way some people hold on to grudges. She had to. It was who she was.

I remember breaking her favorite milk glass vase when I was six. I hadn't meant to—I thought the bouquet of flowers she had picked from our backyard were pretty, and I wanted to smell them. The vase had been placed on the kitchen counter, and I was too short to reach it without stretching up on my tip-toes. I was clumsy and knocked the vase over. It crashed to the floor, shattering. I think Mom was more upset about having to clean up the mess than me stepping on one of those white shards of glass with my bare foot and bleeding all over the kitchen floor. Afterward, any time I did something klutzy, she would remind me of that day, how I'd stood there shrieking like a banshee about the shard in my foot, while she had to sweep up the broken glass and wipe up the blood. As though I'd broken the vase on purpose, and she was the victim.

Mom was either the victim or the heroine in her stories. Sometimes both. She liked to tell me about the sacrifices she'd made to raise me. She never married, didn't finish college. She was stuck living in her dad's rundown house rather than buying the kind of house she always wanted—an airy cottage full of windows that let in the light. A house near the river instead of in the dumpy part of town. She never got to travel, and she had always wanted to tour Europe. There was so much she missed out on because she had set aside her dreams for me. (Not that I had a choice in the matter.) The purpose of these stories was to demonstrate what a wonderful mother she was. Her martyrdom proved her love for me.

I used to believe her, and I internalized the guilt that came with those stories. My very existence had robbed Mother of her dreams. But then I realized something. Those stories weren't true.

Once I learned how much the pearls I grew were worth, I understood that they afforded options for our family. We were bringing in enough revenue that Mother could have traveled to Europe if she'd wanted to. She could have returned to college. She could have sold our old house and bought a better one. But she didn't. Instead, she hoarded the money.

I'm not sure why she did that, but I think it was because she was afraid. She was scared to take the steps she needed to take to change her life. It was easier to blame me for her unhappiness, because if she tried to change, she'd have to examine her own life, her own mistakes. Mom couldn't do that. Her ego was too fragile. If she admitted to her failings, she'd shatter just like that milk glass vase.

She needed me—both to put food on our table and to be able to tell herself she was the one caring for me, that I couldn't survive without her. I wondered what she was doing now that I was gone and she was alone.

As I got older, the story Mother told me most often was how people would abduct me and use me for the wealth I could provide if they ever found out about the pearls. She convinced me I was in danger, and I believed her. I allowed her to keep me prisoner for far too long.

She wasn't entirely wrong. I was a prisoner now, caged by my own stupidity. I'd trusted the wrong person, and he'd hurt me, just as Mom had predicted.

But what Mother never understood—and what Peter didn't know—is a trapped animal is the most dangerous beast of all.

39

Hours passed. I was hungry again, and no closer to finding a way out. I ate another sandwich and took a long swig from the jug of water. With renewed energy and determination, I turned my thoughts to escape. There *had* to be a way out. If I didn't believe that, I'd lose my mind.

I had tried to reach the shelves, to no avail. Chained to a pillar in the middle of the room, I couldn't reach the stone walls that surrounded me to see if there was anything there I could use. I couldn't pull the chain free from the wooden column. But maybe there was a stray rock buried in the soil on the floor that I could use to break it.

I pushed up onto my knees and began sifting through the dirt, searching for something heavy enough to break the chain. The loose soil went down about five inches before it hardened. Slowly, I made a circle around the pillar, exploring the dirt with my fingers. No stones.

Then, at the back of the column, my fingers closed around something straight that was definitely not a rock. I ran my fingers down the length of it. It was a Phillips head screwdriver, small, with a blade of no more than four inches. The handle was made of hard plastic.

I tried inserting the blade into the lock of the cuff first, thinking I could pick it and open the cuff. I'd figured how to pick the lock in the attic of my old house, so I could do it again, right? No such luck. The attic lock had been ancient, and had popped open when I applied pressure to the locking mechanism. That didn't work with this one, or on the padlock securing the chain.

Next, I felt along the chain for a weak link. Perhaps I could pry a link open using the screwdriver. I found a link that had a gap where the metal came together. I inserted the screwdriver and tried to force the link to open wider. I thought I felt it give the tiniest bit, but no matter how hard I tried, I couldn't get the link to open wide enough that I could unhook it from the link next to it and separate the chain. The steel in the chain was too strong.

Frustrated, I leaned back against the column and ran my fingers along the blade of the screwdriver, thinking. I flinched when I felt a sudden pain in my index finger, and then realized the screwdriver had pricked my skin. The end of it had grown sharp from my exertions with the cuff and chain.

That meant the metal in the screwdriver was not as strong as the other metals. I scraped the end of the screwdriver along the metal cuff around my ankle for a few minutes, testing my theory. When I ran my finger over the end of the screwdriver, it had grown even sharper.

I finally had something I could use to help me escape. It was a longshot, and I knew there was a good chance I'd make things worse for myself. Still, I had to try. A risky plan was better than no plan at all.

40

I'm not sure how long I was in that cellar. I judged time by the light filtering through the crack under the door. When it was brightest, it had to be midday. Once it got dark, it was impossible to tell what time it was.

When Peter returned, it was dark. He didn't bother turning on a lantern in the cabin. He used the flashlight in his phone to navigate the stairs and survey the cellar. I prayed he wouldn't find anything amiss. I'd tried to smooth the loose soil back down, once I'd found the screwdriver. I hoped he wouldn't read anything in my face, like the fact that I'd slipped that sharpened screwdriver in my back pocket when I heard his heavy footsteps upstairs.

"You didn't eat all your sandwiches," Peter said, shining the light in my face. I'd eaten the turkey and ham sandwiches and left the peanut butter and jelly ones. I figured I should eat the ones that would spoil, and save the others in case Peter was late. Or didn't return at all.

I blinked against the brightness of the light, which brought tears to my eyes. "I tried to ration. I wasn't sure when you'd be back." My voice sounded rough—like I'd been crying. Really, I was thirsty. I had rationed the water too. I'd made myself drink every few hours, but I was probably dehydrated, given how fatigued I felt. It's not like I slept well either—just in short, fitful jags. And I was terrified—scared of him, scared of what would happen if my plan didn't work.

"I said I'd be back in two days," he reminded me. "And here I am, just as I promised." He stared at me. "Why are you so dirty?"

"I had to sleep on the floor." I hoped I had a neutral expression on my face. I didn't want to sound flippant over what seemed obvious, but I also didn't want to betray my efforts to escape. I looked at my hands, which were shaking once again. They were filthy from the dark soil of the cellar. My flannel shirt and jeans were too, which was good because that hid the blood from the miscarriage. "Can I come upstairs and wash off?"

Peter sat down on the bottom step. "Well, I don't know, Mia. That's up to you, isn't it? Are you willing to do what you need to do to make this relationship work?"

That was my opening. "Yes, Peter." I wiped the tears from my eyes. "I'm so, so very sorry I didn't listen to you. It will never happen again."

He nodded his approval. "That's a start."

"I *really* want to make this work," I told him. "I love you, Peter. You're everything to me, and I'm so sorry I hurt you." I held out my arms, beckoning him to come to me, to enfold me in his embrace.

He relented with a smile, as though he'd won. Like he'd beaten me into submission. I let him think that.

He knelt down, brushing my hair out of my face. "I forgive you, Mia."

That's when I drew the screwdriver from behind me and plunged it into his neck.

Peter yanked the screwdriver from his flesh, throwing it on the dirt floor. Big mistake. Blood gushed from the wound, soaking both of us. I must have punctured an artery.

The look of betrayal on Peter's face almost made me feel sorry for him. He made a choking sound, desperately trying to breathe. He grabbed my arms, but his grip was weak and I shrugged him off.

His hands went to the wound in his neck, trying to stop the bleeding. I focused on finding the key to the cuff, praying he hadn't left it upstairs. If he had, we would both die in this cellar.

I tried the back pockets of his jeans first—nothing. Then I fished in his front pocket and found not one, but two keys—one to the cuff on my ankle and one to the lock he'd used to chain me to the wooden column. Jackpot. No car keys, though. He must have left them upstairs.

Peter sank against me, bleeding out. I pushed him off me, onto the floor, and unlocked the cuff around my ankle. Then I undid the lock on the chain. I snatched up Peter's phone and the screwdriver and stumbled up the stairs.

At the top, I slammed the cellar door, secured the padlock, and left Peter to die in the dark.

41

Peter had gotten rid of my phone *and* my shoes. The realization dawned on me slowly as I searched the dark cabin for them, using his phone as a flashlight. I couldn't unlock his phone to call for help, but at least I had some light. I found his car keys hanging on a nail by the front door, and stuffed them in the pocket of my jeans.

My ankle throbbed—each step I took put weight on it and sent biting pain arching up my leg—but I couldn't stop. I hadn't held out hope he'd leave my phone where I could find it, but I thought he'd at least leave the shoes. How could I hike miles to his car, in the dark, with no shoes? He'd hidden them from me, another way to exert control in case I tried to escape.

It was that small act of cruelty that erased the last of my fear and honed my anger into a fine point. The murders, the threats, holding me captive, the loss of my baby—all that was too much for me to process. If I thought about any of that for too long, I'd freeze up. But the shoes—that was a slight I could focus on. That got me moving.

I'd looked in every room for the shoes, and nothing. Under the bed, in the dresser, in the kitchen cabinets, even in the cooler he used for cold storage. Maybe he'd thrown them away, somewhere in the woods.

Fine. I'd go shoeless, but I was going. I limped back into the bedroom and grabbed an extra pair of socks from my bag, and two pairs of his from the dresser. I needed some kind of protection for my feet.

As I tugged the socks on, it occurred to me that I could simply steal his shoes, but I couldn't stomach the thought of going down those stairs again. I imagined him pretending to be dead, waiting until I was close enough to grab. I shuddered. He *was* dead—there was too much blood for him not to be—but I was not opening that cellar door again. It would stay locked until I was able to bring the police out here. Let them open it.

In any case, his feet were much bigger than mine, and wearing his shoes would only give me blisters. Wearing four pairs of socks wasn't much better, but I'd take it slow, walking through the woods. I couldn't find a regular flashlight or lantern anywhere, but I would have the light from his phone until the battery died. I switched off the light to conserve the battery and set the phone on the kitchen table. I could use the handle of the broom, both as a walking stick to support my sore ankle, and as a cane like a blind person might use, to navigate the path and detect rocks and brambles that would trip me up. The moon was full, so I had that in my favor. Without lights in the cabin, I relied on the moonbeams streaming through the windows to plan my escape.

I hurried around the small kitchen, tugging on my jacket, unscrewing the broom head from the handle, and tucking a granola bar in my jacket pocket. I was surprised to find my wallet was still in my jacket pocket, where I'd left it. I figured Peter would have gotten rid of that too. Maybe he hadn't thought to look there.

As I grabbed a water bottle from the cooler, I became aware of a presence standing at the threshold of the front door. I turned, the hair on the back of my neck rising as I took in the dark, hulking figure filling the frame.

The man ducked his head and took a step inside the cabin. "Amelia?"

I drew the sharpened screwdriver from my back pocket like a dagger, holding it out in front of me.

The man held out both of his hands in front of him and moved forward slowly, as though he were trying to calm a wild animal. As he crossed in front of the kitchen window, moonlight illuminated his face. Gabe.

It felt like a lifetime had passed since I'd last seen him. How much did Gabriel know about Peter's extracurricular activities? He *had* to have known something. Maybe he'd even been part of it.

"Are you all right?" he asked.

"What are you doing here?" I put the water bottle on the kitchen counter so I could hold the screwdriver with both hands. Gabriel was a mountain of a man. If he lunged for me, I didn't stand a chance, but he would not leave this cabin unscathed.

He stopped, eyeing the screwdriver. It was still coated with Peter's blood. Maybe he noticed that. Of course, the blood on my flannel shirt might have given him pause as well.

"I came to rescue you," Gabe said.

I barked out a laugh. "I rescued myself."

He nodded. "I can see that."

"Peter killed people. Did you know? Did you know what he was?" I searched his face carefully, reading his expression, looking for signs of betrayal.

Gabriel looked genuinely shocked. He took a step back, leaning against the wall between the window and kitchen counter. "I thought something was wrong when you didn't show for work. Peter said the two of you argued and you decided to go home to your mother, so he took you to Portland and put you on a bus." He ran a hand over his face, stricken. "I knew that couldn't be true, not after seeing the way your mother treated you. And you didn't even say goodbye. I went to your apartment and peeked in the window. All your stuff was still there." He stared into my eyes. "The painting I did of Tillamook Head. You said you loved that painting. I thought you'd at least have taken that. That's when I knew he'd lied."

My stomach dropped like I was in free fall, plummeting out of control. It was the same kind of lie Peter had told me about Chandra. If he'd told Gabe I wasn't coming back, that could only mean one thing. He really had planned to kill me.

I had known that, deep in my gut, from the moment I saw what was left of Chandra, but I hadn't wanted to believe it. Not when he'd told me he loved me. Not when he'd been so happy about me carrying his child. I guess I'd hoped that would make a difference and he'd let me live. "How long ago did he tell you that?"

"Two days ago. He worked at the museum like everything was normal, even came home and stayed at the house with me and Dad. But when he left town so late tonight, I followed him. I was sure he'd spot me, so I stayed back, keeping to the shadows. I almost got lost—there's not much of a trail to find this place."

"That's exactly how he wanted it. So no one would find him and interrupt him." I leaned back against the kitchen counter, taking the weight off my swollen ankle. Two days—that meant Peter must have gone back to the museum the morning after he locked me up in the cellar. It had been hard to judge time down there in the dark, but the timing felt right based on what little daylight I had seen coming in under the cellar door. And my hunger—I had spaced out my rations based on my sense of time.

In my rush to leave, I'd ignored how hungry I was. Adrenaline and fear will do that to a person, but now I felt weak and shaky from two days of barely eating. I kept my eyes on Gabriel

—still not sure how much I trusted him—and set the screwdriver on the kitchen counter. Feeling ravenous, I grabbed my granola bar, ripped open the packaging, and bit off a chunk, relishing the sweet taste of oats and honey. Gabriel kept his distance, watching me. I'm sure I must have looked unhinged, covered in blood and dirt, devouring food like a starving wolf.

"Where is Peter now?" he asked quietly.

"Dead," I said, not caring that I was talking with my mouth full. I guess I wasn't being terribly sensitive to talk about his brother like that, either. "In the cellar."

Gabe's face was unreadable. He nodded toward my stained shirt. "Is that his blood or yours?"

"His." I crumpled up the granola bar wrapper and threw it on the floor. I took a big swig of water. "He locked me in the cellar, so I stabbed him and got out."

"He hurt you." It was a statement, not a question.

"I fell on the stairs. The wood is rotten. That's how I sprained my ankle," I said. "But, yes. He hurt me."

Gabriel looked down at my feet, taking in the way I was balancing on the left one, resting the right one against the kitchen cabinet. "I'm sorry."

He seemed sincere, so I told him the rest. "I lost the baby too."

He stiffened, staring at me. "I didn't know you were pregnant."

I raised my chin, defiant, daring him to judge me. He didn't need to know that I'd only just found out myself, that I'd lost something precious before I'd even had a chance to get used to the idea of being a mother. "I was. But he took that from me."

Gabriel's eyes went to the dark blood stain on the front of my jeans. He looked away and bowed his head, sadness etched into his features. "I'm so sorry, Amelia. I should have stopped this."

I felt my rage fade. I was taking out my anger on the wrong person. "You didn't know what he was."

He met my gaze. "I didn't. But I should have." He took a step forward, like maybe he wanted to hold me, to offer comfort.

Grief washed over me, and I pushed it back down. I wasn't going to let myself cry, not here in front of him. I waved him off as I grabbed my water bottle and stuffed another granola bar in my pocket. "How about we get out of here?"

Gabriel froze, watching my face as I hid my sadness, like he knew I was shutting him out. Finally, he nodded. "Yeah. We need to get you to a doctor and call the police."

I decided to leave the screwdriver where it was. Gabriel wouldn't hurt me. He was nothing like Peter. I picked up Peter's phone and tried to turn the flashlight back on, but it wouldn't work. So much for conserving the battery. I grabbed the broom handle and used it as a cane to hobble toward the door. Gabriel walked beside me, eyeing my sore ankle and bulky socks.

"You're really going to walk like that, all the way back to the road? You don't even have shoes."

I responded with an angry grunt as I hopped over the threshold. Hell yes, I was walking like this. What other choice did I have?

Gabriel stepped in front of me, blocking my path across the front porch.

I stared up at him, eyes blazing. "Get out of my way, Gabe."

He took my cane from me, gently but firmly, and leaned it against the porch railing. I glared in protest, but he simply turned and crouched down, offering his back. "Get on," he said. "Maybe I wasn't here before, but I'm here now, and I'm not letting you walk with that messed up ankle. I'm carrying you out of here."

I didn't want to give in, but he was right. It didn't make sense to hobble for miles. He was strong, and if he was willing to carry me, why not take him up on his offer? "Fine." I wrapped my arms around his neck and settled onto his back.

He straightened up, his hands behind him to support me. I wrapped my legs around his waist to distribute my weight. He shifted from foot to foot, testing for balance, and then started walking. "You okay back there?"

"Yes," I said. "Thank you, Gabe."

I sensed him smiling in the dark. "You're welcome."

We didn't talk much during the hike. The forest was still, the quiet occasionally broken by the rustling of some nocturnal woodland creature. I thought I heard an owl at one point. The hike was difficult for Gabriel, both because he was walking in the dark and because he was toting me, but he didn't complain. It had rained early in the day, and the ground was damp, not quite muddy under a carpet of moss and pine needles. The moist air was rich with the smell of earth and trees.

Gabe kept trudging forward, picking his way south, navigating by glimpses of stars through the canopy, and the sound of the creek to our right. If it weren't for that, we might have gotten turned around, but the steady sound of flowing water was a comfort. I felt even better when I heard the distant roar of a semi-truck on the highway. We were almost out.

When we reached Peter's car, Gabriel stopped. "My bike is just over there, behind that tree," he said. He set me down gently, letting me lean against the car. He eyed my thin jacket. "It's going to be a cold ride, but the hospital in Seaside is only thirty minutes away."

I smiled at him and retrieved Peter's keys from my pants pocket. "If it's all the same, I think I'll take the car."

Gabriel shook his head, laughing, in spite of the horror of the situation. "People should not underestimate you, Amelia."

At that I grinned.

He held out his hand for the keys. “If it’s all the same though, I’ll drive.”

I dropped them into his waiting palm. “That’s probably for the best, because I don’t know how.”

He laughed again, and then scooped me up in his arms to carry me over to the passenger side of the car. Once I was settled, he went back around and started the car, letting it warm up before pulling around the small clearing, back to the dirt road.

I was glad to be out of the chilly night breeze, but the warm air inside the car felt stifling. It smelled like Peter, the ghost of his aftershave. It should have been a pleasant scent. It wasn’t.

I shifted in my seat, looking at Gabriel. “Are we going to talk about the fact that I killed your brother?”

He winced, but kept his eyes on the road as he turned on to Highway 26. “He wasn’t really my brother.”

“He was though. Legally, at least.”

Gabriel shook his head. “We were never close. At best, we tolerated each other. He—” He hesitated, thinking. “He had a temper. I knew that. I think, deep down, I knew there was something wrong with him.” He glanced over at me before turning his eyes back to the road. “But I never thought he was capable of killing anyone. If I’d thought that, Amelia, I…”

I took his hand and squeezed it. “I know.” I sighed. The warmth of Gabriel’s hand in mine steadied me. He smelled different than Peter, earthier. Like the forest we’d just been in. That was comforting too. “I didn’t think he was capable of murder either. Honestly, I wouldn’t have even dreamed of it. But then I saw those girls, and…everything changed.”

Gabriel looked startled. “What girls? You said he’d killed somebody, but you didn’t say who.”

“Remember Chandra? The girl who played the mermaid before me?”

Gabriel nodded, glancing over at me.

"He killed her. There was another girl—that redhead who went missing in Seaside?" I hadn't paid much attention at the time, but I remembered seeing a story in the paper about a missing girl. Until I'd seen her remains, it hadn't occurred to me that the missing girl was the same woman Peter had flirted with at the museum. "Her too. And two others at least. I didn't look." Four young women dead, as far as I knew. What if there were more?

"You're sure? You saw their bodies?"

"Yes. I did." I had seen *part* of their bodies, but I couldn't talk about that. I couldn't bring myself to speak the words. The moment when I discovered Chandra's lifeless head was burned into my memory, and I would have given anything to forget it. I couldn't share the horror of that with another person, force them to carry that burden too.

Gabriel had a grim look on his face, his mouth set in a hard line. "We take you to the ER, and then I'll contact the police. You don't have to say anything to them until you're ready. I can take them to the cabin if they need me to. You don't have to go back there ever again."

"I'll talk to them. I have to. I have to tell them what I did."

Gabriel held my hand to his chest. "You did what you had to do to survive. It wasn't your fault."

"I know. But still…I murdered somebody."

He looked over at me. "In self-defense. Just like I did."

I'd forgotten about that, the day Gabriel had escaped his own captors and fought off the man who had abused him. That was different than what Peter had done.

All three of us had killed. But only one of us was a monster.

42

Gabriel stayed with me for the exam at the emergency room. A medical assistant named Janine took my vitals and then called in a doctor. The doctor asked me about the blood on my clothes, and I told her about falling on the stairs and having a miscarriage, then fighting off the man who had kept me captive. She eyed Gabriel suspiciously until I told her he wasn't the one who had hurt me, and we planned on talking to the police after the exam.

"That's good," Dr. Danon said, "because I have to make my own report, and too often I see women in here who suffer abuse and try to hide it."

"We don't have anything to hide," Gabriel assured her.

The doctor examined my ankle. "It's awfully swollen," she said, gently probing the skin. She moved my foot at the joint and I let out a sharp breath. "That hurt?" she asked.

"Yes," I said, gritting my teeth.

"I don't think it's broken, but I'm going to want an x-ray to be sure," Dr. Danon said. "Tell me about the pregnancy. Do you know how far along you were?"

"I don't know for sure. Two or three months? My last period was late June."

Dr. Danon nodded, looking at the stain on my jeans. "And after you fell, you started bleeding?" I nodded. "Any cramps or back pains?"

"Yes, but they went away after a day or so," I said. "I felt sore all over. Still do."

"Well, I'm not surprised. You did fall down a flight of stairs," Dr. Danon said. I didn't care for her tone. She made it sound like a mishap, not like I had been fighting for my life.

Gabriel didn't like her tone either. "She was abducted and abused."

Dr. Danon looked over at him. "Yes, abused." She turned back to me. "I'm going to need to do a gynecological exam. Are you okay with him being in the room, or would you prefer some privacy?"

I looked over at Gabriel, my cheeks growing warm. "Um…"

"I'll step out," he told Dr. Danon. To me he said, "I'm right here in the hallway if you need me."

After Gabe left the exam room, Dr. Danon handed me a hospital gown. "Janine and I are going to step out for a few minutes so you can change. Everything off, the opening goes in the back." She gestured to the exam table. "You can sit there, and there's a sheet to drape over your lap."

"Okay." I waited until the door closed and then hurried to change out of my bloody clothes and into the gown. I had just settled on the edge of the exam table when there was a knock on the door. I quickly spread the sheet over my lower half and said, "Come in."

Dr. Danon talked me through the exam before she and her medical assistant conducted it. I was grateful for that. I'd never had a women's wellness check before and I was terrified and embarrassed.

"Hmm," the doctor said. "I see bruising and lacerations on your hips and thighs from where you hit the stairs, but the bleeding you described looks more like spotting, which is actually quite common in the first trimester." Dr. Danon's medical assistant took notes as she talked. The doctor took her stethoscope and placed it on my bare abdomen, listening. "I'd like to do an ultrasound."

"Okay." I'd read the book Peter had given me, so some of what she was saying sounded familiar, but the exam seemed alien to me. I felt unmoored.

The medical assistant wheeled over a machine. She switched it on, and then took a bottle and shook it. "This will feel cold, but it will help us see your uterus."

I nodded my consent and Janine squeezed gel on my belly. Then Dr. Danon took a plastic wand and guided it over my skin. A black and white image appeared on the screen of the machine. It didn't look like anything to me, but Dr. Danon started in surprise, moving the wand back and forth over a particular area of my abdomen.

"We have a heartbeat," she said finally, smiling at her medical assistant before turning to me. "Congratulations, Miss Weaver."

"What?"

"You didn't lose your baby, after all," Dr. Danon explained. "From what I can see, you have a healthy nine-week fetus growing inside you."

I was afraid to move, scared that anything I did would jinx this. "Are you sure?"

"Your baby looks fine," Dr. Danon said, patting my knee. "Of course, we'll want you to have regular checkups with your OBGYN, and you'll need to start taking prenatal vitamins. With your pregnancy, we'll need to be careful about that x-ray, and I'd like to keep you overnight for observation, given the trauma you experienced."

"Yes, okay. That sounds good," I said, letting out a breath. I was so shocked, I probably would have agreed to anything at that point.

"Good," Dr. Danon said. "Janine, why don't we get Miss Weaver settled in a room? Then call Diagnostic Imaging to set up the x-ray." She turned back to me. "There's an extra gown if you'd like to wear it to cover you from the back and you can put your underthings and socks back on. It gets chilly in these rooms, but you can ask for an extra blanket from your nurse if you get cold." Her demeanor had changed—she seemed kinder. Maybe she felt a sense of relief about the baby too.

Dr. Danon and her assistant left to write orders for me, and I pulled on more clothing. I was glad for the extra gown—I hated feeling so vulnerable. I'd been worried the doctor would spot my scars and have more questions. Luckily, she didn't. I opened the exam room door and motioned for Gabriel to come back inside.

"Are you okay?" he asked.

I couldn't help smiling. "I'm still pregnant."

"Oh," he said. "*Oh.*" He took a second to absorb the news. "Is the baby okay?"

"Dr. Danon said she looks healthy," I said.

"She?"

I laughed. "It's too soon to tell, but she feels like a she." I don't know why, but she did. I was still trying to wrap my mind around it. I felt giddy. Thinking I'd lost the baby had hurt more than I thought it would. I hadn't known how much I wanted this until I thought I was having a miscarriage. Now I had a second chance, and it felt good. I silently promised the baby I'd do everything I could to make sure she was born healthy.

There was another knock on the door, and a nurse entered, taking in Gabriel before turning to me. With his height and hairy visage, he did make an impression. "Hello, Miss Weaver. My name is Amy, and I'm here to take you to your room. Once we get you settled, there's a police officer who'd like to speak with you."

"I understand," I said.

"I can talk to him first, if you want," Gabriel offered. "While you get settled."

"That would be good," I said. I took his hand and gave it a squeeze. "Thank you, Gabe."

He nodded and ducked out of the room.

When Officer Jensen came to my room, I was showered and tucked in bed, warm under that extra blanket. Gabriel had given him the gist of what had happened over the last several days, and had drawn a map to the cabin. The officer had Gabriel wait outside as I told my side of the story, probably to make sure our stories matched. I was glad for that. I didn't want Gabriel to hear about what Peter had done to those girls.

Officer Jensen did a fairly good job of keeping his face impassive, writing notes on a slender notepad, but when I got to the part about preserving heads in ceramic gourds, his eyes grew wide. At first, I was scared he wouldn't believe me, but then decided it didn't matter. Once he got out there and saw for himself, he would.

I hadn't realized how tired I was, but once the officer left, I felt like I could finally let go of the tension I'd been holding in. I was about to crash when Gabriel came back in.

"You look exhausted," he said.

"I am. It's after two. We've been up most the night."

He turned to go. "Sleep then, and I'll see you in the morning."

I grabbed his arm. "I don't want you to leave. Will you stay? I'd feel better if you stayed."

He looked toward the door, eyeing the nurses' station. "Yeah," he said. "I'll stay until they kick me out."

43

I slept for nine hours straight. It was almost noon by the time I woke, but I felt better than I had in days. Still bruised and sporting a bad ankle, but optimistic. Gabriel had kept his word, and was snoozing in the arm chair across from my bed. He must have left briefly to visit the hospital gift shop, because there was a trio of red roses and a sprig of baby's breath in a glass bud vase on the table beside my bed. A tiny stuffed kitten sat propped up in the crook of his arm.

As I raised the bed to sit up, he stirred, opening one eye. I smiled shyly, patting down my hair. "Who's your little friend?"

He opened both eyes and looked down at the toy he was holding. "Oh. That's not for me."

"Is it for me?"

He looked a little embarrassed. "The flowers are for you. This is for the baby. I mean, I guess it's a little early for that, but…" He got to his feet and shuffled over, holding out the gray tabby kitten.

He was kind of adorable when he was being awkward. He was a giant, hairy man, but one of the kindest people I'd ever met. I took the stuffed animal from his outstretched hand and tucked it in beside me. "That's really sweet. Thank you."

"I wish I'd danced with you," he said, shoving his hands in his pockets. His back was hunched, like he was carrying a heavy weight.

"What?"

"At Elena and Charlie's wedding. You asked me to dance, and I said no, because I didn't know how and I was embarrassed. I wish I'd said yes." He looked down at his feet. "Maybe if I had, you wouldn't have been with Peter, and you wouldn't have gotten hurt."

I reached up and placed my hands on his cheeks. He stared at me, uncertain. "Maybe." I ran my thumbs along his cheekbones and said, "But then I wouldn't be having this baby, and I *am* grateful for that."

"Oh." He took a step backward, retreating from my touch. "I'm glad the baby is okay. I really am."

"Don't do that," I said.

"Don't do what?"

"Don't pull away from me." I reached over and tried to tug a visitor's chair closer to the bed. I couldn't quite manage it, so he scooted it closer, a questioning look on his face. "Here," I said. "Sit."

He sat down obediently, searching my eyes.

"I want you to stay in my life, Gabe," I said, holding his gaze. "Yes, I'm having his baby, but you're the one who's been there for me. You're the one who really cared."

"I *wasn't* there for you," he said. "But I will be. I'll be whatever you need me to be. If you need me to be your friend, I'll be your friend. If you need space, I'll give you space. If you want me to be something more, I can be that too." He cleared his throat. "And I'm not being trite about the baby. I really am happy for you. I'm here for both of you."

I grabbed his shirt and pulled him close enough to kiss his cheek. "Thank you." He gave me a shy smile.

Someone knocked on the doorframe of the room, and we both looked up to see Vincent standing there, holding an enormous vase of colorful flowers. They dwarfed the roses Gabe had gotten me. Vincent gave us an uncertain smile. "May I come in?"

I froze—I'd been dreading this moment, when I had to see Peter's dad. What do you say to a person when you killed his son? It took me a second to gather the courage to answer. "Of course."

"I wasn't sure if I should come," Vincent said. "When Gabriel called last night and told me what happened, I thought it might be best to stay away and let you rest."

"That was the plan, yes," Gabe said. He didn't look thrilled to see his father. He rose from his chair, ready to boot Vincent from the room at my command.

Vincent stared at Gabriel for a second before turning back to me. He looked as unnerved as I felt. "These are for you," he said, looking around the room for a spot to set the flowers down. He settled on the side table next to the arm chair, carefully placing the heavy vase there.

"Would you like to sit?" I asked.

"Oh!" He waved me off. "Oh, no. No, I won't stay long. I wanted to come and see if you were all right. I am *so* sorry, Amelia. When Gabriel told me what Peter did to you, I was just… well, I was just in shock. I couldn't believe it." His words came out in a rush. "But I do, of course. I believe you, and I know there's nothing I can do to make it right, but I wanted to tell you, I took the liberty of paying your rent for the month, and I intend to pay your medical bills. I hope that's okay."

"That's generous of you," I said, guarded.

A dark look passed over Gabe's face. He sat down and took my hand. "Did you know, Dad? Did you know what Peter was capable of?"

Vincent looked pale. His hands shook, and his eyes had dark circles as though he hadn't slept. If I didn't know better, I would have thought he'd aged ten years in a single night. "I did *not* know, Gabriel. I truly did not." He gripped the arm of the chair for support. "But I should have. I truly am sorry, Amelia, and I don't blame you for…" He hesitated, choosing his words carefully. "For what happened. If there's anything I can do for you, or your child, I hope you will call on me." He gave me a sad smile. "I hope I'm not crossing a line here, but I've begun to think of you as a daughter, as part of this family we've created with the museum, and I was so very happy that you and Peter were together. He finally seemed content—it was like you smoothed out all his rough edges. I just didn't know how rough those edges were."

"Thank you, Vincent," I said, and I meant it. "I'm sorry for what happened too. But I'm not sorry I got to know you, or Gabe, or any of the others."

Vincent looked visibly relieved, like I'd offered some comfort. "I appreciate that, my dear." He started for the door. "I'll let you rest now, but when you're ready, I'd like to talk again." With that, he was gone.

I turned to Gabe. "Do you believe him?" I whispered. "That he really didn't know?"

Gabriel let go of my hand and sat back in his chair. He crossed his arms, thinking. "I do. For all of Vincent's faults—and he has a number of them, believe me—he has a good heart. He always wants to see the best in people. I guess that's why he couldn't imagine his son doing something so horrific. But really, who could? I didn't."

"I didn't either." I had fallen so hard for Peter, I never imagined he had a violent side. I was too caught up in the romance. I simply couldn't see it. And I couldn't understand how a man like Vincent could have a son like Peter. "What was his mother like?"

"Frida? Oh, she was wonderful. Kind, like Vincent. It was cruel that she died so young. We were devastated."

"Is that what did it? Peter lost his mom, and he just…snapped?"

Gabriel shook his head. "I don't think so. That was a tough time—no doubt—but even before that, there was darkness in him. I remember one time, we were at the beach, and he fed a French fry to a gull. Then he kicked it."

My hand flew to my mouth. I know I shouldn't have been shocked, considering everything else that had happened, but I was.

"Vincent and Frida didn't see it, and I never told. I'd only been with them for a year at that point, and I was still learning to trust them. I was a kid—fourteen—and it felt like Peter was so much older," Gabriel said. "It stuck with me, you know? Even so, I wouldn't have thought him being cruel to a bird could translate into something like this." Gabe rubbed his eyes. He looked exhausted—I imagine he hadn't slept well in that arm chair. "And then, with girls he dated…he was never mean outright, but he could be…controlling. Dismissive. If he didn't like a girl, he'd dump her like breaking someone's heart didn't bother him at all."

I nodded. "He didn't have empathy, but he was really good at faking it." I had really thought Peter loved me. I was wrong.

"Yeah. He had zero empathy. But I don't think it was because of how he was raised. I mean, Vincent and Frida raised me too, at least for the latter part of my childhood. Maybe Peter was born like that, or maybe something happened," Gabriel said. "My theory? I think it was because he didn't understand what it was like to struggle."

My eyes widened. "What do you mean?"

"I mean, most of us struggle with *something*. Life is suffering, right? Look at me—all the stuff I've gone through, looking like this, and you, with the pearls…we know what it's like to struggle, so we feel empathy when other people are suffering," Gabe said.

"We understand what pain is, and that makes us want to reach out, to ease that suffering."

"Yeah, I guess so."

"But Peter—he never had to struggle. With anything, as far as I can see. He was handsome, charming—I mean, people *really* liked him. Everything always seemed to come so easily for him—making friends, getting good grades in school, building relationships in business." Gabriel ticked off the list on his fingers. "Vincent paid for the house, college—he even paid for Peter's car. Peter never knew what it was like to be poor, or hungry, or chronically ill. With the family business, he never had to ace an interview, and he sure as hell never had to worry about getting fired. He was entitled, free to do whatever he wanted, without the threat of consequences."

I didn't know if Gabriel was right about why Peter had killed those girls, but Peter had finally faced the consequences of his actions. He'd never hurt anyone again.

44

I couldn't play the role of the mermaid again. Too many memories of Peter, and besides, my clothes were getting too tight because of the baby. There was no way that suit would fit me.

Vincent was gracious and understanding—so much so, I was guarded for a while. I found it hard to believe that he could be so kind when Peter had been so cruel. But the ice around my heart melted, and when Vincent offered me a job helping him with bookkeeping at the museum, I accepted it gratefully. It was hard to go back there. Peter was everywhere. I couldn't look at the door to his workshop without feeling panic grip my heart like a vise.

I had to get past that. I needed a way to provide for myself and save money to care for my child, and since the pearls might never come back, I needed a job with regular income. Benefits too. I'd allowed Vincent to pay my medical bills for my emergency room visit, but I was too proud to let him pay my bills for the pregnancy and delivery—at least directly. He also offered me a room at the house, to stay with him and Gabriel, but I couldn't accept. There was too much there that reminded me of Peter. It was better to have my own place, to maintain my independence.

I let Vincent in, little by little, scared I would regret it, that he'd do something hurtful. He didn't. He approached me like I was a wounded animal, cautious, respectful of my boundaries. Maybe he was scared too. I think he thought of me like one of deer we'd sometimes see grazing near the estuary, ready to bolt at the first sign of danger. He wasn't wrong.

I didn't like the dark. I slept with a light on, buried under a mound of heavy blankets. I had bad dreams—about Peter, the dead girls, my mom—all of them haunting me. I'd dream that I lost the baby, and I'd wake up in a cold sweat, my heart racing. Then I'd lay there on my back, hands resting on my growing belly, holding my breath until I felt the baby kick. Once I knew she was okay, I'd know I was okay too, and I could fall asleep again.

She still felt like a dream—the good kind—like something hoped for, but not quite manifest. She was becoming more real every day. When I went for my first sonogram with my new doctor, I asked Gabe to come with me. He too treated me with care, like he was worried about spooking me, sending me running.

He knew what it was like to walk through hell, the kind of scars that left on a person's soul. Those kinds of scars ran deeper than the scars on my back.

Gabe knew I needed something to anchor me, to keep me steady as I faced fear and uncertainty. I squeezed his hand as I got a glimpse of my child, tears of joy streaming down my face. When I looked over at him, I saw that he was smiling, a look of wonder in his eyes. That's when I knew things would be okay. No matter what happened between us, he'd be there for me.

I made a copy of the sonogram photo and gave it to Vincent. He framed it and hung it in his office, unapologetically goofy about becoming a grandfather, even after everything that had happened. He'd forgiven me, unequivocally, and I realized I'd forgiven him too. What had happened with Peter wasn't his fault, and it wasn't mine either. I had to forgive myself. Only then would I be able to walk past Peter's workshop or visit Vincent's house without a chill crawling up my spine. Only then could I find peace.

The pregnancy wasn't easy. At first, it was a constant reminder of Peter. I couldn't help but think of him as I dealt with morning sickness—the way he'd seemed so happy about the idea of having a child, how he'd been so patient with me as I'd come to terms with what was happening to my body. As the months went by, I thought of him less.

Reminders of him were all around me at the museum and in my apartment, but I was making new memories. My co-workers were my friends—my new family—and they looked out for me. We had an unspoken agreement not to talk about Peter. They had been as shocked as Vincent and Gabriel when they heard what Peter had done.

Together we weathered the storm of bad press—reports that the co-owner of our museum had murdered four girls and assaulted a fifth, who escaped. Vincent made sure my name stayed out of the paper, and I was thankful for that. I didn't want to talk to reporters, and I didn't want to say anything that would hurt our livelihood.

We needn't have worried that the news stories would affect attendance to our shows—if anything, it added to the mystique of the museum. Tourists were fascinated by the idea of a serial killer, and us not talking about it only inflamed curiosity. Business boomed. That doesn't reflect well on the state of humanity, but at least we chose not to dignify nosy questions with a response. We refused to celebrate the horror, even if other people did.

Elena and Charlie threw me a baby shower, which further

restored my faith in people. Charlie even surprised me by knitting a matching cap and booties for the baby. It felt good to be surrounded by friends who cared about me, who wanted to make sure I had everything I needed to care for my child. And she was *my* child.

I worried the memory of Peter would loom over us like a shadow, a specter from my past, but that seemed to be another unspoken rule within this new family. The baby was mine, wholly mine, and we didn't need to talk about who her father had been. I knew, at some point, I'd have to tell her something about Peter—perhaps a sanitized version of the truth until she was old enough to hear the real story. For now, it was enough to focus only on her.

Elena and Charlie were with me when the baby arrived, holding my hands as I labored in the hospital. As the nurse handed me my baby, she asked, "What's her name?"

"Rose Weaver," I said. Rose, because roses are beautiful, but they also have thorns. I knew all too well that thorns can be necessary for survival. I wanted my daughter to be strong enough to protect herself. The name also reminded me of the trio of red roses Gabriel brought me on the day I found out my baby was going to live, and that memory made me smile.

Weaver, because in spite of my affection for Vincent, my baby would have my last name, not Peter's. I didn't put him on the birth certificate either.

Elena beamed down at me and squeezed my shoulder. "You did great, Mia. We'll go tell Vincent and Gabe the good news."

I grinned up at her and Charlie. "Tell them they can come meet her."

As they left, arms around each other's waists, I studied my baby's face. Her tiny nose and perfect rosebud lips, her delicate fingers wrapped around mine. Emotion crashed over me like a wave, a love so deep and fierce, I'd do anything to protect this child. She looked up at me with kitten-round eyes, bright with intelligence.

"You and me, kid," I whispered to her. "You and me against the world."

ACKNOWLEDGMENTS

My appreciation to all the amazing authors at Midnight Tide Publishing who have provided support in my publishing journey. Thank you especially to Elle Beaumont, Melanie Gilbert, Candace Robinson, and Jenny Hickman for your advice and encouragement. My gratitude to my dear friend Jessie Antonellis-John, who always offers invaluable feedback. And finally, my thanks to my husband and boys for their patience and encouragement as I take time to write.

ABOUT THE AUTHOR

Melissa Eskue Ousley is an award-winning author living on the Oregon coast with her family, a neurotic dog, two charming cats, and a piranha. Her suspense novel, *Pitcher Plant*, is set in Seaside, and won a 2018 Independent Publisher Book Award. Her young adult novel, *Sunset Empire*, debuted in a bestselling boxed set. Her short stories have been included in *Rain Magazine*, *The North Coast Squid*, and various anthologies. When she's not writing, she can be found volunteering for her local wildlife center, caring for injured owls and hawks.

Discover more at
www.melissaeskueousley.com

facebook.com/MelissaEskueOusley
twitter.com/meskueousley
instagram.com/melissaeskueousley
goodreads.com/MelissaEskueOusley

ALSO BY MELISSA ESKUE OUSLEY

Pitcher Plant

Sunset Empire

MORE BOOKS YOU'LL LOVE

If you enjoyed this story, please consider leaving a review!
Then check out more books from Midnight Tide Publishing!

Magic Mutant Nightmare Girl by Erin Gramamr

Holly Roads uses Harajuku fashion to distract herself from tragedy. Her magical girl aesthetic makes her feel beautiful—and it keeps the world at arm's length. She's an island of one, until advice from an amateur psychic expands her universe. A midnight detour ends with her vs. exploding mutants in the heart of San Francisco.

Brush with destiny? Check. Waking up with blue blood, emotions gone haywire, and terrifying strength that starts ripping her wardrobe to shreds? Totally not cute. Hunting monsters with a hot new partner and his unlikely family of mad scientists?

Way more than she bargained for.

Available Now

Crow by Candace Robinson & Amber R. Duell

Reva spent the last twenty years in her own purgatory, first as the Wicked Witch of the West, then banished to eternity in darkness. Now that she's returned from oblivion, Reva's out for blood. The Northern Witch, Locasta, destroyed Reva's life out of jealousy over Crow. But Reva's love for him is gone, replaced only with the desire for revenge.

Crow wasted years trying to distract his mind after the Wicked Witch—his true love—was vanquished. He'd thought Reva was lost forever until magic brought her back, though their reunion was anything but happy. Reva hates him now as much as she loved him then. He can't blame her—his former lover cursed them both and stole their daughter away. But he's more determined than ever to earn Reva's forgiveness.

When Reva leaves for the North, intent on destroying Locasta, Crow refuses to lose her to the same magic twice. He joins her on the journey, and, as much as Reva loathes him, she knows it's for the best. Traveling is too dangerous on her own, but spending so much time together isn't exactly safe for their hearts either. Hidden away in her castle, the Northern Witch waits to curse Reva and Crow once more. This time they need to put an end to Locasta, or suffer the consequences of the curse forever.

Available Now

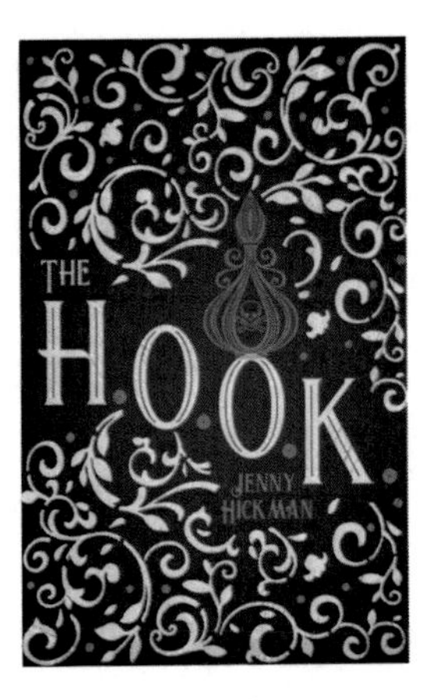

The HOOK by Jenny Hickman

Tomorrow isn't promised, no matter how immortal you think you are.

In the aftermath of Vivienne's capture, she discovers she's destined to become one of the Forgetful P.A.N. The devastating diagnosis leaves her questioning her relationships—and her place in Neverland. While on her second recruitment mission, she ignores a cardinal rule, and one of her fellow P.A.N. pays the ultimate price for her mistake.

Outrage over the death spurs Lee Somerfield's growing rebellious faction to fight fire with fire, leaving H.O.O.K. in ashes and Neverland ripped apart from within.

Navigating new love and old secrets, Vivienne must now face the consequences of her actions … and decide if living forever is worth forgetting everything.

Available Now

9 781953 238238